"Oh...I didn't know you were in here."

Jimmy secured his towel as she remained standing in the doorway. Her nightgown clung to her curves like a second skin.

"Sheri." His voice sounded half-strangled as a wave of immense want roared through him. "You need to back away and close the door."

And still she remained in place, as if waiting. But waiting for what?

"Sheri, if you don't leave now I won't be responsible for my actions."

"I don't think I want you to be responsible for your actions right now. I don't even think *I* want to be responsible for my own actions right now."

She took his hand and placed it on her racing heart.

"What are we doing, Sheri?" he asked.

"I don't know, but I don't want to stop."

Dear Reader,

I've enjoyed my time in Wolf Creek, Pennsylvania, and I hope you've enjoyed it, too. However, I couldn't leave the area without Sheri Marcoli finally finding her prince. Unfortunately, with her aunt Liz still missing and danger closing in, the last thing on Sheri's mind is romance.

Detective Jimmy Carmani is no prince, but he's determined that no harm will come to the gentle Sheri. Even though both of his partners have found love with Sheri's two sisters, he's not looking for a trifecta.

I found my prince years ago. He was shorter than I'd expected, but just the right height for us to fit together perfectly when we danced. He has a perfect falsetto for old fifties songs and makes me laugh more than anyone else in my life. He's my rock when I'm weak and I can't imagine my life without him by my side.

I couldn't do less for Sheri. I hope you enjoy reading about how she found the special man who would be her prince for the rest of her life.

Happy reading!

Carla Cassidy

LONE WOLF STANDING

—

Carla Cassidy

HARLEQUIN® ROMANTIC SUSPENSE

Recycling programs
for this product may
not exist in your area.

ISBN-13: 978-0-373-27877-0

LONE WOLF STANDING

Copyright © 2014 by Carla Bracale

Printed in U.S.A.

www.Harlequin.com

Books by Carla Cassidy

Harlequin Romantic Suspense

Other titles by this author
available in ebook format.

CARLA CASSIDY

is an award-winning author who has written more than one hundred books for Harlequin. In 1995 she won Best Silhouette Romance from *RT Book Reviews* for *Anything for Danny*. In 1998 she won a Career Achievement Award for Best Innovative Series from *RT Book Reviews*.

Carla believes the only thing better than curling up with a good book to read is sitting down at the computer with a good story to write. She's looking forward to writing many more books and bringing hours of pleasure to readers.

To Frank,
My New York Italian prince.
Thank you for loving me.

Chapter 1

The Prince of Philly

Jimmy Carmani was halfway from the police station to his apartment when his radio crackled and dispatcher Erin Taylor's melodic voice filled his car. "Jimmy, where are you?" she asked.

"Just about home. Why? What's up?"

"I just got a call from Travis Brooks and he says he's being held at gunpoint by Sheri Marcoli at her place. You want to check it out?"

"On my way," Jimmy replied, wondering if his voice held the utter shock that swept through him. The idea of Sheri Marcoli holding Travis at gunpoint was stunning. The idea of Sheri holding anyone at gunpoint was ludicrous. It had to be a mistake.

He remembered a year ago when somebody had

called into the station to say that Sarah Fisher, one of the women from the nearby Amish community, was beating a man to death with a hoe.

Jimmy and his partners Frank Delaney and Steve Kincaid had sped to the scene where they found Sarah using a hoe to beat a rug hanging on a clothesline.

This had to be something similar. There was no way that Jimmy would believe that sweet, caring, petite Sheri Marcoli even owned a gun.

His apartment was just off the main drag of the small town of Wolf Creek, Pennsylvania, but he headed in the opposite direction, turning onto a road that would take him up into the mountains where Sheri's small house was located on five acres of thick woods.

Jimmy had only been there once about two months ago and that had been because of the ongoing investigation into the disappearance of Sheri's aunt. It had been a little over three months since Liz Marcoli had disappeared from her home. She'd just vanished and while the case was being investigated as a criminal one, there had been no real clues and it was on its way to becoming a very cold case.

Liz Marcoli was the last thing on Jimmy's mind as he veered onto a narrow gravel road. It was far more likely that Travis Brooks, the owner of the Wolf's Head Tavern, had gotten himself liquored up and was holding a gun on Sheri for some unknown reason.

This thought forced his foot down harder on the gas pedal, making rocks ping against the underside of his car. Of the three Marcoli sisters, Sheri was the youngest and the smallest and although Travis rarely got a snoutful of his own products, it wasn't unheard of.

Jimmy gripped the steering wheel tighter, his Italian blood heating as he thought of Sheri defenseless against a drunk with a gun. He turned right onto a lane that he knew would carry him directly to the front of Sheri's cabin.

Sheri's bright yellow pickup was parked in front of the charming cabin, but there weren't any other vehicles in sight. Jimmy parked and got out of his car, his hand on the butt of his gun as he approached the front door.

He knocked and when there was no answer he called out. "Sheri Marcoli? It's Detective Carmani."

"Around back, Jimmy," her voice came faintly from behind the house. He didn't hear any stress in her tone, but he didn't remove his hand from his gun as he went around the side of the house and toward her backyard.

When he stepped around the corner he froze, stunned at the sight of Sheri with a shotgun to her shoulder and pointed toward the wooded area where in the distance Travis Brooks stood with his hands over his head and a panicked look on his face.

"Thank God you're finally here," Travis exclaimed. "She's gone plumb crazy. She's had that shotgun aimed at me for the last twenty minutes and told me if I moved an inch she'd shoot me."

Although Jimmy gave a faint nod in Travis's direction, his entire focus was on the miniature Annie Oakley. Tight jeans hugged her slender legs and she wore a black T-shirt with Roadside Stop, the name of the store she owned, in gold lettering across her small breasts.

She held the gun with a familiar ease that was both intriguing and appalling, for it was so far out of line with who he'd believed her to be. At her side was a dog, a black mix of breeds that was the size of a small Shetland pony.

"He's got a crossbow at his feet," Sheri said, as if that explained everything. "I warned him the last time he was hunting on my property that the next time I caught him I'd shoot him."

"I was on the trail of a feral pig, the biggest damn piece of pork I've ever seen," Travis replied. "That swine has been tearing up crops and some of the locals want it killed. I didn't realize I'd crossed onto your property, Sheri."

She kept holding the gun steady. "I've got No Hunting signs posted everywhere. How can you see a big pig and not see one of my big signs?"

"Sheri, you need to put the gun down," Jimmy said softly. "You know you aren't going to shoot Travis."

"Why shouldn't I? He's trespassing and he knows how I feel about hunting. My land is a sanctuary for animals."

"Sheri, I was on my way home from the station when I caught this call. If you shoot him then I'm going to have to arrest you and there will be tons of paperwork and I won't get home until after midnight and I do need my beauty sleep," Jimmy replied.

A hint of a smile curved her lips. The late evening sun sparkled in her chestnut-brown hair and when she looked at him her amber eyes held a hint of amusement that let him know she'd never intended to use the weapon.

She turned her gaze back to Travis and her eyes narrowed. "This is your last warning, Travis Brooks. Stay off my property with that crossbow of yours."

"I promise I'll be more careful in the future and the next time you come into the tavern your tab is on me," Travis answered.

Sheri lowered the shotgun so it pointed to the ground. "I wouldn't want to mess up your beauty sleep," she said to Jimmy.

"I appreciate that." Jimmy waved at Travis. "Get your crossbow and get out of here fast in case the lady changes her mind."

Before the words were completely out of Jimmy's mouth Travis had grabbed his crossbow and vanished from his shadowed spot in the woods. Jimmy turned back to Sheri, this time the smile gone from his face.

"Are you crazy?" he asked. "Do you have any idea how dangerous a gun can be? It might have accidentally gone off. You could have killed Travis or yourself."

"No, I couldn't have." Sheri stepped back toward the concrete patio and leaned the shotgun next to the back door. "It isn't loaded."

She moved to one of the patio chairs, the dog following at her side and sitting next to her as she sat. She motioned Jimmy to a chair as he continued to stare at her in surprise.

He walked to the chair next to hers and sank down. She pointed to the small patch of mowed lawn before them and the woods that surrounded it.

"These five acres are not just my sanctuary, but

a safe home to any wild creatures that come here," she said.

He'd never been in her backyard and now he found himself studying it with interest. It was common knowledge that Sheri loved animals, but knowing it and seeing it were two different things.

Bird and squirrel feeders hung from trees limbs; a blooming flower garden surrounded a big birdbath. A salt lick was mounted on a post to attract deer and a tin tub at the very edge of the yard he assumed was used to put food scraps to feed bear, raccoon and any other scavenger in the vicinity. It was definitely an animal's paradise.

There was also a brightly striped hammock and a wrought-iron table next to it...a perfect place to spend a lazy afternoon or lounge for a while before bedtime.

"No hunters allowed," she said firmly.

"Sheri, it's a dangerous practice to threaten a man with an unloaded gun," he said, and tried not to notice the heady floral scent that wafted from her and rode the light breeze to tease his nose.

"Would it be better to threaten a man with a loaded gun?" she asked.

"It would be better if you got rid of that gun altogether," he replied. He eyed the dog who sat like a statue next to her. "He's a big guy and very well behaved."

"His name is Highway and he's very well trained," she said as she stroked the top of the dog's head. "Highway, make nice," she said.

Jimmy tensed as the behemoth dog got up and approached where he sat. Highway opened his mouth, appearing to grin when he sat down and offered his paw.

A surprised laugh escaped Jimmy as he shook the dog's paw, and then Highway returned to sit at Sheri's side. "Did Jed train him?"

Sheri nodded. "I found him on the side of the highway between Wolf Creek and Hershey a little over a year ago. There were two of them, puppies about four weeks old, tossed out and abandoned. I picked them up, brought them home and tried to keep them alive. I lost one, but Highway was a fighter. Once he was old enough I took him to Jed for some special training. Highway would kill somebody if they threatened me. All I'd have to do was give the right command."

Jed Wilson was a talented dog trainer who lived in Wolf Creek and worked with search and rescue and cadaver dogs. He also trained tiny poodles not to piddle on the rug and apparently big dogs to protect and defend.

"I'd prefer you not give that command right now," Jimmy said drily.

Sheri smiled. "Don't worry. You're no threat to me. Highway is the main man in my life until my prince comes along."

"Prince?" Jimmy raised an eyebrow.

She nodded, her shoulder-length thick hair swaying with her head motion. "You know, my golden-haired, blue-eyed prince who will share this enchanted cottage in the woods with me for the rest of my life."

"And when, exactly, are you expecting this prince to show up?" Jimmy asked, his mind working to keep up with the conversation that had gone from guns, to killer dogs and now to a prince with blond hair who would provide her with her happy-ever-after ending.

She shrugged her slender shoulders. "Could be tomorrow, could be in a year. Who knows, but I'm a patient woman and I'm only twenty-six. I have time. I'm willing to wait until fate blows him in my direction. Forgive me, I'm being a bad hostess. Would you like something to drink? Maybe some iced tea or a cold beer?"

What he'd like to do was to sit here and talk to her forever, to get to know the woman who had captured his attention from the moment she and her two sisters had walked into the police station three months ago to file a missing-persons report for their aunt.

Instead he stood and shook his head. "Thanks, but I should probably head on home." He had a feeling if he spent too much time with Sheri he might like her even more than he already did, and one of the few things Jimmy was certain of was that he wasn't any kind of a golden-haired prince.

Sheri stood, the dog rising to all fours, as well. "Thanks for coming so quickly, Jimmy. I really just wanted to scare Travis. This is my property, not his personal hunting grounds and he needed to be reminded of that fact."

"I'll remind him again the next time I'm in the tavern," he replied. On impulse he reached into his pocket and took out a pad and pen. He scribbled down his personal cell phone number and handed it to her. "Just in case you get the urge to hold somebody at gunpoint again. Call me first and I'll see if I can talk you down."

She smiled at him, her eyes twinkling with amusement. "Night, Jimmy."

She headed inside the house as he walked around the side and back to his car. Minutes later as he made the drive to his apartment, he thought of what Sheri hadn't asked. She hadn't asked for any updates on her aunt Liz's case.

That indicated to Jimmy that she'd already given up hope of the woman ever being found and that was a tragedy. Jimmy couldn't imagine what it must be like to have a missing loved one.

Of course, Jimmy had no loved ones in his life. Despite the fact that she'd just held a man at gunpoint, Sheri Marcoli was a caring and gentle woman who deserved a prince and a happy ever after.

No matter how attracted he was to Sheri, he knew he was the antithesis of that prince. Black-haired and dark-eyed, Jimmy also sported two tattoos, had literally fought his way through life and had only known love for a brief period of time when he'd been eight years old.

As he pulled into the parking space in front of the small apartment he rented, he dismissed thoughts of Sheri Marcoli. He was a man apparently built to be alone, as he had been through most of his life.

What he needed to concentrate on was the mystery of Liz's continued disappearance and the most recent case of an armed robbery at a local convenience store.

Work. That's what Jimmy did best. Solving crimes was his talent, his passion. He was good at it and he had a feeling he'd be very bad at loving and being loved.

* * *

"Okay, Highway, you be a good boy while I'm gone today," Sheri said as she opened the oversize doggie door that had been cut into a side wall of the kitchen. The door led into a large fenced area where Highway could enjoy coming and going from the inside to the outside, without having the full run of the backyard and the woods.

When she was home all day she allowed him the freedom of the yard, but when she was gone, he spent his time using the doggie door and was confined to the large pen or inside the house.

As he ambled out into the mid-June sunshine, Sheri grabbed her purse from the kitchen counter and headed toward the front door.

Minutes later she was in her pickup headed for the roadside store she ran along with her sister Marlene. Unfortunately, she had a feeling the days of her sister working there were limited.

Marlene was in the process of realizing her own dream of owning a bakery on Main Street. She'd already found the perfect storefront and with Detective Frank Delaney's love and support, her dream was slowly becoming a reality.

Sheri couldn't be happier for both of her sisters, who had found the men of their dreams and were working to build a future filled with love and commitment.

Sheri's one foray into a relationship with a man had been a disaster. Her hands tightened around the steering wheel as she thought of Eric Richards. They'd dated for three months before he'd shown his true colors.

She hadn't realized at the time they were dating that Eric was just like the kids who used to bully her at school. He'd only shown that side of himself to her when he'd gotten angry and once had been enough.

A sudden vision of Jimmy Carmani filled her head. He was definitely a hot piece of work with his thick black hair and dark chocolate-colored eyes. Nobody in the entire town of Wolf Creek wore a pair of black slacks and a tailored white shirt quite as well as Jimmy.

She didn't know much about him except that he was one of three detectives that served the small town of Wolf Creek. She also knew he had a reputation for being brilliant and devoted to the job and she had to admit feeling a small tug of attraction toward him.

She dismissed thoughts of Jimmy as she pulled in front of the store where signs advertised Amish cheese and furniture, fresh produce and nuts, and a variety of other items that would appeal to the tourists that came through the area on their way to the bigger, more popular tourist city of Hershey.

This was the kind of place Sheri had always envisioned working. She loved doing business with the nearby Amish community and visiting with travelers who passed through the store on their way to new adventures and family fun.

She was always the first to arrive and open the doors for the day. She'd work alone until ten at which time Jennifer Fletcher would come in to help out. Marlene would arrive between noon and one along with Sheri's other part-time help, Abe Winslow.

Sheri wasn't planning on replacing Marlene when she stopped working at the store and instead devoted all her time to her bakery. Sheri, Jennifer and Abe were a good team and would hopefully be able to manage the store during the hours it was open.

They were like a little family and since Aunt Liz had gone missing and her sisters had become romantically involved with their men, a sense of family had been missing for Sheri.

Her evenings were quiet with just Highway and her woodland creatures for company, and yet she knew there was somebody special fate had in store for her…her prince who would banish her loneliness and love her as nobody ever had before.

Once inside the store all thoughts of princes and loneliness vanished as she got to work stocking shelves, checking the produce to make sure it was still fresh and attending to all the duties to be ready for a day of business.

She hadn't been open long when seventeen-year-old Jason King walked in carrying one of his mother's handmade quilts. "Good morning, Jason," she greeted him with a gentle smile. She had a special soft spot for the young Amish man. His mother, Mary, had died six months ago, leaving Jason and his father, William, the burden of caretaking for five little Kings ranging between the ages of seven and two.

Jason cast her a tired smile as he set the quilt on the counter. "Good morning to you, too."

"I see you've brought me another of your mother's treasures." Sheri placed a hand on the lovely, close-stitched patchwork quilt. "We sold the wedding ring quilt almost the same day you brought it in. What design is on this one?"

"Mom always called it her field of flowers." Jason's gaze lingered on the quilt, as if remembering special moments with his mother.

Sheri's heart squeezed tight. She wished she had any memories of her own mother, but her mother had dropped her off for her aunt Liz to raise when she'd been a couple months old.

"Same price as we put on the other one?"

Jason lifted his gaze back on her. "Yes, that would be good." He leaned against the counter as if reluctant to leave. He was a good-looking kid with dark hair beneath his requisite straw hat. But his eyes held concern and dark circles rode beneath, making him appear much older than his age.

"Everything all right?" Sheri asked softly.

Jason shrugged slender shoulders. "Okay, I guess, although I'm worried a bit about my da."

"Worried about what?" It wasn't right for a child to worry about his father, she thought.

Once again Jason shrugged, a faint pink stain coloring his cheeks. "He's just not been himself the last couple of months. He leaves the fieldwork and disappears and I don't know where he goes. He's distant and isn't part of the family like he used to be." Jason flushed again. "I shouldn't be talking about this."

Sheri reached out and covered his hand with hers. "Don't worry, Jason. You know I'm not a gossiper. Maybe your father is still grieving and he's dealing with it by isolating himself." She pulled her hand from his.

"I know he misses my mother a lot, and dealing with the younger ones is difficult. Thankfully, Sarah Fisher is watching them for me this morning for a couple of hours." He gave her a small smile. "I love my family but sometimes a little break away from them all is not a bad thing."

"You have a lot of responsibility on your shoulders, Jason. Just try to find some time for a little fun, too," Sheri replied.

At that moment Jennifer arrived and the private conversation between Sheri and Jason halted. With a wave of his hand he left the store as Jennifer came around the counter to stand next to Sheri.

"Everything okay?" she asked.

Sheri nodded. "Jason brought in another of his mother's quilts to sell. I feel so sorry for him. Since Mary died he's had so much to deal with."

"You know the old saying, 'What doesn't break you makes you strong,'" Jennifer replied.

Sheri eyed her wryly. "Ah, words of wisdom from a twenty-two-year-old who still lives at home with her parents who treat her like a princess."

Jennifer laughed. "I'm the first to admit that I'm hopelessly spoiled."

"Now that we agree on that, take thy spoiled bottom into the storage room and unpack the boxes of Wolf Creek souvenirs that came in yesterday," Sheri said.

Jennifer gave her a saucy salute and then disappeared into the big back room that provided storage space and a picnic table for lunch breaks.

The morning seemed to fly by, with more business than usual for a Wednesday. She hoped it was a portent of a busy tourist season. Spring and summer business was great, but when the snow flew she shortened her hours and lived mostly on what she'd made during the busy season.

There were only three places where Sheri was happy—here at the store, at her cottage with the surrounding woods, and at her aunt's home that had always smelled of cinnamon and apples or rich chocolate and dough.

Liz Marcoli was a talent in the kitchen when it came to baking sweets and desserts. Marlene had inherited her natural talent for baking. Roxy also had a genuine talent in the kitchen, but Sheri was hopeless when it came to cooking anything but the simplest of dishes.

A blur of tears misted her eyes as she thought of her missing aunt. She knew the law enforcement in Wolf Creek had done everything in their power in an attempt to find Liz, but there had been no leads to follow, no breadcrumbs of clues.

Three and a half months had passed and the hole in the fabric of their little family had been ripped right from the center. Aunt Liz had been their mother-figure, their support system, their snuggle buddy on dark stormy nights when they'd been children.

And now she was gone…vanished from her home, seemingly vanished from the entire world.

The tears that had been about to fall as grief attempted to take hold of her vanished when a car pulled up to the front door and a family of five tumbled from the doors.

It was one o'clock when Sheri's cell phone rang and she saw Marlene's number light up. "Hey, sis, what's up?"

"I feel really, really bad calling at the last minute like this, but can you get by without me today? I've got an appointment at three to meet an electrician at the store and I have a feeling it's going to be a long meeting."

"It's not a problem," Sheri assured her sister. "In fact, if it's time for you to stop working here to focus solely on the bakery, it's all right. Jenny, Abe and I can handle things here and if I find myself short-handed, I can always hire a new part-timer."

There was a long silence from Marlene. "Are you sure?" she finally asked. "I really am excited to get the bakery up and running as soon as possible."

Sheri smiled into the phone. She knew between the work on the bakery and her relationship with Detective Frank Delaney, Marlene had finally found all the pieces she needed for her happiness. Working in the store had never really been part of Marlene's dreams.

"I'm positive," Sheri replied. "I don't want to see you here unless you're shopping for something you need to create culinary magic."

"Sheri, you're the best," Marlene said, her relief evident in her tone.

Sheri laughed. "Just build that bakery and invite me as a special guest on opening day."

"You know that goes without saying."

The two spoke for another few minutes, talking about their eldest sister, Roxy, who had moved in with Detective Steve Kincaid and his seven-year-old son. Roxy ran a successful restaurant called the Dollhouse and specialized in hearty breakfasts and delightfully fresh and original lunch fare.

Neither of them mentioned Aunt Liz or the stalled case that had all three sisters barely clinging to any hope that she would be found alive.

When the call finally ended, the rest of the day remained busy. Thankfully when it was time for Jennifer to leave, Abe Winslow had arrived to take up the slack.

The two of them stayed busy with customers until seven. By eight Sheri decided it was time to close up shop. She locked up the front door and then together she and Abe left through the back.

"Busy day," he said as they stepped outside into the warm night.

"Hopefully we're just going to get busier."

"I could work more hours if you needed me to," Abe said.

Sheri smiled at the older man. He'd taken the job of working here in the late afternoon and evenings after his wife had died. He'd told Sheri that the silence of their cabin had been overwhelming after she was gone.

"I might need you to work more hours. Marlene isn't going to be working here anymore. We'll see how things go. Good night, Abe."

"See you tomorrow," he said and headed toward his old Chevy parked in the lot next to her pickup.

As she pulled out of the lot, she thought about Abe. He'd initially been a suspect in Liz's disappearance when he'd told Sheri and Marlene that he'd asked Liz out and she'd turned him down.

But he'd quickly been cleared of any wrongdoing. At the time Liz had disappeared Abe had been spending the night at his brother's home in Hershey. The brother and several other family members had confirmed his alibi.

Thoughts of Abe halted as Sheri noticed car lights

behind hers. She slowed to allow the car to pass, but the car slowed, as well. She sped up and the vehicle behind her mirrored the action.

No reason to believe anyone is following me, she thought. And yet when she turned off the highway and onto the narrow gravel road that would eventually lead to the lane that was her driveway into her cottage, the car made the turn right behind her.

An edge of apprehension crept up her spine. There were few people who used this road and she couldn't remember the last time any vehicle had shadowed her from the shop to her home.

Stop being silly, she told herself. There were other people who lived in this area. She didn't own the road that continued past her driveway and on up the mountain. It was probably just the thought of somebody kidnapping Aunt Liz that had her unusually on edge.

She couldn't tell the make or color of the car that was behind her. Darkness had fallen and all she could discern was the brilliance of the headlights.

As she turned into the lane that led to her cottage, she could have sworn that the car behind her came to a near halt, and then zoomed on and disappeared from sight.

Sheri hadn't realized she'd been holding her breath until it expelled out of her in a deep whoosh. She parked her truck and when she stepped out, a sense of uneasiness settled over her again as she heard the sounds of Highway barking raucously from his pen.

Nerves jittering, she quickly unlocked her front door, stepped inside and then locked the door behind her. She went to the kitchen and looked out the window where Highway was at the back of his fenced pen facing the forest and barking the kind of sound that indicated danger.

The dog was well trained not to bark at four-legged creatures or any of the wildlife that populated the area. Highway only acted this way when there was a two-legged predator in the woods.

Sheri opened the window above her kitchen sink, her heart beating an abnormally rapid rhythm. "Highway…inside!"

The dog turned in her direction, looked back toward the forest and gave a sharp bark, and then headed to the doggie door.

As he entered the kitchen, Sheri flipped the latches on the door that would keep anything else from crawling inside. She hurried back to the window and peered outside, wondering who or what had set Highway off.

The darkness betrayed no movement, no discernible figure, but that didn't slow the frantic beat of Sheri's heart. She tried to tell herself she was overreacting.

Still, she went from room to room, turning on lights and checking windows for any sign of an intruder. Her blood chilled as she found an unlocked window open an inch in the spare bedroom.

Had she unlocked the window last week when the weather had been so nice? Had she opened the window to let in some fresh air? She couldn't remember. All she knew for certain was that she didn't want to be here alone.

She wasn't even aware that she had memorized Jimmy Carmani's phone number until she punched it into her phone. He answered on the first ring. "Jimmy, can you come to my house?"

"On my way," he replied, and hung up.

Chapter 2

Jimmy had been at home when he'd gotten the call from Sheri. He hadn't bothered to run a comb through his thick, unruly hair. He hadn't taken the time to change from his jeans and polo shirt. He simply grabbed his gun and car keys, jumped in his car and headed out.

As he tore out of his driveway, all he could think of was the faint simmer of stress he'd heard in Sheri's voice. She hadn't specified anything wrong, but the phone call directly to him was definitely an anomaly.

He hoped he didn't find her holding a shotgun on somebody again. She was obviously territorial about her property, but her going up against a hunter's loaded gun with her useless shotgun was not just foolish, it was suicidal.

If that was what this call was about he intended

to leave her home tonight with that shotgun of hers safely locked away in his trunk.

He thought about calling her back to find out what was going on, but figured by the time he pulled over and made the call he could be at her place. He couldn't imagine why she'd called him, but as he rolled to a stop in front of her cottage every light in the house radiated outward and she opened the front door.

He breathed a sigh of relief, just now realizing how tense he'd been on the drive here. "Are you okay?" he asked as he got out of his car. He'd pulled his gun, but kept it by his side, ready for any situation.

"I'm fine, just a little freaked out." The smile she offered him was slightly shaky as she opened the door wider to allow him inside.

Jimmy had never been inside her house before and he was instantly embraced by the warmth of the earth-tone furniture, the pop of vibrant colors of scattered throw pillows and the various scents of candles here and there. A variety of healthy-looking plants added greenery, as if it was her attempt to bring the outside in. It was exactly how he'd imagined her living space would be.

What he didn't see in the room was anything to give him pause. He turned back to look at her as she closed the door and locked it, and then faced him once again. The sight of her slightly pale face made his stomach clench.

"What's going on?"

She motioned him to the sofa and she curled up in a chair nearby. "I think maybe I overreacted," she said.

"About what?"

It was obvious she was still not herself as she clasped her shaking fingers in her lap. "First I thought I was followed home from the store. A car followed me off the main highway onto Timberline Drive and then when I pulled into my driveway, it appeared to stop for a moment and then sped off."

Jimmy frowned. "Did you get a make or color?"

She shook her head. "No, it was too dark. All I could see were the headlights. I slowed down to allow them to pass, but they didn't and when I sped up, they did the same. It just felt…slightly sinister."

Jimmy's concern grew as she continued to tell him about Highway's frantic barks and the unlocked window in the spare room. "Where is Highway now?" he asked when she'd finished telling him everything.

"He's in my bedroom. I didn't figure you'd want to mess with him."

"As long as he doesn't eat me I'm fine with him." Jimmy was rewarded with the first genuine smile from her.

"I already told you he wouldn't hurt you unless you were hurting me or I gave the command." Her smile fell and she worried a strand of her long shiny hair between her slender fingers.

"He was just acting so out of character when I got home, like he knew somebody was in the woods."

"Maybe Travis?"

"Possibly," she conceded. "But when I noticed the unlocked window in the spare room I just got totally creeped out. That's when I called you, because I was afraid to be here alone. Now I'm just feeling rather foolish."

Jimmy got up from the sofa. "Better safe than sorry. Let's check out that window." As always whenever he was around her he experienced a hyperawareness of not just her, but himself. He suddenly wished he'd taken the time to run a comb through his hair and maybe pulled on a different shirt. He frowned at the inappropriate thought.

She led him down the hallway and he tried not to notice the tempting sway of her slender hips in her tight jeans. He followed her into a small bedroom that held a double bed neatly made up with a purple flowered spread, and a dresser that sported a purple vase filled with an arrangement of white flowers.

He caught the pleasant scent of lilac and wondered if it was coming in through the partially opened window or wafted from her.

"The screen appears to be solidly in place. Are you sure you didn't crack the window open at some point or another and have simply forgotten it?"

She hesitated for a long moment and then nodded. "I suppose that's possible. I'm sorry, Jimmy, that I called you out here on a wild-goose chase."

He smiled. "It wasn't a goose chase. You were scared and that's when you're supposed to call the law."

"How about I make a short pot of coffee for us to share before you head out?" Her amber eyes simmered with emotion and Jimmy realized she was still slightly freaked out and not quite ready to be left alone.

"Sure, some coffee sounds great."

He followed her back down the hallway and into a kitchen that was pristine clean, cheerful and bright in sunshine-yellow and yet had the appearance that it was rarely used.

The only thing that sat on the countertop was a coffeemaker. The table was a small two-top that would make it difficult for her to be the entertaining type.

"Cook much?" he asked once the coffee had begun to drip into the glass carafe.

"Almost never." She reached up into the cabinet to grab two mugs. "Cream and sugar?"

"Black is fine."

"Marlene and Roxy got the cooking genes in the family. At any given time there's usually more animal food in this house than people food."

"So, what do you do for food?" Jimmy realized he was enjoying this time with her, learning a little bit more about her as a woman and not as the worried relative of a victim.

"There's a lot of produce at the store. Sometimes I bring things home for a salad or occasionally Roxy will show up with a doggie bag of whatever the special of the day is at the Dollhouse. To be honest, food just isn't that important to me. I eat to stay strong, but I don't eat because I love any specific food."

"Food is definitely high on my priority list," Jimmy replied as she poured the coffee and joined him at the table. He didn't mention that for much of his life he never knew if he'd get a meal or not. There had been far too many nights he'd gone to bed hungry.

"I suppose you're a steak and potato man."

"And pizza and burritos and pancakes… Just a food man, that's me."

She leaned back in the chair, looking relaxed for the first time since he'd arrived. "They say the way to a man's heart is through his stomach. I'm hoping when my prince arrives he's also a professional chef and can cook the meals."

He grinned at her. "You have lots of ideas about this prince of yours."

"I've spent most of my life forming his image in my head." She took a sip of her coffee and then set the cup back down. "At first I thought I was fantasizing about my father, but as I grew older I realized it was the man I wanted to love me as a woman, not as a child."

"You don't know your father?"

"None of us does, although I'd say it's obvious by how different Marlene and Roxy and I look from each other that our fathers were three different men. I doubt that our mother knows who our fathers are."

"And we still haven't found a trace of your mother." Jimmy knew that the three Marcoli sisters had been dropped off at different times at their aunt's house by their mother who was strung out on drugs and apparently incapable of raising her children.

He took a sip of his coffee. "At least you know who your mother is. When I was two weeks old I was found in a cardboard box in front of a Philly police station and I immediately went into the foster care system."

Sheri's eyes widened and he noticed for the first time the sinfully long length of her brown eyelashes. "And nobody ever found out who your parents were?" He shook his head and she continued, "Then how did you get the last name of Carmani?"

"The police station was located in a heavily populated Italian neighborhood and the cop who found me said I looked like an Italian. His name was Jim Carmani, so he named me Jimmy Carmani and that's been my name since."

She stared at him thoughtfully. "I've heard the foster care system can be brutal."

He took another sip of coffee before answering. "I had some great experiences and I had some bad ones, but that was then and this is now. So how is business at the store?"

The last thing he wanted to do was journey back into his past where pain resided and faint memories of love lost stirred. He'd survived and ultimately made the right decisions that had led him to a job he loved in a town that finally felt like home.

As Sheri talked about the store, he enjoyed the emotions that played across her face. It was obvious she loved interacting with the people who visited there and shared a close relationship with the Amish from the settlement.

He liked looking at her and he'd discovered that the lilac scent came from her, not from the open window in the bedroom. When was the last time he'd enjoyed the scent of a woman? The pleasure of sitting and listening to a woman talk about what she liked?

Certainly the last time had been long before he'd come to Wolf Creek three years ago. Since coming to the small town he'd focused solely on work, knowing that as a twenty-eight-year-old detective he had a lot to prove to everyone, not just his co-workers, but the people of the small town, as well.

Now he felt solid in his position as the youngest

detective of three and suddenly realized his desire to be more sociable, but he knew this was not the time and Sheri was not the woman.

As she poured him a second cup of coffee he told himself he was just doing her a favor. It was obviously she wasn't yet ready for him to leave and if he looked deep within himself, prince or not, he definitely wasn't ready to call it a night.

"So, you spent your whole childhood in Philly?" Sheri asked. She'd never noticed before that Jimmy's eyes weren't just a plain chocolate-brown but rather like caramel swirled chocolates that might have pulled her into places she'd never been if she allowed them.

"What brought you to Wolf Creek?" She sat back in her chair as if unconsciously needing some distance from him. He smelled like clean male and a woodsy cologne that appealed to her senses.

"The job. I saw an advertisement for a deputy for Wolf Creek and decided to apply. I was tired of the city and ready for a different experience." He grinned at her and the warmth of his smile filled her stomach.

"I never dreamed that my different experiences would include checking out reports of wolves eating small children, hunting down a woman throwing knives at your sister and disarming an unarmed woman holding a shotgun on a clueless man chasing a pig."

She felt the warmth that swept into her cheeks. "You aren't going to let me forget that, are you?"

"Probably not," he replied easily.

"So, you like it here?"

"I feel like I've finally found home. Eventually

I'd like to build a house in the woods, maybe get a dog for company and spend my days crime-fighting and my nights relaxing in a big recliner." He nodded, his black hair shining in the overhead light. "Yeah, I definitely like it here."

She cupped her hands around her half-empty mug, knowing that the two cups of coffee would probably have her awake half the night. "It's funny, I've never been anywhere else but here and Hershey, but I've never had any desire to go anywhere else. The minute I saw this cottage and the surrounding forest, I knew I was home."

"And from the looks of your backyard you have a lot of creatures depending on you."

"The store is my job, but this place and those creatures are my passion." Her eyes sparkled brightly with that passion. "There's nothing more peaceful than seeing a deer walk without fear across the backyard. The raccoons and squirrels can be as entertaining as any movie playing on television and the birds add the music to my life."

"It sounds nice, but a little bit lonely."

"It is," she agreed. "Especially since Steve and Roxy and Marlene and Frank have hooked up. With them so busy with their own lives and Aunt Liz still missing, there are definitely moments when I feel a touch of loneliness."

She fought back the grief that always threatened to grab her by the throat when she thought of her missing aunt. Besides, the last thing she wanted to do was get upset because then she might start to stutter, an affliction she'd had since she'd been a young girl but had almost mastered now.

She couldn't get emotional and start stuttering in front of Jimmy. She'd be mortified. She'd spent a lifetime of torture being bullied by peers and most recently by the man she'd thought she loved, who had obviously not been the prince of her dreams.

Jimmy finished the last of his coffee and stared down into his empty cup. "You know, I was just thinking about that song by Air Supply, the one where there are two less lonely people in the world."

He looked up at her, his eyes dark and soulful and once again beckoning her to fall into their depths. "Since I've been in town I really don't hang out much with people other than other cops. I haven't made a lot of friends and I was just thinking maybe you and I could hang out…just while you wait for your prince…you know as friends."

He gave her an awkward smile. "Or maybe it's just a dumb idea."

She studied him intently, noting the faint hint of color that filled his lean cheeks, the insane length of his dark lashes as he cast his gaze back down into his empty cup.

She wasn't sure if it was her own loneliness she felt or his, but a hollowness welled up inside her. "I think that would be nice…as friends," she quickly added.

She wanted to make certain that he understood that she wasn't agreeing to actually date him. Heck, she wasn't even sure that's what he intended anyway.

"Great, then maybe some night we could get a drink at the tavern or see a movie or something."

"I'd like that, and now I know I've kept you here too long." She rose from the table as he did the same.

"Are you sure you feel all right about being here alone now?" he asked as she walked him to the front door.

"I'm fine. Maybe with Aunt Liz's situation I just overreacted to normal circumstances." She frowned thoughtfully as she thought of Highway's frantic barks in the backyard. "Still, there's no question in my mind that somebody was in the woods. That's the only thing that would have set off Highway."

"I'll talk to Travis first thing tomorrow morning and see if maybe he was still on the trail of that feral pig."

"Knowing it was him would definitely make me feel better." She opened the door, surprised to find she was still reluctant to tell him good-night, but it was getting late and this hadn't been a social call. "Thank you, Jimmy, for coming at a moment's notice."

He stepped past her and out the door. "Anytime, Sheri. Anytime you feel uncertain or afraid, don't hesitate to call me."

By the time Sheri closed the door behind him a warm glow infused her. There was no question that she liked Jimmy. She would even confess that she was physically drawn to him, but certainly the attraction had nothing to do with anything other than friendship.

She could use a friend, she thought as she locked the door and then began to turn out all the lights in the kitchen and living room.

There were plenty of people who were regulars at her shop, acquaintances but not real friends. With Marlene and Roxy and Aunt Liz, Sheri had never really missed having friendships with other people. Family had filled her up, but now that family had been fractured.

She entered her bedroom, where Highway lay on a rug at the foot of her bed. He raised his head, his tail beating a happy rhythm against the floor at the sight of her.

She sank down beside him and wrapped her arms around his thick, muscled neck. It was like holding a living, breathing teddy bear.

"You're a good boy, Highway," she said. He turned his head and gazed at her with adoring eyes. She released her hold on him and stood to change out of her clothes and into her nightgown. "I just wish I knew who you were barking at when I got home tonight."

As she went into the adjoining bathroom to finish getting ready for bed, she hoped Jimmy found out that it had been Travis in her backyard.

She reminded herself that there was no reason to feel uneasy. Throughout the years there had been times when hunters or hikers had accidentally come onto her property.

She left the bedroom and got into bed and shut off the light on the nightstand. Within minutes she heard the soft sound of Highway snoring.

Jimmy. She had a feeling he'd be a good friend and it would be nice to fill some of the empty evening hours with human conversation instead of the one-sided monologues she shared with Highway.

She closed her eyes and tried to bring a vision of Jimmy into her head, but instead her thoughts drifted to her missing aunt, the sound of Highway's frantic barking and the window she didn't remember opening. Had somebody followed her home or had she simply been freaked out by a car that was coincidentally going in the same direction she'd been traveling?

Despite the lingering warmth of Jimmy's visit, it took her a very long time to finally allow the uneasiness that plagued her to dissipate enough that she could fall asleep.

Something had to be done about the damned dog. The man stood in the deep cover of the woods, the only illumination a faint beam of moonlight that managed to find its way through the leafy trees that surrounded him.

The dog was like a hound from hell and had to be neutralized before he could get to Sheri. He leaned his back against a tree trunk as he stared at the now-darkened cottage.

And what had the detective been doing out here?

He'd been watching the cottage for weeks now, pleased to realize that Sheri was definitely a creature of habit. She returned home from the store about the same time each day, spent her spare time alone and often in the backyard.

She would have been an easy target, but the appearance of the detective tonight had confused him. Had the dog barking at him made Sheri afraid enough to call the law?

Surely the dog barked all the time when he was outside. That's what dogs did, they chased squirrels and barked at the wind and chased their own tails.

Maybe Detective Jimmy Carmani and Sheri were starting some sort of a relationship? If that was the case, then he'd have to move fast to take Sheri to his underground bunker where hopefully she would be a far better candidate for his intentions than her aunt and the woman before Liz.

Liz. He frowned and clenched his fists at his sides. He'd been so sure that she was the right one, so certain that she would break and become the woman he needed her to be.

But she'd proven to be too strong, too bullheaded. After three and a half months of captivity she still showed no fear, no hint of weakness. She would have to be disposed of, as Agnes Wilson had been eliminated before her.

He focused his attention back on the small, moonlit cottage. There was his future. Sheri was the right one. He knew it in his heart, felt it in his very soul.

She was sweet and soft and he had a feeling it wouldn't take her long to understand that her true destiny was to be his wife, to care take for him as she did all the wild animals in the forest.

She was the right one to take the place of his dutiful, submissive wife he'd lost. A man could only be alone for so long.

Now all he had to figure out was how to get past the dog and take what he knew belonged to him.

Chapter 3

Jimmy caught up with Travis at ten the next morning at the Wolf's Head Tavern. The place wouldn't open officially for business until noon, but Jimmy knew the owner was usually in about this time of the morning to start prepping for the day.

Jimmy knocked on the back door and Travis opened up to allow him inside the kitchen that served up mostly fried appetizers.

"I hope you've come by to tell me you've taken that shotgun away from Sheri," Travis said as he led Jimmy into the main area where mounted wolf heads glared from the walls next to booths and tables. Jimmy opted for a stool at the bar and Travis moved behind the long polished wood.

"I've got to tell you, she scared the living hell out of me the other night. There's nothing more terrifying than a woman with a gun."

Jimmy grinned. "Your chauvinism is showing, Travis."

"Yeah, well, I'm just saying women are emotional and unpredictable. I could have been killed if she'd flinched the wrong way."

"Yeah, you could have been," Jimmy agreed, not spilling to Travis that Sheri's shotgun had been unloaded. "I stopped by to see if you might have been hunting that feral pig again last night on Sheri's property?"

"No way," Travis replied, his green eyes emitting earnest truth. "You couldn't pay me enough to go out there again. Seriously man, I really thought she was going to shoot me."

"So, you weren't in her woods last night," Jimmy said to confirm the matter.

"Nope." He shook his head. "If somebody was out there it definitely wasn't me."

Jimmy believed him. He and Travis had always had a good relationship and he knew that if Travis had been in Sheri's backyard the night before he would have confessed to it. "That's what I needed to know." Jimmy slid off the stool.

"Is Sheri having some sort of problems?" Travis asked, genuine concern in his expression.

"She just thought somebody was skulking around her place last night and naturally we thought of you."

Travis frowned and shook his head once again. "As if that family hasn't been through enough already. First Liz's kidnapping and then Steve's ex-girlfriend trying to kill Roxy. Then his ex's boyfriend trying to kill Marlene... You'd think enough was enough for that family."

"Hopefully enough is enough and there's no danger in Sheri's future. At least something good has come out of all this. Both of my partners have found the loves of their lives and are happier than I've ever seen them."

Travis snorted. "Women don't do anything but complicate your life. I'd rather hunt a feral pig than deal with a woman's drama."

Jimmy laughed. "I guess we're all built differently when it comes to dealing with the opposite sex. Thanks for your time, Travis."

Together the two men returned to the kitchen where Jimmy went out the back door. He got into his car and sat, oddly upset to discover that Travis hadn't been the person in the woods Sheri had been convinced was there. It would have not only eased Sheri's concern to discover it had been Travis, but it would have also eased some of his own.

Travis was right, the Marcoli family had been through more crime and drama in the past three and a half months than any family should ever experience in an entire lifetime. Although the threats to Marlene and Roxy had been deemed not connected to Liz's disappearance, the last thing Jimmy wanted was for anything else to happen to any of the Marcolis.

Especially Sheri. A tiny thrill shot through him as he thought of spending more time with her. She'd surprised him by agreeing to hang out with him. Oh, she'd made it clear that it was a temporary thing just until she found her prince.

But he'd enjoy whatever time she was willing to give him. It definitely beat his usual evenings after work, having a few beers with other cops and talking shop, or flopping on his sofa to watch a couple of hours of mindless television shows.

Jimmy had spent most of his life with a loneliness deep inside him, but lately the feeling seemed to gnaw a bigger hole in his gut.

He thought often about a desire to have what his partners had found: love and commitment with women who would stand by their sides for the rest of their lives. But at his very core he didn't believe he'd ever have it, and he knew with certainty that the woman, if she really existed, wouldn't be Sheri.

At least he was finally dipping his toe into social waters rather than being an all-work, no-play kind of guy. Even if he wasn't a forever kind of man, that didn't mean he couldn't date.

He headed to the police station located on Main Street. Stores were opening their doors and a variety of people had taken to the sidewalks. It was easy to spot the unfamiliar faces of tourists who were visiting for the day and it was mostly the tourist industry that kept the small town of Wolf Creek alive.

The town boasted a long history that was highlighted in many of the quaint restaurants and bed-and-breakfasts. Specialty shops lined Main Street, like The Treasure Trove, an antique junk store where Marlene Marcoli had lived in the upstairs apartment, a taxidermy shop that displayed a variety of stuffed animals that were indigenous to the area, and it wouldn't be long before Marlene's Magic Bites would add confectionery delights for both tourists and locals.

He parked and headed into the station, where he

greeted Officer Wade Peterson who stood duty in the common area. "Morning, Wade," Jimmy said.

"A little late this morning, aren't you?" Wade teased as he buzzed open the door that led to the large area where police desks and officers were the decor. "Hot date last night?"

"Yeah right, because I do that so often," Jimmy replied drily. He pushed open the door that led to the inner office and immediately spied his two partners at their desks.

Steve Kincaid shot him a lazy grin. "Ah, look what the cat finally dragged in."

"Nice of you to join us this morning," Frank Delaney added.

Jimmy sat at his desk between the two. "I've been working already, interviewing a potential suspect."

Frank frowned. "A suspect for what?"

Jimmy quickly explained first his call to Sheri's house and finding her holding Travis at gunpoint and then his subsequent visit the night before. "Travis swears it wasn't him on her property last night."

"It could have been anyone or it might have been nothing more than her imagination," Steve said. "Maybe with everything that has happened with all the other members of her family she's feeling particularly vulnerable right now."

"Maybe," Jimmy agreed reluctantly. "But she was pretty sure somebody was out in those woods by the way Highway was reacting when she got home from the store."

"Maybe Highway was just acting like a normal dog and barking just to bark," Frank said.

"According to Sheri, Highway isn't a normal dog. He's been highly trained by Jed."

"Then maybe Sheri just wanted to see you," Steve said with a sly look in his blue eyes. "After all, two of the three detectives in town have found love with her sisters. Maybe she's looking for a trifecta."

Jimmy laughed and shook his head. "No way. I'm the antithesis of what she's looking for in a man."

"What does that mean?" Steve asked.

"Sheri is waiting for a blond-haired, blue-eyed prince to ride into her life, and if he's a prince you know he'll be tall. She's definitely not looking for a short meatball like me."

His partners laughed. "You aren't round enough to be a meatball," Frank protested.

"And you aren't short, you just aren't overly tall," Steve added.

"I'm average," Jimmy said. "And if Sheri is looking for a prince, she's definitely not interested in an average kind of guy like me."

"You definitely aren't an average guy, Jimmy," Frank said. "Average guys don't have black belts in martial arts training and they don't have a brain like a computer that stores even the most minute detail of a crime."

"This is a stupid conversation," Jimmy said. "What's going on with our armed robbery case?" He was more than ready to change the topic of conversation.

It didn't matter what Sheri thought about him. Jimmy wasn't made for any kind of a long-term love and Sheri definitely wasn't the type of woman to be a "friend with benefits" or a drive-by, hit-and-run kind of woman.

As the three men began to discuss the details of the armed robbery, Jimmy shoved thoughts of Sheri out of his head. He was a detective and that was all he would ever be. He'd never be a husband or a father and he'd made peace with that fact a long time ago.

"Go home," Abe said to Sheri at three in the afternoon. "I've got you covered for the rest of the night and I know that you usually like to spend some time in the later afternoons and evenings with your critters."

"Thanks, Abe, but I think I'll go ahead and hang out until closing," Sheri replied.

"With Marlene not working here anymore you should probably hire on somebody. You can't keep showing up early in the mornings and working until closing. You have to have a life outside of the store."

"You're right," Sheri conceded. "I'll put a sign in the window tomorrow and see who shows up." She frowned thoughtfully. "Maybe I should give Michael Arello another chance."

Marlene had fired the young man when she'd caught him stealing food, but it was later learned that Michael was trying to feed three young orphans who were holed up all alone in a mountain cabin. Their grandmother had died of a heart attack in town and nobody had known that she was raising her three grandchildren.

Abe grunted. "His heart was in the right place but he made some bad choices. He's not a bad kid, he's just young."

"He's old enough to need a job. I think I'll give him a call." Sheri went into the small office in the back room and pulled up her employee records, both past and current. It took her only a minute to find Michael's contact information. She called and left a message on his voice mail.

That finished, she returned to the front of the store and with Abe standing behind the counter she wandered over to the four quilt racks that displayed beautiful handmade quilts, including the one Jason King had brought in two days ago.

"I hope this one sells quickly," she said as she touched the colorful patchwork. "I have a feeling the King family is in crisis. Jason was in the other day and said his father isn't doing much work in the fields, that he disappears from the family for long periods of time and Jason doesn't know where he goes or what he does."

"That poor kid has more on his shoulders than most men twice his age," Abe replied. "But at least they won't go hungry. The community will always help their own."

Sheri nodded. That's what she admired about the Amish, their sense of community, of family. Like she'd had with her aunt Liz and Marlene and Roxy before the rug had been pulled out from beneath them with Aunt Liz's disappearance.

It frightened her just a little bit that the grief that had been with her for the past three months each time she thought of her missing aunt had begun to dissipate, as if the last vestiges of hope had left her and resignation had moved in to reign.

She felt as if she was moving on with the unspoken knowledge that she'd never see her aunt again. There was no rational reason for Liz's absence other than foul play that had ended in her death.

It would be nice at this point to have some closure, to have remains to bury, to know the reason everything had happened. She would never, ever be able to guess why anyone would want to harm somebody as kind and as loving as Liz Marcoli.

Part of the reason she was reluctant to call it a day and head home was that she was still a little nervous about the events of the night before.

She knew she was probably being silly, but danger had come too close too often to everyone in the Marcoli family except her. Last night before Jimmy had arrived she'd instinctively felt threatened, sensed danger lurking nearby. A case of the heebie-jeebies or some sort of primal feminine survival instinct?

All thoughts of danger and family disappeared as the door to the shop swung open to admit two adults and three small children who instantly began to run wild among the aisles.

"Jerry, Richard and Susan, come back here right now," the harried mother exclaimed, and then shot an apologetic smile at Sheri. "Sorry, cooped up in the car too long."

"We're going to Hershey Park!" A little boy about six raced up to stand next to his mother, his slender body vibrating with excitement.

"And we're going to see how they make chocolate." The little girl joined the discussion.

"That will be such fun. Where are you coming from?" Sheri asked. She noticed that the man had taken the other little boy to the restroom.

"Indiana. It's been a long drive," the mother replied.

Sheri smiled. "The good news is you're almost there. Hershey is less than thirty miles from here."

"That's great. We just couldn't drive by this place without stopping in to see some of the Amish things you have for sale."

Sheri led the woman to the area where Abraham Zooker's beautiful furniture was displayed and then to the special cheeses that Isaaic, Abraham's brother, provided. There were fresh herbs provided by Sarah Fisher, who had the best herb garden in the county, and the quilts and embroidered sacks and bags that several of the women in the Amish community brought in to sell.

They finally left with bags of chips and sodas and all three children sporting Wolf Creek hats complete with stuffed little wolves on the top.

"I've just been reminded why I never had kids," Abe said. "I don't think I ever had the energy for them."

"I can't wait to have children," Sheri said, her heart warming at the very thought. Her head filled with a little boy with dark curly hair and she frowned. No, that wasn't right. Her children would all be blond, like their father.

"You might want to find a man before you think about having any children," Abe observed.

"I don't have to find him. He'll find me when the time is right."

Abe eyed her in bemusement. "He's not going to find you as long as you're holed up in the store ten hours a day."

"You never know who might walk through that door," Sheri replied. "One of these days it will be the man of my dreams."

At that moment Michael Arello walked in. Sheri grinned at Abe. "Definitely not the man I was looking for."

"I got your message that you wanted to talk to me." At twenty-one years old Michael Arello was a handsome young man when a sullen cast to his lips wasn't present. At the moment there was no sign of the sullenness, just a wary glint in his brown eyes.

"Come on back to the office and let's have a talk," Sheri said.

It only took fifteen minutes of speaking with Michael to pin down the hours he'd work, talk about what had happened when he'd worked before and been fired, and elicit a promise from him that he'd be a good employee.

"You sure you know what you're doing with him?" Abe asked when Michael left the store.

"Probably not, but I believe everyone deserves a second chance and I think at heart he is a good kid."

"You're a good woman, Sheri. You've got a heart just like your aunt Liz. Of the three of you girls I see her in you more than in Roxy and Marlene."

Sheri smiled, touched by his words. "Thanks, Abe."

"That Roxy, she's got firecracker in her and Marlene has always seemed kind of cool and distant. But you have all the qualities Liz had." He flushed, as if realizing he'd spoken of her in the past tense.

"You have to remember that Roxy lived with our real mother, Ramona, for the first seven years of her life, and the experience was the stuff of nightmares. Even Marlene spent four years in Ramona's care before she showed up at Aunt Liz's and left her there."

"And you?" Abe asked.

"I was just a couple of months old. I have no memories of anyone else as a mother other than Aunt L...L...Liz." She bit her tongue and swallowed against the sudden emotion that threatened to prompt the stuttering.

"I'm sorry, Sheri. Damn, I'm sorry," Abe said, his blue eyes growing darker in hue.

She shook her head. "It's fine. I'm fine." She stiffened her shoulders and pasted a smile on her face as the door opened and an older woman walked in. "Welcome to the Roadside Stop. Just let me know if I can help you with anything."

The woman nodded, a long salt-and-pepper ponytail swaying across her lower back. "Thanks, I'm just browsing."

Sheri moved behind the register as Abe went to the storage room to take care of cleaning shelves and checking stock. Sheri watched the skinny, older woman checking out the items for sale and her thoughts suddenly filled with a vision of Jimmy Carmani.

Yes, it would be nice to have a friend to hang out with, to spend a few hours a week chatting with him and enjoying his company. He appeared to have a fairly laid-back personality, as did she, and neither of them were in the market for anything romantic, so it could be an ideal friendship.

The older woman carried a cold canned drink to the register and pulled several dollar bills from a purse that looked worn. "This should do it," she said, her chocolate-brown eyes intent on Sheri.

"Just traveling through town?" Sheri asked as she rang up the drink.

"I haven't decided yet. The town seems quite charming. I may decide to hang around." She smiled.

"It's a wonderful place to live with terrific people," Sheri said as she handed her the change.

"Thanks, maybe I'll see you around." Without a backward glance the woman went out the door with her cold drink in hand.

By eight that evening Sheri felt a dread creeping over her and was stunned to realize it was the anxiety of going home. It was an emotion she'd never known before. Normally she was eager to head back to her cottage and snuggle with Highway.

On impulse she pulled out her phone and punched in Jimmy's number. He answered immediately. "Hey, Jimmy, it's Sheri. Are you still at work?"

"Actually I am," he replied. "But not for too much longer. What's up?"

"I was just wondering if maybe you'd like to meet me at the tavern for a cold beer in about a half an hour or so." Her stomach clenched. She'd never initiated a date with a man before. No, she corrected herself. It wasn't a date, it was just two people getting together for a little conversation and a beer.

"Sounds perfect to me. I might even indulge in some of Travis's hot wings with that beer. Shall we make it around eight-thirty?"

He sounded ridiculously pleased that she had called and a sweet wave of answering pleasure swept through her. "I'll see you at eight-thirty," she agreed.

The store had been quiet for the past hour, so she sent Abe home, locked the front door and then went into the bathroom with her purse in hand.

She stared at her reflection in the mirror and then dug a brush from her purse and quickly pulled it through her shoulder-length hair. There had been a time when she'd been jealous of Roxy's rich black curls, of Marlene's cool blond strands, but as she'd gotten older she'd made peace with her chestnut-brown hair. At least it was thick and required little more than a daily brushing.

She thought about lipstick, but never wore it. She also considered mascara but again, makeup had never been her thing and she wondered why she was even thinking about it now. It wasn't like she was going to meet the man of her dreams. She was just going to hang out with Jimmy. She settled for a quick spritz of her purse-size bottle of her favorite perfume and then left the bathroom.

It was almost eight-twenty by the time she got into her truck to head to the Wolf's Head Tavern. Twilight had fallen, painting the landscape in deep purple shadows as she pulled out of the parking lot.

Almost immediately she saw the car that pulled out of a wooded area near the road and fell in behind her. Every nerve in her body tensed. With the sun low in the sky it was impossible to tell if the car was black or blue, but it was definitely pacing her.

When she slowed, it slowed. When she sped up, it also sped up, keeping enough distance that Sheri couldn't tell anything about the driver. She didn't know if the driver was male or female, but she knew for certain that just like the night before, somebody was following her.

What was going on? Why would anyone be interested in her movements? With everything that had happened with her aunt and her sisters over the past three and a half months, Sheri was definitely feeling freaked out even though the driver of the vehicle did nothing to present imminent danger.

She was grateful she wasn't going home alone to her little cottage where she only had a well-trained dog and an empty shotgun if she needed protection.

At least she was headed to a public area where a detective was waiting for her and there would be other people around. Her fingers were tight on the steering wheel, her back stiffened as if bracing for a blow.

Even though she hadn't seen the color of the car the night before, the headlights looked the same and she was certain the car behind her now was the same one from the day before.

A sigh of relief shuddered through her when she turned into the Wolf's Head Tavern and the car continued on, disappearing into the gloom of the coming night.

She pulled into a parking space, cut her engine and dropped her forehead to the steering wheel as she waited for her heartbeat to slow to a more normal pace.

Was she looking for a bogeyman who didn't exist? Had the car really been following her or was she taking innocent coincidences and making them into something nefarious?

Was she looking for trouble when there was none?

She supposed it was possible that the events of the past few months were finally catching up with her, making her paranoid when she shouldn't be.

She raised her head, checked her reflection in her rearview mirror and then headed inside the tavern, trying to ignore the faint simmer of fear that still remained deep inside her.

Chapter 4

Jimmy sat at a big round table for six. He wasn't going to lie, he was immensely disappointed that Steve and Frank had invited themselves and Sheri's sisters to join Sheri and him.

He'd hoped for some quiet time, just him and Sheri alone, but maybe this was fate reminding him that he shouldn't want anything but a friendship with Sheri, and that meant all his friends gathered together.

He sensed her presence the moment she walked into the dimly lit room. At first glance the look on her face radiated something akin to fear and Jimmy tensed in response. Then their eyes met, a warm smile curved her lips and he instantly relaxed.

He started to rise, but Roxy beat him to the punch, jumping out of her chair and running to Sheri. She grabbed her sister's hand and pulled her to the table.

"Isn't this fun?" Roxy said as she gestured Sheri to the empty seat next to Jimmy. "When Steve heard Jimmy was meeting you for a drink, he decided to make it a little family reunion for us, since we've all been so busy with our own lives lately."

"Where's Tommy?" Sheri asked, referring to Steve's young son, as she sat.

"At my place with grandma babysitting," Steve replied. "My mom still can't believe he's back and she can't get enough time with him."

"Which hasn't been a bad thing for us," Roxy replied as she grinned at Steve.

"She's spoiling him rotten," Steve added. "As is Roxy, as well."

"Children are meant to be spoiled," Marlene said. Frank's hand covered hers on top of the table and Jimmy knew they both were probably thinking of the baby Marlene had lost in her previous abusive marriage. The only reason Jimmy knew about it was because Frank had confided in him that Marlene's ex-husband had been abusive and when she'd been pregnant had kicked her down a flight of stairs. She'd lost the baby as a result. Travis ambled over to the table with a lazy smile on his face. "I'll take orders from everyone, but whatever Sheri wants is on me tonight."

"That's not necessary," Sheri protested.

Travis shook his head to indicate he wasn't taking no for an answer. "That was my offer when you let me go the other night without putting a bullet in my black heart. Now, what can I get for everyone?"

After taking orders for hot wings, mozzarella sticks and pitchers of beer, Travis left. Marlene arched a perfectly plucked eyebrow. "A bullet through his heart? What did I miss?"

"Absolutely nothing," Sheri said and turned to focus on Jimmy. "Have you had a good day?"

"It's good now," he replied, then leaned closer to her so the others couldn't hear him over the din in the room. "Although it could have been better if it was just two friends getting together rather than the men I've already spent way too much of my life with today."

"I have to admit I was looking forward to a little quiet time with you," she confessed. Between the heavenly scent of her that drifted to him and her words, Jimmy warmed from head to toe.

"Hey, what are you two whispering about?" Roxy asked. "Do I smell a little romance in the air?"

"Absolutely not," Sheri replied. "Jimmy and I have just decided that it would be nice to have some friend time together."

"Just friends," Jimmy reiterated.

"That's good, because Ninja Jimmy has told us a hundred times that he never intends to do the wife thing," Frank said.

Sheri looked at Jimmy again. "Ninja Jimmy?"

Jimmy's cheeks grew hot. "Have you noticed that my partners are jerks? Frank is just referring to the fact that when I was younger I was pretty heavy into the martial arts."

Sheri smiled at him, her whiskey-colored eyes sparkling bright. "That's not a bad thing. You never know when you might need a ninja."

They all laughed and at that moment Travis and a waitress arrived with frosty glasses and the pitchers of beer. "Food will be up in just a few minutes," he said.

Beers were poured for everyone and the conversation swirled around the table as Roxy talked about the business at the Dollhouse and Marlene spoke about her work on the new bakery.

Jimmy fought against a wealth of disappointment. When Sheri had called him to meet, this definitely wasn't what he'd had in mind. However he only had himself to blame as he'd been the one who had mentioned having a drink with Sheri to Steve. From that moment on the evening event had exploded out of Jimmy's control.

Still, while he sipped his beer he enjoyed watching Sheri interact with her sisters. He liked watching the play of a variety of emotions that crossed her pretty features.

She had a heart-shaped face that emphasized her large beautiful eyes and small impish nose. Her lips were cupidlike, slightly plump and inviting. She would never make a good suspect in a crime. Her features were too expressive and he had a feeling a lie crossing her lush lips would immediately be obvious.

By the time Travis had delivered their food to the table, the conversation had turned to the painful subject of Liz Marcoli's disappearance and the case that had gone stone-cold.

Two days before the sisters had been told that the search of mountain cabins had finally been called off. For weeks a team of officers had searched lean-tos and cabins and any other structures hidden in the thick woods up the mountainside, but finally Chief of Police Brad Krause had called off

the search as he could no longer justify the over-
time and manpower used without further evidence.

"And nothing ever came from comparing Agnes
Wilson's disappearance to Aunt Liz's?" Sheri asked.

"Agnes was a few years younger than Liz and
other than the connections we would have expected
to find with the two living in a small town, there
was really nothing to tie the two women together,"
Jimmy explained.

Agnes's case was much like Liz's. The sixty-four-
year-old woman had simply vanished from her home
two years before.

"I didn't realize Jed Wilson was Agnes's nephew
until recently," Roxy said.

"I didn't realize that until now," Marlene replied.

"We questioned him at the time of Agnes's disappearance," Frank said. "The two weren't very close.
Jed said they just drifted apart after Jed's mother's
death. He had a solid alibi for the time Agnes disappeared and there was no motive to believe he had
anything to do with it, so he was never a suspect."

"We never really had any suspects in Agnes's
case," Steve added.

"I still think Edward Cardell had something to do
with Aunt Liz's disappearance," Roxy exclaimed, her
dark eyes flashing with anger.

Edward had been Liz's secret boyfriend at the time
of her disappearance. Jimmy and his partners had
looked hard at the man for the crime, but ultimately
had come up with no evidence to tie him to anything.

"I can't believe he's dating Treetie now. It sure
didn't take him long to move on with his affections,"
Roxy continued, her voice filled with distaste.

Jimmy thought of Patricia Burns, aka Treetie. She'd been Liz's best friend and like a beloved auntie to the three sisters as they'd grown up. But Treetie's decision to date Edward following Liz's disappearance had fractured any relationship the Marcoli sisters had had with her.

Edward and Treetie were still on a persons-of-interest list that the three detectives had on file, but no evidence, no real motive had come to light to take it any further.

A glance at Sheri let Jimmy know the conversation was upsetting her. He fought a sudden impulse to reach out and cover her small hand with his, to somehow comfort her without stepping out of bounds.

Instead he did the only thing he knew to do, he shoved his basket of hot wings toward her. "Try one," he said. "Travis might not know how to read No Hunting signs, but he makes a mean hot wing."

He was pleased by her smile as she reached for one of the appetizers. "Frank, anything happening with that house of yours?" he asked in an attempt to get the conversation off the missing woman.

"Got the for-sale sign up, and Marlene and I have already found a potential place to buy off Maple Circle," Frank replied.

"That beige two-story one with the red shutters and the sweeping wide veranda?" Roxy asked.

"That's the one," Marlene replied, her blue eyes lit with excitement. "It has a huge kitchen and everything has been updated."

"That definitely wouldn't excite me," Sheri said ruefully. She turned to Frank. "But, I hope it all works out for the two of you."

"No matter what, it's going to work out for us," Frank declared. The loving look he gave Marlene welled up an ache deep in Jimmy's soul. What was it like to feel that way about another human being? What was it like to know with such certainty that the other person loved you as much?

He'd experienced it only once many years ago and it had been such a fleeting thing that he had known in his heart, in his very soul he'd never have the opportunity again.

By ten o'clock both Steve and Roxy, and Frank and Marlene finished up the last of their beers and snacks and prepared to leave. Jimmy stood, assuming the night was over for him as well, but Sheri touched his arm and looked up at him.

"Could you stay a little bit longer?" she asked.

"Of course," he replied, realizing he was far too pleased by her request. "I'll see you two in the morning at Roxy's," he said to Frank and Steve. At least three times a week the detectives began their days with a big breakfast at Roxy's Dollhouse restaurant. "And, Marlene, I can't wait for that bakery to open."

She smiled as she twined her arm with Frank's. "I'm working on it. I've got electricians and plumbers and Sheetrock people all working together to get me up and running as quickly as possible."

Within minutes they were gone, leaving Sheri and Jimmy alone. Friends, just friends, he reminded himself as she scooted her chair closer to his and his heart beat just a little bit faster than normal.

"That was a surprise," Sheri said when everyone was gone. Truthfully she wasn't sure if she'd been happy to walk in and see the whole gang or slightly disappointed that it wasn't just Jimmy.

"When I mentioned that I was meeting you here after work, the last thing I expected was for Steve to invite not only himself but Roxy, Frank and Marlene, too." Jimmy cupped his hands around his half-empty beer mug. "To be honest, I was looking forward to a little time just with you."

"It's definitely hard to get a word in edgewise when Roxy is around. As much as I love my big sister, she talks too much," Sheri said ruefully.

"And you don't talk enough," Jimmy replied.

"You're right, I don't, especially not if I'm in a group. I do much better one-on-one." She looked up as Travis appeared at their table.

"More beer?" he asked.

Sheri shook her head. "Not for me, but I would take a diet cola."

"Make that two," Jimmy said, and shoved his beer mug aside. As Travis left them, Jimmy turned his gaze back to her. Sheri had meant to talk to him about the fact that she believed she was being followed, that she was afraid to go home alone.

But with his beautiful brown eyes focused intently on her the last thing she wanted to discuss was the fact that she might be overreacting to anything. "Tell me about your life in Philly," she said. "You know so much about my life and I feel like I know so little about yours."

"There isn't a lot to tell. I already told you that I was abandoned as a baby in a shoe box outside a police station and spent most of my youth being shuffled from one foster home to another. I was what they considered a difficult placement." His eyes darkened as if he'd touched a memory nerve that was still exposed and painful.

He gave a small shake of his head and then grinned at her, displaying his beautiful straight teeth. "By the time I was kicked out of the system at eighteen I fell into some bad company. At that time my goal was to become the biggest badass in Philly."

"Is that when you started the martial arts training?" She leaned slightly toward him, finding herself interested in all the things that had gone into forming the man he had become. Now that she'd decided he was going to be a friend, she wanted to know everything about him, past and present.

He nodded, a strand of his dark hair slipping forward across his forehead. Sheri fought the desire to reach up and shove it back, to feel the texture of it beneath her fingers.

The very idea spoke of the uneasiness that still gnawed in her stomach. Surely the impulse to touch him in any way was driven by her desire to be distracted from her own thoughts, she assured herself. It had nothing to do with the fact that she found him far too attractive.

"At first I started training just to get tough, but it didn't take me long before I realized I loved it. I loved the discipline and I developed a strong relationship with my sensei, who encouraged me to use my powers for good, not evil. As a result when I turned twenty-one I went into the police academy and that eventually brought me here."

At that moment Travis returned to the table with

their soft drinks. "Sheri, we're square, right? You forgive me for the other night."

"I forgive you, but I might not be so forgiving if it happens again," she warned.

"Trust me, it won't," he promised, and then left their table.

Sheri looked at Jimmy expectantly, wanting him to continue to tell her about himself.

"Actually, that's enough about me," he said. "To be honest, I don't know that much about you, aside from being a close relative of a victim of a crime and that you have two sisters, one who tends to talk too much."

She had a feeling there was much more in his past to explore. He had some darkness about him that had momentarily deepened the hue of his eyes and tightened his handsome features with tension. But he'd shared what he was comfortable sharing and she wouldn't push him for more.

"You know our mother abandoned us with Aunt Liz when we were just kids. But I had a wonderful childhood as far as having my aunt and my sisters beside me. It was a little less wonderful when I started school."

She paused to take a drink of her soda. She rarely told people about her stuttering issue, but if she and Jimmy were going to be good friends, then she thought she should tell him about it, especially since it still raised its ugly head occasionally.

"For most of my school years I was a terrible stutterer. The favorite saying of my peers was, 'Sheri, stupid stutter Sheri, she'll never find a boy to marry.'" Her cheeks warmed at the memories of those horrible days. She had been tormented into being a silent, withdrawn student at school who had no friends.

"Kids can be crazy cruel," he replied. "If I'd been there I would have beaten up those jerks."

Sheri smiled. "I had Roxy to do that for me. I can't tell you how often she was in trouble for threatening some kid who'd been teasing me."

"But you don't stutter now."

"Yes, I do, if I get overly emotional or upset or frightened. I'm just warning you in advance that it's a part of me. If we're going to be friends, then you should know about it."

"Oh, we're definitely going to be friends," Jimmy said and there was a glimmer of promise in his eyes that made her heart leap expectantly. "I already like everything I know about you."

"You don't know everything," she countered, half-teasingly.

"Then tell me everything I don't know, especially the bad things, so I know what I'm getting myself into." His eyes had lightened to a dark caramel as he teased her.

"No way," she replied with a laugh. "That's what friendship is all about, getting to know the positive and negatives about each other as the relationship grows."

"Since I'm new to all this, I didn't know there were rules to being friends."

"There are definitely rules, like you have my back and I have yours. Friends forgive each other their flaws and they want only the best for each other. They share secrets and can be trusted without question."

"That sounds easy enough," he said.

"Actually good friendships are hard to maintain They're like little flowers that have to be fed and watered all the time in order to flourish."

"I'll be glad to feed and water you whenever you need it." His grin teased her and she realized again that she liked this man.

"I like you, Jimmy. I liked you when you were helping us with Aunt Liz's case and I like you now," she said with the refreshing honesty she was known for.

"I liked you when we were actively working the case, but I thought you were very quiet and shy."

"I was always in the police station with Roxy and Marlene, and Roxy especially has never known a silence she doesn't want to fill. I'm usually pretty quiet when they're around, but I'm not really shy. I couldn't be and run the store."

"Business is good?"

"We're heading into the best part of the tourist season, so yes, things are going well at the store. Marlene has quit working there to focus on her bakery and today I rehired Michael Arello as a part-time worker."

Jimmy raised a dark brow. "Do you think that's a good idea?"

"I guess only time will tell. At least we all know why he was caught stealing food first from Roxy's restaurant and then from my store. He had bad judgment but good intentions."

"Last time I checked on the three kids he found in that mountain cabin they were doing well with their foster family in Hershey. I think the foster parents might be considering adopting all three of the kids."

"That's nice to hear. Those kids deserve to have a happy ending." Sheri frowned as she suddenly thought about the car she believed had followed her here. It was getting late and they both had to get up and work the next morning. She really should call an end to the evening, but she was reluctant to get back into her truck and head home.

"Are you okay since the scare last night?" he asked, as if he could read her thoughts.

She hesitated before replying. "Actually, I got a little freaked out driving here from the store. I swear the minute I hit the highway, a car pulled off the side of the road and followed me." She gave a little unsteady laugh. "I think maybe last night freaked me out a bit more than I admitted."

Jimmy didn't return her laugh. Instead he leaned closer to her, his eyes once again a deep, dark brown. "Somebody followed you when you left the store? Somebody who pulled out of the woods?"

"That's what it looked like to me." Her heart thrummed anxiously as she realized he wasn't scoffing at her words, but rather appeared to be taking her quite seriously.

"What kind of vehicle was it?"

She could tell he was in full cop mode now, the relaxed lines of his face taut with tension, making him only more handsome with a small hint of danger sculpting his features.

"Definitely a car, but I couldn't tell if it was black or dark blue. I think it was a car that followed me last night, too."

"Did you get a tag number?"

Sheri looked at him, stricken by her stupidity. "No, I didn't even think about it. I was just so scared. When I turned in here the car went on down Main and I thought maybe I'd just imagined that I was being followed because of what happened last night."

"I don't like it. I don't like the idea of somebody following you and I definitely don't like the idea of you being afraid."

She wasn't sure why, but his concern made her feel better. At least he wasn't accusing her of being some kind of a hysterical female jumping at her own shadow.

He looked at his watch. "It's getting late. Let's get out of here and I'll follow you home and make sure you're safe and sound."

She opened her mouth to protest, but then closed it and nodded. "I'd appreciate that."

It didn't take long for them to leave the tavern and for Sheri to pull out of the parking lot with Jimmy's car on her tail.

There was no question that there was comfort in the sight of his headlights just behind her, in the knowledge that he was watching her back.

She had no idea if she'd mistaken the car's intent on the way to the tavern. She only knew that with the two incidents in two nights, she was more than a little on edge.

Maybe it was because Aunt Liz was missing, or because Roxy had nearly been killed by Steve's former girlfriend and Marlene had found her life in danger by that girlfriend's crazy lover.

Perhaps she was looking for trouble where none

existed. She felt almost embarrassed as Jimmy pulled up next to her truck in front of her cottage.

As she stepped out of her truck the only sounds that greeted her were wonderfully normal…the faint whisper of the wind through the treetops and night insects singing their comforting, familiar songs.

Jimmy joined her and together they walked to the front door. "Why don't I come in and look around just to set your mind at ease?" he suggested.

"I feel like I've already taken advantage of you by having you follow me home," she protested.

He smiled and lightly touched the tip of her nose with his index finger. "You can't take advantage of a friend."

She gave him a warm smile and then turned and unlocked her front door. She didn't want to think about how her nose burned with a pleasant heat from his simple touch.

Highway stood just inside the door, his tail wagging as he caught sight of Sheri. She grabbed hold of Jimmy's hand. "Highway, zocar." She released Jimmy's hand. "I just told him you were safe."

Jimmy eyed her curiously as Highway sniffed his leg, then his hand and then wagged his tail once again. "What language did you use?" he asked curiously when Highway returned to Sheri's side.

"No real language. It's something Jed makes up when he trains a dog for protection. It's nonsensical and specific to each dog. It's so that bad people can't command the dog because they can't guess the right commands."

"So, if you or I said 'attack' to Highway?"

"He doesn't know that word," she replied, and

scratched Highway behind an ear. "There's no need
for you to look around. Everything is fine here,"
she said as the dog lay down at her feet. "Otherwise Highway would be acting differently. But I can't
thank you enough for coming here tonight. I don't
know, maybe I'm just now processing the horror of
the last couple of months."

"Maybe," he agreed. "You've definitely had plenty
of excitement in your life lately. Is it permissible for
a friend to give another friend a hug good-night?"
he asked.

Sheri realized at that moment how badly she
wanted to be held, how hungry she was for big, solid
arms to surround her. She'd thought she'd managed
to tamp down the disquiet that had simmered inside
her for the past two days, but she'd been wrong.

"I think a hug would be a great way to end the
night."

Before the words were completely out of her
mouth he had her in his arms. And they were big and
strong and surrounded her with warmth and a sense
of protection and security she'd never felt before.

As he held her around the waist, she reached
up and wound her arms around his neck, melting
against him for just a brief delicious moment before
she broke the embrace and stepped out of his arms.

"Good night, Jimmy."

"Good night, Sheri."

The instant he stepped out of the door, a sense of
loneliness immediately gripped Sheri's heart. In the
shelter of Jimmy's arms she'd forgotten all about any
potential danger that might be near. More unsettling
was the fact that as she'd smelled the woodsy scent

of him, cuddled into his firmly muscled chest, she'd also momentarily forgotten about any blond prince that held her future.

Chapter 5

"Detectives, in my office," Chief of Police Brad Krause yelled across the room.

Frank stifled a yawn as he got up from his chair and Steve grabbed his mug of coffee to carry into the chief's office with him. The three of them had only walked into the building minutes before. They'd started their Monday morning as they usually did, with a big breakfast at Roxy's restaurant and then had headed here.

Jimmy wondered what was up. It was rare for Krause to call an early morning meet, especially when there were no real pressing cases on their desks. Even though Liz was still missing, the case was cold enough not to be pressing anymore.

"Shut the door," Krause said once the three were inside. He motioned them to the chairs in front of his desk.

Brad Krause was relatively young for a chief of police. He was in his mid-thirties, with shaggy brown hair. It was only when you looked into his intelligent green eyes that you recognized he was an old soul.

"I got a phone call this morning just after six from our good mayor." Krause frowned and Jimmy wondered if he was irritated because he'd been awakened from sleep or if he and Ralph Storm were butting heads again, which they did on a regular basis.

"He's worried that we're in the middle of a crime crisis that might affect tourism for the town," Brad said.

The three detectives looked at each other and then back at their boss. "A crime crisis?" Jimmy repeated with more than a hint of disbelief.

Brad nodded. "With everything that has happened in recent months concerning the Marcoli family and now this armed robbery at the convenience store…"

"Solved," Steve replied. "At least we think we've solved it."

"We just need one more interview with the clerk who was on duty during the robbery and then we should have it all cleared up," Frank added.

"Does one of you want to catch me up on who you're arresting?" Brad asked drily.

"We believe it was an inside job. The clerk and her boyfriend cooked up the whole scheme," Jimmy explained. "We're pretty sure another round of questioning of her and she'll break."

"Isn't she like sixteen?" Brad asked.

"Seventeen and six-months pregnant, and her boyfriend, Ned Manning, is twenty-two. We're going to tell her we intend to charge him with statutory rape unless she talks to us about the details of the robbery," Frank said. "And then we're going to arrest him for statutory rape anyway."

"Sounds like a plan," Krause said with a satisfied nod.

"As far as the latest cases concerning Roxy and Marlene Marcoli, they've been cleaned up. The only two unsolved we've got on our desks are Agnes Wilson, which has been a cold case for some time, and Liz Marcoli," Steve said.

"And we've run out of leads on that case," Jimmy added.

Chief Krause frowned once again. "I don't know why but that case has Storm chewing on my butt with a frenzy. His wife was friendly with Liz."

"We've explored every avenue possible at this point," Jimmy said. "Unless we get some new evidence or leads our hands are pretty well tied. There's no place else for us to go."

"Keep looking," Krause said. "Keep digging. Ralph is looking for reelection in November. He doesn't want any more crimes in town to give somebody an opportunity to use them against him when voting time comes. He wants a nice, quiet summer."

"Don't we all," Steve replied.

With that, the three detectives were dismissed. They left the office and pulled chairs up to Steve's desk. "So, we don't just have to worry about solving crimes, we've also got to be concerned about Ralph Storm's election chances?" Jimmy said with disgust.

"Ralph Storm is a pompous jerk," Steve added.

Neither Frank nor Jimmy objected to Steve's assessment of the mayor. There was nothing worse than a big fish in a little pond and forty-year-old Storm thought he owned the town of Wolf Creek.

His one saving grace was his wife, Julia. She was a pretty blonde with a generous spirit and a sense of community service. She was always putting together charity events for a variety of worthy causes or out visiting the sick and the elderly. People put up with Ralph, but they adored his wife.

"Either of you have any fresh ideas on where to find Liz Marcoli?" Steve asked wryly.

"I'm still trying to find Jimmy Hoffa's body," Frank joked.

Jimmy grinned, although the situation wasn't particularly funny. In fact his heart ached as he thought of the continued torture for the Marcoli sisters and their loss, their lack of answers or closure where their aunt was concerned.

As always when he thought of the sisters, his head filled with the memory of the hug he'd shared with Sheri three nights before.

She had fit so perfectly in his arms, against his chest. He'd been almost breathless by her nearness, so that for a moment he'd forgotten it was just supposed to be a friendly hug. He'd forgotten that he wasn't, that he would never be, the man she wanted in her life on a romantic basis.

Still, just thinking about her now made him want to see her again. They hadn't spoken since the night they'd all met at the tavern, but she'd certainly been on his mind.

Maybe it was time for him to call and see if she might be interested in having dinner at the local pizza place. This time he wouldn't make the same mistake of mentioning anything about it to Steve or Frank.

Frank and Jimmy headed to their own desks and Jimmy made the call, pleased when Sheri agreed to meet him that night at The Pizza Place at six-thirty. Although he assumed that with their schedules, late night dinners would be the norm for their friendship, she insisted she'd be able to get away early tonight, and unless something popped on the criminal end of things, Jimmy had no problem leaving work by that time.

Thirty minutes later the three detectives were on their way to Susan Thompson's home. The young clerk who had been robbed at gunpoint in the convenience store still lived with her parents, who had been cooperative so far in the investigation.

They had been livid to discover that their just-turned seventeen-year-old was pregnant by a twenty-two-year-old loser and had encouraged law enforcement to pursue the statutory rape charges.

At the moment all Jimmy was interested in was getting a confession from the young teen that it had been her boyfriend behind the ski mask and he'd probably been holding a toy gun on her when she'd given him all of the money in the cash drawer.

The surveillance film from the store had shown only the back of the robber, indicating that he'd probably known where the camera was located. He was the right height and weight to be Ned Manning and in playing and replaying the film, they'd noticed that Susan had looked at the door as if in anticipation seconds before the robber had burst inside.

Susan was a rebellious teenager who had given

her parents fits over the past two years. Apparently things had only gotten worse when she'd hitched her star to Ned, who had a reputation as a tough guy who dabbled in selling and using dope.

Jimmy had a feeling Jack and Lorraine Thompson loved their daughter and not only feared for her, but actually feared her temper and violent outbursts. Twice in the past two years officers had been sent to the address to settle an issue between the parents and their daughter that had become physical.

It took the detectives two hours of intense grilling to finally get Susan to break and confess that she and Ned had cooked up the scheme for some quick cash. She sobbed and fought them as they put her in cuffs and placed her in the back of their car.

"What will happen to her now?" Lorraine asked as she wrung her hands and tears spilled down her cheeks.

"We'll talk to the D.A.," Jimmy said. "We'll see if we can get her a fairly light sentence. If we push forward on the statutory rape issue, then a defense attorney can argue that she is a minor and was under Ned's control when the robbery took place."

Lorraine nodded as her husband placed an arm around her shoulder and silently led her away from the officer's car.

Once they had deposited Susan at the police station, they got back into the car and headed out to find Ned Manning.

Ned Manning lived in an old trailer on a plot of overgrown land just outside town with three other young men, all of them with criminal records of one kind or another.

As the three detectives got out of the car in front of the trashy place, they all had their guns pulled. They had been out here several times before for a variety of reasons and never knew what to expect. They had no idea who might be inside besides Ned and they had no idea how Ned or his buddies would react to Ned's arrest.

It was quickly decided that Steve and Frank would go in the front and Jimmy would head around back in case the suspect decided to dive out the back door.

Hurriedly Jimmy stepped through weeds and brush thigh-high as he made his way around the trailer. He stood just to the side of the back door that had two small wooden steps leading up to it.

The trailer emitted the smells of garbage and urine and booze. He was grateful he was the one standing outside rather than having to go in.

A cool calm swept over him while he waited for the action to begin. It didn't take long to hear the sounds of shouts coming from inside the trailer and a moment later the back door flew open and Ned Manning raced out.

He got only three feet away from the door when he was halted by Jimmy. "Put your hands up and slowly turn around," Jimmy instructed. Ned hesitated. "I've been in the mood to shoot somebody lately, it might just as well be you," Jimmy said.

Apparently Ned heard something in Jimmy's voice that made him believe him, for he slowly raised his hands and turned to face Jimmy, his features twisted into a dark rage. "Whatever that little bitch told you, it isn't true. The convenience store gig was all her idea. She wanted to get money for the baby."

"Whatever," Jimmy said before he read the man his Miranda rights and pulled a pair of handcuffs from his pocket. By that time Steve and Frank had joined him and together they got Ned in their car.

"Productive afternoon," Steve said once they were back at the station.

"It was so productive I think I'm going to take off." It was just after five and officially they were all off duty. Jimmy wanted to go home and take a shower, wash the day of crime dirt off his body and soul before he met with Sheri for pizza at six-thirty.

It was five forty-five when he stepped out of the shower and heard the ring of his cell phone. The caller identification indicated it was Sheri. He hoped she wasn't calling to cancel.

"Jimmy, I—I just left the store to head to my house and that s-same car is following me." Her voice held more than a tremor of fear. She'd told him she only stuttered when she was anxious or under tremendous stress. She was afraid.

"Where are you now?"

"About five miles from my driveway."

"Just keep heading up the mountain. I'll catch up with you and we'll find out who is in that car. Drive slow and I'll be there as soon as possible."

He clicked off, pulled on a pair of jeans and a T-shirt and then grabbed his gun and keys and took off. He used his siren to get him down the length of Main Street and onto the mountain road that led to Sheri's place.

He shut it off as he traveled the two-lane road and instead punched the button on his steering wheel that would allow him to make a hands-free phone call.

"Sheri," he said when she answered. "Are you on a hands-free phone?" The last thing he wanted was an accident caused by her using her cell phone talking to him.

"I am." Her voice held a tense fear.

"Is the car still following you?"

"Yes. I've slowed down several times and pulled over as far as possible to allow it to go around me, but it just keeps pace with me."

Jimmy stepped on his accelerator. "I can't be too far behind you. I just passed the turnoff to your place."

"I'm about ten miles up the mountain from there," she replied.

"Hang tight, drive slow and I'll be there in a minute or two." He murmured a goodbye and then focused on the road and once again sped up.

Within minutes he saw taillights in the distance and his heart began to beat wildly. Who was following Sheri? It was definitely a car. He could tell by the shape of the taillights. Why were they pacing her and what did they want from her?

He'd know in just a few minutes. As he drew closer he saw not only the black vehicle but also the shiny yellow cab of Sheri's pickup truck just ahead of it.

When he was close enough, he turned on his siren and held his breath, hoping this all didn't result in some kind of mad chase through the narrow, winding mountains roads.

He released a sigh of relief as the car pulled as far off the road as possible and shut off its engine. Jimmy pulled right behind it, noting that the license plates were from Arizona and that Sheri had also pulled over some distance in front of them.

He called in the license plate to dispatch, who got back to him within seconds that the car was registered to a Louis Harper, from Phoenix. The vehicle had not been reported as stolen.

So, what was it doing here in Wolf Creek, Pennsylvania, following behind Sheri? Jimmy opened his car door and placed a hand on the butt of his gun. Traffic stops always had the potential to be dangerous and cold washed over him. Steadying his nerves he mentally prepared for any scenario to play out.

Sheri watched in her rearview mirror as Jimmy approached the driver's side of the car behind her. Twilight had begun to fall deeper, darker here where ancient, thickly leaved trees crowded the sides of the road and absorbed the last of the day's sunshine.

Jimmy looked as if he meant business, with his hand on the butt of his gun as he stepped up to the dark sedan behind her. She tightened her hands on the steering wheel, wondering who he would find in the car that she was certain had now followed her more than once.

Would he be met with a gun? Shot before he could even react to the danger? She restarted her engine, ready to make a run for it if necessary.

Papers were handed out the driver's window to him and he took a step backward, as if surprised. Sheri's tension grew. He walked back to his car and her phone rang once again.

She punched the button on the steering wheel to allow her to answer. "Who is it? Why have they been following me?" she said before he got an opportunity to speak.

"She doesn't have a driver's license, but she does have a birth certificate and some other forms of identification."

She? Sheri frowned. The fact that it was a woman took away none of her fear. It had been a young woman who had nearly killed Roxy on the second floor storage room in her restaurant.

"Sheri? It's your mother. It's Ramona."

A rivulet of shock swept over her. Her mother? Why was she here after all this time? What did she want? Did she have something to do with Aunt Liz's disappearance?

"Sheri? What do you want me to do?" Jimmy's deep voice pulled her from her thoughts. "I can arrest her right now for driving without a license."

"No...no, I don't want her arrested. D-did she say what she wanted? W-why she's been following me?" She grabbed hold of the steering wheel and drew several deep breaths, trying to get control of the stutter that threatened to erupt in full force.

"She said she's been trying to get up her nerve to make contact with you," he replied.

Make contact? Why now? Sheri didn't know how to feel. Ramona wasn't her mother. Aunt Liz had held her when she'd cried as a baby, she'd bandaged every scratch with a kiss. Aunt Liz had been safety and security and love—all the things a mother should be and all the things Ramona had not been.

Make contact... Exactly what did that mean? She wanted to do lunch? She wanted to step into her role as mommy now that Liz was missing?

"Sheri?"

"Tell her to meet me at the store in the morning around eleven," she finally said. "And, Jimmy, can we postpone pizza until tomorrow night? I have a feeling by then I'm really going to need a friend."

"You got it."

She watched in her rearview mirror as Jimmy returned to the side of the car. He was there only a moment and then the black car pulled away from the shoulder and passed Sheri, the taillights disappearing into the encroaching darkness.

Sheri unclenched the steering wheel as her phone rang once again. "I'll follow you back to your place and then see you tomorrow night at The Pizza Place at six-thirty," Jimmy said.

"Thanks." It was all she could muster as she turned her truck around and headed back to her cottage, her brain in a freeze of stunned surprise.

She was still numb when she walked into her cottage and Highway greeted her with his usual enthusiastic tail-thuds. "Hey, boy," she said, and absently scratched the top of his head affectionately.

Ramona was here in town. What could she possibly hope to achieve after all these years? Sheri flopped on the sofa, her brain still working to make sense of things. She patted the cushion next to her and Highway jumped up and made himself comfortable next to her.

As she stroked his thick fur, she consoled herself that at least she now knew who had been following her. Had Ramona done more than that? Was she the person who had been standing in the woods, watching, waiting for the perfect opportunity to introduce herself to Sheri?

There was no question that she felt relief at the thought that her spooky man stalker was actually the mother who had been absent from her life since she'd been a baby. She was probably out there in the woods trying to get up the nerve to approach Sheri and that was what Highway had gone crazy about.

She should call Roxy and Marlene and share this latest development, but she wasn't going to, not until she spoke with Ramona in the morning and learned what her intentions were.

If she expected some warm and fuzzy family reunion she was sadly mistaken. Roxy made no bones about the fact that she hated Ramona and Marlene wasn't far behind Roxy in that sentiment.

Sheri didn't know what to feel. Certainly the woman had given birth to her, but she was also a stranger and according to the stories Sheri had heard about Ramona, she'd been a drug addict and loser for most of her life.

She had a feeling Jimmy and the other two detectives would be speaking to Ramona before morning to find out where she'd been and if she had anything to do with Aunt Liz's disappearance.

Sheri's gut instinct was that she hadn't. A criminal didn't put herself in a position to be stopped by a cop and questioned. At the moment Sheri had to take what Ramona had said to Jimmy at face value… that she wanted to reconnect, although Sheri couldn't imagine why.

She must have fallen asleep, for when she awakened it was to the dawn of morning seeping in through the windows. Highway had abandoned the sofa for the floor at some point during the night. Sheri sat up with a moan as her back protested not spending the hours of sleep in the comfort of her bed.

Today I meet my real mother, she thought minutes later while she stood beneath a hot shower spray. She didn't feel particularly excited about the prospect, nor did she feel any real dread. The truth was that today she was meeting a stranger. It happened all the time when she was working in the store.

She dressed no differently than she would for a day at work. A pair of jeans and a light blue T-shirt that advertised the Roadside Stop in bold navy letters.

She didn't put on makeup or fix her hair in anticipation of meeting the mother who had abandoned her years ago. She wasn't sure what Ramona's intentions were, but she also wasn't sure of her own. She'd lived a long time without Ramona Marcoli in her life and she wasn't sure she needed her in her life now.

It was just after nine-thirty when she finished up filling bird feeders, checking the corn that the squirrels loved to munch and headed for the store.

It was only then that a fluttering of nerves shot off in the pit of her stomach. She was going to meet the mother she'd never known, the woman who had given her life and then had given her away without a backward glance.

Sheri had never really wondered why Ramona had given her to Aunt Liz, not after Roxy had shared with her some of the details of Roxy living with Ramona for the first seven years of her life.

According to Roxy, living with Ramona had been hell on earth and Aunt Liz had been her salvation after years of chaos and terror. Marlene had been raised by Ramona for four years and even she had some pretty terrible memories of that time, although not as many as Roxy.

What Sheri didn't understand was why Ramona had continued to have children after Roxy and lived a lifestyle that was wrong on every level for a child.

She had specifically set the time for meeting with her birth mother at eleven when Jennifer would be in the store and Sheri and Ramona could have a private conversation in the back room while Jennifer took care of the front of the store.

Sheri's nervous tension only increased as she made a pot of coffee, poured herself a cup and then officially opened the store by changing the sign in the window from Closed to Open.

She sat at the stool behind the register, her hands cupped around the warmth of her mug as she waited for the first customer to arrive. It would be another hour or so when Ramona would show up, if she showed at all.

There was really no reason to believe for sure that Ramona would be any more dependable or responsible today than she'd been years ago. It was quite possible that eleven o'clock could come and go without any sign of her. It was possible she'd chicken out and disappear for years to come.

Jennifer came in at ten-thirty and Sheri told her that she had a meeting set up for eleven that would take place in the back room. She didn't confess that the meeting was with the mother Sheri had never known.

"Not a problem. I can handle things," Jennifer assured her. "Tuesdays are usually pretty slow anyway."

Sheri nodded absently, realizing that she wouldn't even recognize her mother when she walked in the door. Certainly she didn't believe that some special sixth sense would make a daughter recognize a mother. Sheri didn't believe that some magical genetic bond would make bells ring and doves fly at the mother-and-daughter reunion.

And what do you say to a woman who had given birth to you and then virtually thrown you away? If Ramona had shown up because she'd heard that Liz was missing and thought her daughters might need her for some sort of emotional support, she was sadly mistaken.

At precisely eleven o'clock the door to the shop opened and the slender, older woman with the long salt-and-pepper hair who had been in the store a week before walked in and gave Sheri a small smile.

Sheri returned the gesture and then watched her curiously as she meandered up and down the aisles for a few minutes and then finally headed back toward the counter.

Sheri's stomach clenched as she saw the chocolate brown of the woman's eyes…so like Roxy's, and the delicate line of her jaw that resembled Marlene. "Ramona?" Sheri asked tentatively.

The woman nodded. "Hi, Sheri. Long time no see."

Things had changed.

Over the past couple of days Liz Marcoli had become even more afraid than she'd already been and she wouldn't have thought that possible after finding human bones in the earthen wall at the back of the bunker where she had been held for what felt like a lifetime.

She'd been keeping track of the days she'd been held captive by using the tine of a fork to scratch a line in the wall that was made of earth…until she'd made a line in the dirt and had found the human hand.

She'd lost track of time since then. But, in the past couple of days the routine of the days since she'd been here had changed and the simmering terror that had been her constant companion threatened to wail out of her in primal screams.

Despite her circumstances, she had become oddly comforted by the routine established by her captor over the past weeks or months.

Each morning the small doggie-like door opened and a food tray was pushed in. Breakfast was usually oatmeal and coffee. Lunch came some time later, a sandwich and slaw or potato salad. Dinner was a hearty meal of meat and potatoes and a vegetable. The meal deliveries had been a way for her to keep day and night right in her head and had spoken of somebody who cared about keeping her alive.

But over the past couple of days, meals had been sporadic. There had been no lunch two days ago, no dinner last night and no breakfast yet this morning.

It was as if her captor was losing interest in her, that his top priority was no longer providing the basics of keeping her alive.

She'd never been able to figure out who had taken

her or why, but now she was terrified that whoever it was didn't want her anymore. And if that was the case, then she feared she would wind up another skeleton in the dirt in this hellhole that had been her home for months.

Chapter 6

Sheri had been on Jimmy's mind from the moment he'd awakened that morning. At eleven he wondered if Ramona had shown up at the Roadside Stop and how well Sheri was holding up.

It had to be unnerving after all these years to have a mother who'd been absent for twenty-six years of your life suddenly show up.

He'd discovered last night that Ramona had been in town for several weeks and staying at the Sleepy Eye Motel, a relative dump on the east side of town.

Later this afternoon Steve and Frank intended to visit Ramona at the motel to learn what she'd been doing in town for so long and what, if anything, she knew about her sister's disappearance. They had a vested interest in her plans and movements because of their intimate relationships with the women Ramona had hurt so much.

Jimmy had decided to excuse himself from that particular interview. He didn't want to blur personal and professional lines and in the case of Ramona and Sheri, Jimmy already knew what side he was on. It was best to leave Ramona to his partners so he could be a support for Sheri if she needed him to be.

He looked up from his desk as Jed Wilson walked in, bringing with him the scent of fresh pine, a spicy cologne and the faint odor of dog.

"Hey, Jed." Jimmy greeted the dog trainer and waved him into the chair before him. "Nice to see you again."

"I was in town for some supplies and thought I'd stop by," Jed replied.

"I met one of your star students the other night."

"Oh, yeah? And who would that be?" Jed folded his lanky frame into the chair.

"Highway."

Jed smiled, crinkles appearing like starbursts at the outer corners of his eyes. "One of the smartest dogs I've ever worked with. When Sheri brought him in for training after a week I tried to buy him from her, but she refused. That dog loves her and she loves that dog."

"Hmm, is that roadkill I smell?" Officer Chelsea Loren looked at Jed from her desk across the room. She wrinkled her nose as if smelling something bad.

"I'm surprised you can smell anything since you got that nose job," Jed returned easily.

"I had a deviated septum," she said with a coolness to frost the entire room.

"You had a big bump on your nose," Jed replied.

To Chelsea's credit, she didn't say a word. She

expressed her irritation at Jed by jumping out of her chair and heading to the back break room.

"I don't think she likes to talk about her...uh... enhancements," Jimmy said.

"I've known Chelsea since grade school. There was never anything wrong with her that needed to be enhanced," Jed revealed. "Except maybe something wrong with her brain."

Jimmy laughed. "Trust me, there's nothing wrong with her brain. She's smart as a whip."

"If she's that smart then she'd know her nose was fine and those lip injections just look plain ridiculous," Jed scoffed. "But I didn't come here to talk about Chelsea's foolishness. I heard this morning that Ramona Marcoli has been here in town."

"That's right."

"I just wanted you to know that if you need my dogs to sniff out her motel room or anywhere else she's been staying for signs that Liz Marcoli was there, we're available."

"Thanks, Jed, we appreciate your working with us so closely."

Jed raked a hand through his dark brown hair. "You know, even though I wasn't very close to my aunt Agnes, there are days I still wonder what happened to her. Her disappearance two years ago only reconfirmed my commitment to my search-and-rescue work."

"What you do is important." Jimmy gave him a sly grin. "Even if you do smell like roadkill."

Jed returned his grin. "Chelsea has hated me since sixth grade. She was the first woman in my life to tell me I was a jerk and I've had plenty of women since the sixth grade tell me the same thing and worse."

Jimmy knew that Jed was thirty-five years old and seemed content for the most part in running his business and working with his dogs. Jimmy had never heard any gossip about him and any women in town.

"You want some coffee or something?" Jimmy asked.

"Nah, I just stopped in to offer my services if you need them." He got to his feet.

"Besides, in half an hour I've got an appointment with Mrs. Neddles's poodle. According to her the pooch has suddenly developed a refusal to piddle outside and much prefers the Persian rug in her dining room."

"Hmm, sounds like a mystery for our resident dog whisperer." Jimmy stood, as well.

"I'm on it." Together the two men walked toward the door that would lead Jed back out to the reception room.

"Thanks for stopping by," Jimmy said.

"Not a problem." Jed cast a quick glance across the room where Chelsea had returned to her desk. "And don't tell her I said this, but she wears a uniform better than anyone I've ever seen."

With that Jed left the office. Jimmy ambled over to Chelsea's desk. "Why was Satan's spawn here?" she asked.

"Now, now, is that any way to talk?" Jimmy chided teasingly.

"When we're talking about Jed Wilson it is," she replied.

"He was here to offer his help with his dogs if we

want to check out where Ramona Marcoli has been staying to see if they can scent that Liz was there."

Chelsea frowned. "I wonder what Steve and Frank have found out about that lowlife Ramona?"

"Yeah, I wonder, too." Jimmy checked his watch. It was after four. He had no idea when either of his partners might check in, but he was anxious to meet Sheri later that evening to see how she was holding up.

"You realize if Agnes Wilson and Liz Marcoli were taken by the same person, then it's possible we have a serial killer someplace here in town," Chelsea said softly.

Jimmy winced. "I don't even want to think about it. Besides, at this point we have no reason to believe that the two things are related or that Agnes Wilson or Liz Marcoli is dead."

"They're related," Chelsea said with a confident lift of her chin. "And you know the odds are that both Agnes and Liz are dead. Let's just hope no other woman suddenly disappears from her home."

Jimmy frowned, mentally chewing over her words as he went back to his desk. He pulled out his cell phone and laid it on his blotter.

Several times throughout the afternoon he'd thought about calling Sheri, but figured since she hadn't called him she was probably busy at the store or not yet ready to share anything with him about her meeting with Ramona. She might not share much this evening.

After all, this friendship thing of theirs was new, and while he'd managed to solve the issue of who had been following her, that didn't mean she'd automatically be prepared to trust him with her innermost feelings.

He certainly wasn't ready to share with her the pain of his own personal tragedy, a loss that had been so immense it had made him reluctant to ever hope for love or a family again.

He didn't know if he'd ever be ready to share that with anyone. Even now a flicker of the love-starved little boy he'd once been sprang to life, bringing with it a pain that was visceral.

He consciously willed away that childhood trauma and walked back to the break room for a cup of coffee, eager for the next hour or so to pass so he could go home, freshen up and then meet Sheri.

He shouldn't be looking forward to seeing her as much as he was. He shouldn't be anticipating the sweetness of her smile, the warmth in her eyes. More than anything he shouldn't be thinking about the hug they'd shared.

At five foot ten, Jimmy was never going to be her six-foot prince, but there was no question that his lack of height and her short, petite frame had fit perfectly together. The top of her head had brushed the underside of Jimmy's jaw and her breasts had pressed against his chest. No, he definitely shouldn't be thinking about how great they'd fit if they made love.

He jumped as his phone rang. He grabbed it and saw that it was Steve. "What's up?" he asked his partner.

"We've finished up our interview with Ramona and we're heading on home. We'll have a report for you ready in the morning."

"That works for me," Jimmy said. He knew if his partners had learned anything pertinent to Liz's case, they'd be heading back into the station instead of to their homes.

"I'll see you both in the morning and I'll want a full update then," Jimmy said, although he had a feeling he'd get at least a little bit of an update from Sheri in a matter of hours.

"You got it," Steve said.

Jimmy hung up and looked at his watch again. "I think I'm going to go ahead and take off," he said to nobody in particular.

If he left now he'd have time to shower and change and relax a little bit before meeting Sheri at six-thirty. It took him only minutes to drive down Main Street to the Wolf Creek Apartments.

When he'd first arrived in town three years ago he'd rented a studio apartment, figuring when the time was right or he had a reason he'd look for something bigger, something more permanent.

There was no sense of welcome when he walked through the door. This had always been a sort of temporary holding place for him. He'd collected few items of value over his past and the apartment was void of any real personality.

The kitchenette was rarely used and the black sofa served as his bed at night. He had an easy chair and a television and that was pretty much the sum of his living space.

It was supposed to be a place to start and now only served to remind him that his personal life here in

Wolf Creek hadn't progressed much since he'd arrived here as a stranger, a new hire.

He headed straight to the tiny bathroom where he stripped and got into the shower. As he washed off, he thought of the night ahead.

Meeting a friend for pizza shouldn't set off a tingling sense of anticipation. There was no reason for a burst of adrenaline to flood through him as he thought of spending time with Sheri.

During the past three months he'd worked with her and her sisters, she'd certainly never given off any indication that she might entertain a romantic interest in him. In fact, she'd made it more than clear that he was not what she was looking for in a life partner.

And even though he'd never believed he'd have a life partner, a wife, it was difficult not to want something more than what he had, especially when he glimpsed the way Steve looked at Roxy, when he saw the shared love and bond between Frank and Marlene. He wanted that, but he was also afraid to wish for it. He never wanted his heart broken again.

A pizza date with a friend. That was all tonight would be. A friend, that was all he'd ever be to Sheri. Despite the fact that he was drawn to her in a way that was distinctly more than friendlike, he'd spent years learning discipline and control in martial arts training and he'd draw on that to keep himself in line with Sheri.

He'd have to use that training to keep himself in check…otherwise he knew he risked enjoying any kind of relationship with the pint-size, golden-eyed woman who stirred him like nobody had before.

* * *

"I don't care what her story is, I have zero desire to see her, to talk to her or to interact with her in any way," Roxy said with vehemence.

It was four o'clock in the afternoon and Sheri had called a sister meeting to let Roxy and Marlene know about Ramona being in town and wanting to reconnect with all of them. The three were the only occupants in the "green" room at the Dollhouse restaurant.

It was a room that was supposed to bring peace and tranquility with its lush plants and wooden plantation ceiling fans and wicker tables. But at the moment the room held the tension of Sheri's news.

"How long has she been clean?" Marlene asked, her blue eyes simmering with uncertainty.

"Four years. For two of those years she was an inpatient at a place called Tranquil Home in Arizona and after her treatment finished, she stayed on there as a volunteer."

"How would she be able to afford that kind of treatment?" Roxy asked, her voice still holding anger and more than a hint of disbelief.

"Louis Harper. He's a successful businessman who fell in love with Ramona and wanted to help her. He wanted to save her. He sent her to treatment and encouraged her to stay and volunteer there."

Roxy snorted, distinctly unladylike but also displaying her utter disgust. "Just another man taking care of poor Ramona."

"This is different, Roxy," Sheri protested. "He's been beside her for the last four years. It was him who encouraged her to come out here and try to seek forgiveness from us."

"I'll never forgive her," Roxy said defiantly. "I don't need to forgive her to have a wonderful life."

Marlene worried a strand of her blond hair between two fingers. "What does she want from us?"

"According to her, nothing. She just wants us to know that she's sorry for the choices she made through the years. She wants us to understand that even as messed up as she was, she knew being with Aunt Liz would be far better for us than being with her," Sheri explained.

Roxy narrowed her eyes as she looked at her younger sister. "And Miss Gentle Soul is just ready for us to forgive and forget, to send Mother's Day cards and share precious moments together."

"I never said that," Sheri replied evenly, refusing to be baited into a spat with her overly emotional sister. "I don't know what to think, what to feel about any of this. All I wanted to do was tell you both she's here in town and staying at the Sleepy Eye Motel. She'd like an opportunity to talk to both of you, but that's between you and her."

"Are you going to see her again?" Marlene asked Sheri.

Sheri frowned thoughtfully. "To be honest, I don't know. I'm still a bit numbed by it all."

"I'd hoped Aunt Liz was with her," Roxy said, the anger gone from her eyes and instead a deep grief there. "I'd hoped that Ramona had gotten herself into some kind of a mess and Aunt Liz had rushed off to save her."

"Apparently that's not the case," Sheri said softly.

She didn't say out loud what they all knew to be true—even if that had happened, Aunt Liz would have contacted them long before now. At the very least she would have needed to get money from her account to live on and her finances still remained untouched.

"So now I'm stuck with a mother I don't want and without an aunt I desperately need," Roxy said.

Sheri reached across the table and grabbed Roxy's and Marlene's hands. "And you have two sisters who love you dearly despite all your flaws."

Roxy choked out a laugh and squeezed Sheri's hand.

"We'll get through this, Roxy…just like we've always gotten through everything…together. And now I've got to get out of here." Sheri rose from the table. "All I'm asking you both is to open your hearts to Ramona just a little bit and see what happens."

"Last time I did that I got Steve."

"And I got Frank," Marlene added.

"My point exactly." With a wave of her hand, Sheri turned and exited the room. She'd dreaded this conversation from the moment Ramona had left the store, but she'd known she needed to give her sisters a heads-up.

As she stepped outside the Dollhouse she breathed a sigh of relief. Now she could look forward to a pizza night with Jimmy. But first she wanted to head home, take a relaxing bubble bath and get rid of the stress the day had brought.

She had known going into the Dollhouse that Roxy would have the most issues with Ramona. Roxy had lived the longest with a drug-addicted, neglectful Ramona. Roxy remembered the gut-wrenching fear of strange men, of filthy dope houses and trashy motel rooms. She had memories of rib-gnawing hunger and a constant fear that no child should ever experience.

Thankfully, Marlene had few memories of the first four years she'd spent in Ramona's care and Sheri had none. Ramona had a tough task ahead of her in breaking through the wall Roxy had erected around her heart where her birth mother was concerned.

Things would be so much easier if Aunt Liz were here, Sheri thought as she got into her car to head to her cottage. Liz would have words of wisdom for all of them. She would understand their reluctance to get involved with the woman who had thrown them away, and yet would speak of the power of forgiveness.

Roxy would be more prone to listening if the words came from the woman she loved, from the aunt who had taken her in and transformed her life with love.

She dismissed all thoughts of her mother and her sisters as she turned on to the mountain road that would take her home. All she wanted to do for the rest of the evening was enjoy some pizza, a beer and conversation with a friend.

Luckily, the case of her stalker had been solved and the sense of unease that had been with her for the past week was gone, as well.

Highway greeted her with a happy bark as she walked through her front door. She fell to her knees and hugged the dog around his neck.

This was unconditional love. Highway didn't care

if she stuttered when she got too excited or upset. It didn't matter to him if she was in a foul mood or had fought with one of her sisters, or had made a mistake at the store. Highway loved her despite her shortcomings.

When she and Eric Richards had broken up and Sheri's heart had been in tatters, it had been Highway's presence that had comforted her.

She'd buried her head in his neck and wept like a baby, needing the warmth of him, the solidness of him to keep her from slipping off the end of the world.

This time her hug was of sheer happiness. She released her hold on him and stood. "I'm going to take a nice long bath and then we'll let you run a bit in the yard."

Highway followed her into the bathroom, where she started the water running in the tub. As she waited for it to fill she went into her bedroom and stood in front of her closet, trying to decide what to wear.

She knew the red sundress showcased the gold-and-red highlights in her hair, but she'd also been told that her navy sundress did amazing things for her amber-colored eyes.

She frowned, irritated with herself. This wasn't a date. This was pizza with a friend. She pulled out a clean pair of black jeans and a red T-shirt that advertised her business in bold black lettering. That was the appropriate attire for the night.

By that time her bath was ready and she sank down into the warm sudsy water with a sigh of bliss. Today had not only been the first time she'd met her mother, but it was also the first day of Michael Arello's second chance at working for her. Abe and

Michael were closing the store together this evening for Sheri.

When Marlene had been sharing the responsibility for the store, Sheri usually took off for home around three or so, but now that Marlene was no longer there, Sheri had resigned herself to early mornings and late nights.

If Michael proved himself trustworthy, then she and Jennifer could work the morning and midafternoon hours and Abe and Michael could work the late afternoon and evening hours. That would definitely make things easier on Sheri.

It was just after five-thirty when she'd finished getting ready for her evening with Jimmy. She opened the back door to allow Highway the run of the yard rather than the confinement of his pen.

She stepped outside with him, surprised to see dark clouds had usurped the evening sunshine and transformed the backyard into a false twilight. It definitely looked like a storm might be approaching the area.

She laughed as Highway ran circles in the lush grass and fell to his back, wiggling with all four legs in the air as if scratching his back. "You're a goof, Highway," she exclaimed.

He got back to his feet and raced around the perimeter of the lawn at the same time Sheri heard the ring of her landline phone from inside the house.

With a quick glance at Highway, who was once again enjoying the feel of the grass as he rolled over and over, she hurried back into the kitchen and picked up the receiver of the phone on the edge of the counter.

It was Roxy. "I called to tell you I'm sorry for yelling at you today."

Sheri smiled into the receiver. "You weren't yelling at me. You were yelling about the situation."

"Marlene said I got a little out of control."

Sheri laughed. "That's your nature, Roxy, but in any case you don't owe me an apology. We're good and whatever you decide to do about Ramona is between you and Ramona."

"I don't know what I'm going to do about her," Roxy admitted, an unusual uncertainty in her voice.

"You don't have to make any decision tonight. Just think about things for a day or two. Ramona doesn't appear to be in any hurry to leave here right now."

The sound of Highway barking moved Sheri to the kitchen window where she saw no sign of the big dog. "Roxy, my mutt is outside and he's going crazy about something and I can't see him from here. I need to go check it out. I'll call you tomorrow."

"Talk to you tomorrow," Roxy said.

Sheri carried with her a niggle of worry as she walked back outside. In the distance she could hear Highway continuously barking, a frantic kind of noise that stood up the hairs on the nape of her neck.

The darkness had grown deeper as the clouds thickened overhead. "Highway," she called. "Inside."

Normally whatever he was doing, wherever he might be on the property, he would instantly obey the command. This time his sharp barks continued. Sheri started in the direction of the raucous noise and then halted as there was a sharp yelp and then silence.

The silence screamed through her heart. "Highway?" She started moving quickly toward the woods.

Had he stepped into a hunter's trap? Been attacked by a coyote or the feral pig Travis had been chasing? The feral pigs that were in the area had sharp tusks that could easily pierce through a dog's hide.

"Highway," she cried desperately as she entered the darkness of the woods. "Where are you, boy?" She paused and listened, needing to hear a cry, a doggie moan that would indicate where he was in the vast dark forest.

The sound of that yelp shot a terrifying fear through her. Something had hurt Highway. She had to find him. She didn't know what she'd do without him.

A crunch of leaves to her left gave her hope. "Highway?" If he was moving, then that meant he was still alive. She took several steps in the direction where the noise had come from.

A tall, dark figure rushed out of the darkness. Even in the shadows she could see the ski mask that hid his facial features.

Danger!

Escape! Her brain screamed the words as a sob escaped her and she turned to run deeper into the forest.

Her only thoughts were that the man was responsible for whatever had happened to Highway and she had no idea what he wanted with her. But as she ran, she could hear the crashing of the brush behind her, indicating that he followed her.

Grief for Highway mingled with a new kind of terror she'd never felt before as she attempted to elude the danger that was far too close behind her.

Chapter 7

The Pizza Place located at the far end of Main Street was a popular hangout spot for teenagers and young adults on the weekends, but on a Tuesday night it was relatively quiet.

A family of four took up one of the red booths in the back of the cheerful place that smelled of spicy tomato sauce, simmering sausage and yeasty crust. A table in the center was occupied by a young couple who were definitely more interested in each other than the pepperoni pizza in front of them.

Jimmy slid into a booth up front by the windows where he could see Sheri when she arrived. He was early by about fifteen minutes and when the waitress appeared he asked for a beer and indicated that he was waiting for someone else to arrive before ordering pizza.

Minutes later with a cold beer in hand, he leaned back against the red upholstered booth and wondered how things had gone between Sheri and her mother. How would he react if one day a stranger walked up to him and introduced themselves as his mother or father? In all honesty, he didn't know how he would react or if he would want to make a connection at all.

At the time of his abandonment as a newborn, police had scoured the area in search of a woman who had just given birth, but they'd never found the woman or a man who would claim him as their own.

He'd long ago made peace with the fact that for some reason his parents had given him away into a system that wasn't always good and wasn't always bad.

He took a sip of the beer and then checked his watch. Five minutes. He had a feeling that Sheri wouldn't be one of those women who was perpetually late. She couldn't run a successful business without being the punctual type.

Outside the window it appeared as if night had already fallen as dark storm clouds brewed overhead. So far he'd seen no lightning or heard any thunder, although as he'd left his house he'd noticed the distinctive fresh scent of approaching rain. Many times storms developed overhead, but then were blown away by mountain winds without dropping any rain on the small town of Wolf Creek.

He checked his watch again. It was exactly six-thirty. Nerves in the pit of his stomach gave a little jump as he anticipated seeing her at any moment.

He'd dressed in a pair of jeans and a short-sleeved navy polo, grateful that the sleeve length hid the two tattoos that rode his upper arms. If Sheri was looking for a prince he was pretty sure she wasn't into tattoos.

One of them was his shame, and the other one represented what, at the time, had been a dream that he had finally achieved.

By 6:45 the waitress checked in on him to see if he wanted to go ahead and order or if he wanted another beer. He declined both offers, telling himself that Sheri should be walking through the door at any moment.

Maybe he had misjudged her. Maybe she was one of those people who were usually late to any event. In Philly he'd had a partner who had never been on time and it had driven Jimmy half-crazy.

After another five minutes passed he began to wonder if maybe he'd been stood up. Surely if she hadn't intended in coming she would have called him. He couldn't imagine her being the kind of callous woman who would just keep a man waiting indefinitely without an explanation or a simple call to put him out of his misery.

So, where was she?

By seven he pulled his cell phone out of his pocket and called her. Her cell phone rang four times and then went to voice mail.

"Sheri, I thought we were meeting tonight at The Pizza Place. Did I get my time or day screwed up? Call me back and let me know if I should wait for you."

He repocketed his phone and tried to ignore the uneasiness that flittered at the edges of his mind. No reason to think like a cop. No reason to believe she was in any danger.

They'd solved the mystery of who had been following her and he suspected Ramona had been watching her house from the woods the night that Highway had gone crazy. There was absolutely no reason for his stomach to start to twist into a knot of uneasiness.

It was far more likely that she'd just decided that since he wasn't the man she wanted as her forever after there was no point in pursuing a friendship with him.

Still, it didn't feel right that she hadn't called him, that she hadn't told him. In the months he'd known her she'd struck him as a straight shooter, a woman who didn't play games with anyone.

Once again he pulled his phone from his pocket and called her. Voice mail again. He frowned as he stared at his phone, wondering if he should continue to hang around or leave and write off the night, write her off.

Maybe she'd gotten hung up at the store. He called the Roadside Stop and Abe answered. "Abe, it's Jimmy Carmani. Is Sheri there?"

"Sheri? No, she left much earlier this afternoon, said something about meeting her sisters at the Dollhouse to have a sit-down about their mother showing up here in town."

"Thanks, Abe." Jimmy ended the call with a sense of relief. She had probably gotten hung up with her sisters talking about the sudden appearance of Ramona.

The minute he disconnected from Abe, he called the Dollhouse and got the automated response that the restaurant was currently closed but was open from seven to five every day except Sundays.

He immediately called the number again, hoping that if the sisters were still there Roxy would pick up the phone, but there was no answer.

He hung up, fighting not just a level of frustration, but a genuine concern. If she wasn't at home and she wasn't at work, if she wasn't with her sisters, then where could she be?

She was now over thirty minutes late and his cop instinct was definitely starting to rear its head. He finally got up from the booth, threw enough money on the table to pay for his beer and then left the restaurant.

Something wasn't right. He knew it in his heart, in his very soul that Sheri wouldn't just stand him up. There was a reason she hadn't made it to The Pizza Place and the only way he'd rid himself of the unease that rippled through him was to find her right now.

Sheri raced through the thick woods, branches slapping her face and shoulders as her breaths came in frantic gasps. She felt as if she'd been running forever, dodging tree trunks, nearly falling over roots and into holes, and still her pursuer continued to chase her.

It was like a scene from a nightmare, a flash of coming attractions from a horror film, but it was real and terrorizing and she knew she couldn't keep running forever. She was slowly running out of steam.

She now stopped behind a tree and held her breath, hoping, praying that she'd finally lost him. Had she managed to evade him? She heard no sounds, even the wildlife of the forest seemed to hold their breath with her.

The darkness grew profound, making it more difficult to maneuver through the thick woods. Who was chasing her? And what did they want with her? Certainly she didn't intend to confront a person hiding behind a ski mask and ask what his intentions were.

She leaned her head back, grateful for a moment to catch her breath, to rest. She had no idea where she was at the moment. Hopefully he was far away from her and lost in a tangle of bramble bushes.

She only prayed he didn't have a flashlight. If he didn't then they were equal in the darkness and if she couldn't see him, then the odds were good that he couldn't see her.

Tears burned at her eyes as she thought of Highway. Had the man killed her precious dog? Did he intend to kill her, too? Why?

She'd thought the stalker in her woods before had been Ramona, but she'd apparently been wrong. Somebody was after her and twice during the mad dash through the woods he'd gotten close enough to her for her to smell his sweat, to hear his labored breathing.

She tried to meld into the tree, her hands raised to cover her mouth so that her pursuer couldn't hear the sound of her fear, the terrified gasps of breath that desperately needed to be released.

She knew these woods. She and Highway had spent hours rambling through the brush, finding overgrown trails long forgotten and forging new ones in their exploration.

In her race for her life, she'd made a big circle and

wasn't that far from her house. But, whoever was after her apparently knew the woods as well as she did, for he hadn't faltered until now.

She remained frozen, afraid to move, fearful that the man was someplace close by, playing possum like she was doing at the moment.

If she left this tree, could she run fast enough to make it back to the house and lock the doors? If she did make it to the house, would he follow her and break through a window? Barrel through a door?

Damn. In the house the only real weapon she had was a shotgun with no shells. There were knives in the kitchen drawers, but she couldn't use any of them to protect herself unless she could somehow manage to get back inside.

She had to do something. She couldn't stay trapped here until the light of dawn would be upon them. If she was going to make a move to reach the house, it had to be now.

Drawing a deep breath, still not hearing anything that might indicate the man was near, she darted away from the tree, and instantly screamed as her arm was grabbed by the man who must have been hiding just on the opposite side of the huge tree trunk.

She whirled to face him, kicking her legs, her other arm extended in an attempt to poke at his eyes, scratch at his skin. But his skin was hidden by the ski mask and his eyes were only tiny holes in the material.

Frenzied, she thrashed with a force and energy she didn't know she possessed, knowing her life depended on it. She was small, yet strong for her stature.

She finally managed to break free but stumbled

over an exposed root. Once again she kicked out and then rolled away and sprang to her feet.

She raced like the wind, her heart feeling as if it was going to burst out of her chest. Get away. She had to get away. She'd smelled the evil on him, felt the firm grasp of the devil on her.

"Sheri?"

The familiar voice came from someplace in front of her. Jimmy! There was safety, if she could just get to him in time. Like a wild woman she flailed through brambles and thickets, running in the direction of Jimmy's voice as he called her name again.

"Jimmy," she shouted.

She broke out of the woods and into the clearing where the spill of the back porch light illuminated him. She didn't stop running until she banged into him and grasped him tightly around his waist.

"A m-man…in the woods…ch-chasing me."

Jimmy pulled out his gun with one hand as he wrapped his other arm around Sheri's shoulder. "Where?"

"I d-don't know now. He's been chasing me through the woods forever."

"Where's Highway?"

She buried her head in Jimmy's broad chest. "I—I think he k-killed him." She began to weep.

Jimmy withdrew his arm from around her only long enough to pull his cell phone from his pocket. Sheri was vaguely aware of him speaking to Steve and then he'd hung up the phone and led her toward the house.

Once inside he kept her next to him as he cleared the house room by room, his gun like an extension of his fingers. Once he knew they were alone in the house, he locked the doors, and then sat with her next to him on the sofa.

"W-we have to f-find H-Highway," she said, unable to control the stutter that had taken full control of her speech.

"I've got men on their way, Sheri. We'll find Highway as soon as they arrive. Right now I need you to tell me exactly what happened."

She swiped at her tears and drew several deep breaths in an attempt to get her emotions locked down. "W-what are you doing here?" she asked.

"Six-thirty? Pizza date? You don't strike me as the type of woman who would simply stand a friend up with no explanation, so I decided to come and see if you were here. When I saw your truck in the driveway and walked around back and saw the door open and you and Highway weren't anywhere around I got a bad feeling. Now tell me what happened."

She leaned into him, noting the pleasant scent of his cologne, the faint smell of beer on his breath, despite the terrible circumstances. "I let Highway out to r-run. Then Roxy called and I ran back inside to a-answer the phone. When I got off the phone Highway was g-going crazy barking someplace in the woods. He barked and barked and then he yelped and then there was silence."

She gulped back fresh tears as Jimmy pulled her more closely against his side and she thought of that moment when she'd heard that terrible yelp and then the ensuing terrifying quiet. "I thought maybe he'd gotten caught in a hunter's trap. No matter how often I check my property, there's always a chance some creep has put a trap out there. So I went to look for him and then a m-man j-jumped out of the darkness and tried to grab me."

Jimmy's arm tightened around her. "A man?"

"A t-tall, big man dressed all in black and wearing a ski mask." She couldn't halt the shudder that swept through her. "He started chasing me and I ran like I've never run before."

"Did he say anything to you?"

She shook her head. "Not a word."

"Did anything about him appear familiar?"

"No. H-he was just big and scary and he was trying to c-catch me."

"And you don't know why?" Jimmy's voice was soft, but with a steel undertone.

"I have no idea. I j-just knew that a man in a ski m-mask wasn't anyone I wanted near me. Highway's probably d-dead, isn't he?" She looked up into his dark brown eyes, needing him to tell her differently, but seeing in the depths of his gaze that he believed her words.

Before he had an opportunity to give her a verbal response that she knew would break her heart, a knock fell on the door. "Our backup has arrived." He gave her shoulder a reassuring squeeze and then got up from the sofa to answer the door.

Steve and Frank came in first, followed by officers Chelsea Loren, Joe Jamison and Wade Peterson. All of them were armed with both guns and high-beam flashlights.

Sheri remained on the sofa, fighting against a wave of chills as Jimmy quickly filled in the others on what had happened.

Joe, a big man with shoulders the size of mountains, walked across the room and crouched down in front of Sheri. "We're going to figure out who chased you tonight and we aren't going to leave here until we find Highway."

Sheri placed a hand on his shoulder. "Thanks, Joe."

He rose and Jimmy took his place, holding out a hand to her. "Come on, we'll wait in the kitchen while the others search the area."

It took only minutes for the team to go out the kitchen door and quickly disappear into the woods, the only sign of their presence the illumination of their flashlights flittering around like fireflies on steroids.

Sheri sat at the table, Jimmy next to her. Now that the danger had passed, all she could think about was Highway and whatever had happened to her faithful companion.

"I can't imagine my life without him," she said, fighting back a fresh spill of tears. She got up from the table and moved to the back door where through the screen door she could hear the sound of the officers as they not only searched for her dog, but also for any sign that her pursuer might have left behind.

She was aware of Jimmy getting up from the table and coming to stand just behind her, the nearness of his body warming her skin, but unable to pierce through the icy chill that still held possession of her heart.

"What are the odds?" she said more to herself than to him. "What are the odds that Aunt Liz would disappear, that Roxy and Marlene would be attacked by unrelated assailants, and now somebody chased me through the woods in an attempt to grab me?"

Jimmy placed his hands on her shoulders and squeezed gently. "We'll figure this out, Sheri."

She knew he meant to reassure her, but at the moment she was less afraid for herself than what the searchers would find of Highway.

Her enchanted cottage would no longer feel magical without Highway's presence. He'd been her companion for the past year. Her vision blurred with tears as she continued to stare outside.

"Can you think of anyone who might want to harm you? Had any problems at the store lately?"

"No, no problems with anyone either at the store or out of it. I can't imagine anyone who might want to hurt me." But she'd experienced the determination of the man who had chased her, she had felt his desperation to get her. What she couldn't imagine was why.

If he'd managed to grab her what would he have done with her? Would he have sliced her throat? Strangled her? Or would he carry her off someplace to keep, making her just another woman who had vanished from the small town of Wolf Creek?

Once again her body shivered uncontrollably and Jimmy's hands on her shoulders tightened. She breathed in through her mouth and out through her nose in an attempt to slow her heartbeat to a more normal pace, but it didn't seem to be working.

What she wanted to do was turn around, to fall back into Jimmy's arms and find some kind of comfort. She was just about to do that when a voice cried from the woods.

"I found him."

Joe Jamison appeared from the woods, Highway limp and appearing small in the big man's arms.

Sheri raced out the door, Jimmy right behind her. "Is he...?" She couldn't bring herself to finish the awful sentence.

"He's alive," Joe said. "At least he's breathing, but he's unconscious."

"We need to get him to the emergency clinic," Sheri said, tears splashing down her cheeks as she saw Highway's tongue lolling from his mouth, the utter stillness of his body and an unnatural bend in one of his front legs.

Jimmy took Highway from Joe. "You all keep searching for any evidence you can find. I'll check in with you later."

Sheri hurried after Jimmy as he headed for his car, her heartbeat racing so fast nausea twisted in her stomach. Were they already too late? Was Highway already lost to her?

Jimmy placed the dog carefully in the backseat and then he and Sheri were on their way to the emergency animal clinic just off Main Street.

"I'm going to buy bullets for my shotgun and if Highway doesn't make it, I'm going to find out who did this and kill him," she said passionately.

Jimmy was smart enough not to reply.

Chapter 8

Only once in Jimmy's life had he briefly felt the bond of intense love and that had been years ago when he'd been a child. Since that time he'd never really bonded with anything or anyone, but he felt Sheri's love for the dog that remained unmoving in the backseat of his car as he sped to the clinic.

He also experienced a burn of anger deep in his gut, felt the uncertainty of the entire situation sitting like a ton of bricks on his back.

Somebody had attacked Sheri. That somebody had first rendered her protection dog unable to come to her aid and then he'd gone after Sheri.

Who and why?

Somebody had been in the woods, clad in dark clothes and a ski mask. He'd obviously been waiting for the opportunity to kidnap or kill Sheri. If the chase hadn't occurred in the woods, he might have come through a window in the house or burst through the front door. Who had been in those woods just waiting for an opportunity?

He shoved these thoughts aside as he turned into the parking lot of the animal clinic where veterinarian Dr. Chris Cusack and a technician manned the overnight hours.

Sheri was once again weeping silently as Jimmy gently picked up the limp Highway. He was grateful that the dog was still breathing, but he showed no signs of consciousness.

They hurried into the quiet, antiseptic-scented waiting room where Dr. Cusack took one look at them and quickly motioned them into a back operating area.

"What happened?" he asked tersely as Jimmy laid Highway on the steel table.

"We aren't sure," Sheri replied, her voice trembling.

"Somebody tried to attack Sheri. She heard Highway yelp, but didn't see what was done to him."

Dr. Cusack was a short, thin man with thick black-rimmed eyeglasses that gave him the appearance of a meek, mild bookworm. His appearance had nothing to do with his dynamic, authoritative personality.

"Out," he bellowed at them, and pointed to the door that would return them to the waiting room.

Jimmy sensed Sheri's hesitation, so he took her by the hand and physically pulled her from the room. Together they sat side by side on the uncomfortable plastic chairs in the waiting room.

"At least he's still alive," Sheri said as she twisted her hands together in her lap.

"He's a tough cookie and Dr. Cusack is a great vet." Jimmy fought the impulse to take one of her hands in his, to somehow give her the strength to get through whatever news the doctor might have when he appeared again.

As the minutes ticked by and Jimmy knew he was helpless to do anything to aid in Highway's condition, his thoughts went to the most troubling aspect of the night.

Who had been after Sheri and why?

"Maybe Travis was angrier than we initially thought about me holding him at gunpoint," she said, as if she could read his thoughts. "Maybe he just wanted to scare me by chasing me through the woods."

"Maybe," Jimmy said dubiously. "But I can't imagine Travis having anything to do with what happened tonight. I also can't imagine him doing something to hurt Highway. He might be a hunter, but he usually only hunts for what he eats."

Sheri looked at him, her eyes filled with a distrust he knew was probably alien to her character. "Maybe he was back there hunting again and when Highway alerted to his presence he just freaked out."

"We'll check him out, Sheri. I told you, I won't rest until we get to the bottom of this."

She frowned. "I just hate not knowing who to trust. It's a little weird, isn't it? My mother shows up for the first time in years and suddenly there's a man chasing me through the woods."

"I don't see how to tie those two things together,"

Jimmy said. "She would have had to hire some man to chase you, and in any case why would she want to hurt you?"

"I don't know...crazy thoughts." The distrust in her eyes transformed to a comforted warmth. "There's one thing positive, it's good to·have a detective as a friend."

Jimmy nodded, although he was beginning to think that this whole friends thing had been a stupid idea from the very beginning. He had definitely been having more than "friends" kinds of thoughts about her in the past couple of days.

He jumped when his phone rang. It was Steve. "Have you found anything?" Jimmy asked.

"Nada," Steve said. "Oh, there are plenty of broken tree branches, indications of a chase going on through the woods, but we haven't found a scrap of material or a single piece of evidence that might point to the culprit. We plan on coming back first thing in the morning to take another look. We'll have more light then and maybe can spot something we've missed in the darkness."

"I appreciate it," Jimmy said.

"How's Highway doing?"

"We don't know. He's in the back with Dr. Cusack. We're waiting to hear something. I'll let you know what we learn first thing in the morning."

"Until then," Steve said, and they hung up.

Jimmy pocketed his phone and this time he didn't fight the impulse to take one of Sheri's hands into his. He'd feared she might pull away, but instead she squeezed his tightly.

"Let me guess, they didn't find anything," she said miserably.

"It's dark, Sheri, and searching an area that large with flashlights is difficult. All the officers plan to be back in those woods first thing in the morning to see if they can find something to help us identify the man who was after you."

She leaned her head back against the pale green wall. "I feel like this is all a terrible nightmare and I just need somebody to wake me up."

"I wish it were a nightmare," Jimmy agreed. "I'd be the first person to wake you. But what we have to figure out now is who would want to hurt you. I need you to think long and hard about it."

"At the moment all I can think about is Highway." She focused her gaze on the door that separated the waiting room from the operating room. She narrowed her eyes, as if by sheer willpower alone she could send healing vibes to the dog she loved.

"Okay, right now you think about Highway, but sooner than later you need to think about who that man in the woods might be," he told her.

She nodded and once again leaned her head back, this time closing her eyes. Jimmy took the opportunity to take in each and every one of her features.

She was so unlike either of her sisters. Roxy was a sexy, fiery Italian with bold features that screamed of sensuality. Marlene was like an old-fashioned movie star, with her blond hair, blue eyes and glamorous sense of style.

But as far as Jimmy was concerned, her older sisters paled when next to Sheri's quiet, natural beauty. Her whisky-colored eyes were fringed by long dark-brown lashes. Her nose was straight with just enough upturn at the end to be slightly impish, and her lips were full and made to smile…or to kiss.

He shouldn't think about kissing her. He shouldn't even want to kiss her, yet he did. The desire to taste her mouth had been on his mind for days.

She even looked pretty with her red T-shirt grass-stained and twigs and leaves tangled in her thick hair. Yes, he definitely wanted to kiss her.

He yanked his gaze from her and instead focused on a wall across the room that contained a bulletin board with photos of dogs needing homes.

Maybe that was what he needed…a dog. He immediately dismissed the idea. His hours were too erratic to have a pet. Besides, he saw the way Sheri was bonded to Highway. He wasn't sure he knew how to bond with either animal or a human so closely. He wasn't sure he wanted to.

"What's taking so long?" Sheri asked, her voice laden with gut-wrenching worry.

"Be grateful that he hasn't come out and told us he can't do anything more to help Highway," Jimmy said.

"You're right. The doctor has to be doing something and that means he believes there's hope, right?"

Those beautiful eyes of hers gazed at him, obviously seeking confirmation. At that moment with her eyes looking so trustingly into his, he would have told her the moon was green if that was what she needed to hear.

Thankfully the door to the operating room opened and Dr. Cusack walked out. Sheri bolted up from her chair as if she'd been hit by lightning and Jimmy stood with her, bracing himself not so much for what the doctor might say, but for how what he said would affect Sheri.

"I took a complete set of X-rays and discovered his front leg was broken. Thankfully it was a clean break and easy to set and cast," Dr. Cusack explained.

"Is that why he's unconscious?" Sheri asked.

Dr. Cusack shook his head. "I've drawn blood to do a series of tests. I think he's either been poisoned or tranquilized in some way. At this point I'm leaning toward some sort of tranquilizer as he isn't exhibiting the normal symptoms of poisoning."

Sheri stiffened and Dr. Cusack continued. "I won't have all the test results until morning. Right now he's resting easy. I have him hooked up to fluids and I think it would be best if he stays right here for a couple of days."

"But, he's going to be all right," Sheri pressed.

"I think things look encouraging. Go home, Sheri. I'll do what needs to be done to help Highway and there's nothing more right now that you can do for him."

"Just please let me know when he's conscious, no matter what time of day or night it is, promise you'll call me and let me know."

Dr. Cusack smiled at her. "Of course I'll call you. I've seen you with that dog since he was a malnourished puppy. I know what he means to you."

"Come on, Sheri," Jimmy said gently. "Let's get you home."

Her shoulders slumped in defeat beneath his arm as he led her out of the building and to his car. "He looked more tranquilized than poisoned to me,"

Jimmy said once they were back in his car, hoping to lift her spirits somehow.

"That's better than being poisoned, right?"

When he pulled out of the animal clinic parking lot, he was aware of the weight of her intense gaze on him. "I'm no veterinarian, but I would think that definitely it's better to be tranquilized than poisoned." He shot a glance in her direction.

She frowned. "That man in the woods broke his leg. I don't know how he managed to do it, but I know in my gut he probably broke the leg and then somehow injected him with something. Highway would never take anything to eat from anyone but me, no matter how tasty the food might look or smell. Jed and I trained him too well."

They drove for a few minutes in silence. "Sorry about the pizza plans," she finally said.

He flashed her a quick smile. "Nothing to apologize for. I'm guessing you didn't plan for a man to attack your dog and then chase you in the woods tonight. I think I can forgive you for not meeting up with me for a slice of pizza."

"Thank God you came to find me." She wrapped her slender arms around her shoulders, as if chilled despite the warmth of the night. "If you hadn't shown up when you did, I think he would have caught me. I will tell you this, he seemed to know the woods as well as I did, so it has to be somebody local."

"We'll figure it out." He seemed to be saying that a lot lately. "Maybe in the daylight tomorrow we'll find a piece of his clothing snagged on a tree branch, or something he dropped while he was chasing you."

"I hope you all find something." Her voice was

slightly husky with undisguised fear. "I felt his malevolence, Jimmy. I smelled his sweat."

"You're safe now, Sheri and we're going to keep it that way. Highway is going to be fine and we're going to get to the bottom of this."

"S-so, what happens now?" she asked.

"Since we didn't get our friendly meeting for pizza, we're going to do something else I've heard that other friends do," he replied.

"And what's that?" she asked.

He flashed her a bright smile as he pulled in front of her cottage. "We're going to have a slumber party."

Together they got out of the car and were greeted by Officer Joe Jamison. "I figured I'd hold down the fort here until you got home. How's Highway doing?" Joe looked at Sheri sympathetically.

"That creep in the woods broke his leg and Dr. Cusack thinks he was either poisoned or tranquilized." Anger seethed up inside her, binding to the fear that still bubbled deep in her heart.

"Dr. Cusack is going to keep him for a while and we're hoping he'll be just fine," Jimmy informed him. "Shouldn't be long before he's back home where he belongs," he added optimistically.

"He definitely will be fine," Sheri said firmly, needing to believe it. She absolutely refused to believe that fate would take something else away from her.

"He's a tough mutt," Joe said. "And now that the two of you are here, I'm heading home. We'll be here early in the morning to take another look through the woods. It's fairly easy to figure out where you ran with all the broken branches along the way. Hopefully with daylight we can find something we couldn't see tonight."

"Thanks, Joe," Sheri said. She sank down on the sofa, a deep weariness stealing over her as Jimmy walked Joe to the door. A glance at the clock hanging above the fireplace mantel let her know it was almost eleven.

She was exhausted and as she gazed down at herself she realized she was also filthy. Her jeans and T-shirt were covered in dirt and grass stains and a rake of her hand through her hair found twigs and leaves entangled in the strands.

Jimmy locked the front door and then turned to look at her. "So, let's get this slumber party started," he said with what sounded like forced enthusiasm. "Although I have to confess I really don't know what goes on at slumber parties."

"Both Roxy and Marlene had a couple of them while we were young. The girls painted each other's fingernails and giggled a lot. They gossiped about other girls, listed the guys they wanted to go out with and then watched a scary movie and ate popcorn between squeals of terror."

"You never had a slumber party?" He remained across the room.

"No." She attempted a small smile. "I figured everyone came to Roxy's because they were afraid to tell her no. They came to Marlene's because she was easily the most beautiful girl in town. I had a feeling if stuttering Sheri tried to have a party nobody would show up, so I never tried." She wasn't looking for sympathy, but rather was simply stating the facts.

"Sounds to me like you didn't miss out on much." He took a step closer to where she sat. "Fingernail polish has always been overrated and we both know that scary movies are really kind of silly."

"Jimmy, you don't have to stay here tonight." All she really wanted was a long hot shower and the blessed release of sleep.

"Unfortunately, princess, this isn't your call. Somebody tried to get you tonight and they failed. Right now you don't have Highway as your first line of defense. All you have is a shotgun without shells."

He moved closer to the sofa. "This place is relatively isolated and has plenty of cover for somebody to approach the house and break inside. Even if you managed to call for help it would take fifteen minutes or so for a patrol car to get here. I'm not going anywhere tonight, Sheri. Consider me your personal watchdog while Highway is away."

"I hope you don't need your belly rubbed as often as Highway does," she said ruefully, and then released a deep, trembling sigh, realizing that she did want him here. She wanted to sleep, but she also didn't want to be alone in the house.

"I don't need anything but maybe a sheet and a pillow to sleep on your sofa," he said.

"I think I can manage that." Logically she knew that bad things happened in the daytime, but nights were for evil and there was no way to be sure that the evil that had chased her through the woods wouldn't return tonight. There was still plenty of darkness left before morning.

She rose from the sofa, once again struck by the bone-numbing tiredness of too much adrenaline

spent, too many emotions played out and the gnaw-
ing worry about Highway. "I'll get you a couple of
sheets and a pillow, and then I'm going to take a hot
shower. You know you don't have to sleep on the
sofa. I do have a spare room."

Jimmy sat in the spot she had just vacated on the
sofa. "I'll be more comfortable here. I can hear anyone trying to get into the front or back door and I
don't intend to do much sleeping anyway. The sofa
will work just fine."

She hated that he intended to stay up all night but
couldn't help but feel relieved that he would be guarding her place, herself until morning came.

She left the room and headed down the hallway to
the linen closet where she pulled out two pale blue
sheets and then went into the guest room and grabbed
a pillow from the bed.

When she returned to the living room his gun
and car keys were on the coffee table. "Go take that
hot shower," he said as he took the bedding from
her. "And then get a good night's sleep because unfortunately I'll have more questions for you in the
morning."

She nodded, grateful that he wasn't going to in-
sist on any more questions tonight. She headed for
the bathroom and within minutes was standing beneath a hot spray of water, using the bar of soap she'd
ordered from an online store that smelled of lilacs
and lavender.

Jimmy might have questions for her in the morning, but she feared she wouldn't have any answers.
She had no idea who the man in the woods was or
what he wanted with her. She had no idea who would

want to hurt Highway in an effort to neutralize his duty and desire to protect her.

She squeezed her eyes tightly closed and leaned weakly against the glass enclosure as she thought about her beloved companion. The idea that somebody had intentionally broken his leg and then poisoned or tranquilized him shot a pain through her heart that was nearly debilitating.

What kind of person attacked an innocent animal? A monster, that's who. It had been a monster chasing her through the woods.

Tears fell as she raised her face to the spray. They were tears for Highway and for herself. Tears of relief and of the fear of danger still too close.

She finished rinsing off and then shut off the water and grabbed the towel she had waiting for her. Drying off, she said a small prayer for Highway and grabbed the short lavender nightgown and matching robe that hung from a hook on the back of the bathroom door.

Brushing her wet hair into some semblance of order she noted that her skin was unusually pale and she appeared not just tired, but stressed. Her eyes looked hollow and her mouth trembled slightly.

The only thing that made her feel a little bit better was the fact that one of Wolf Creek's finest was sitting in her living room and would remain there until morning.

Tomorrow she intended to get ammunition for her shotgun and if anyone attempted to get into her house without a personal invitation she'd shoot first and ask questions later.

As she exited the bathroom she smelled the scent

of pizza baking and realized Jimmy must have found the frozen pie she had in her freezer.

He was just pulling it out of the oven when she stepped into the kitchen. He placed the pizza stone on a pot holder in the center of her table and smiled. "I hope you don't mind. I figured since we didn't get pizza out, we could get it in instead."

She was surprised by the pang of hunger that stirred in her stomach. In anticipation of her meeting Jimmy for pizza, she'd skipped lunch that day. "Actually, I don't mind at all. I guess life-threatening drama makes me hungry." She slid into one of the chairs at the table. "No need for silverware or plates," she said.

"What about drinks?"

"There's cold soda in the fridge."

"Perfect." He grabbed two colas from the refrigerator, ripped off a couple of paper towels from the holder on the counter and then joined her at the table.

For the next few minutes they ate in silence. It was a comfortable quiet, as if words were not necessary between them. She was spent, emotionally and physically and he appeared to not only recognize it, but respect it, as well.

"Not as good as the Pizza Place fare, but it definitely is hitting the spot," she finally said as she reached for her second piece.

"Tastes great to me, but I was starving, too. Besides, you'll sleep better with a full belly. And you need a good night's sleep."

His eyes were dark pools of compassion and for just a moment she wanted to fall into the depths, forget the pizza and curl up on his lap. She wanted him to wrap her in his big strong arms and take away the taste of terror that still lingered in the back of her throat.

Instead she looked down at the pizza in her hand and took a bite. Jimmy was here not just as a friend, but as a detective doing his job, and his duties didn't involve holding her so close that she felt his reassuring heart beating against her own.

By the time she'd finished her second piece, her eyes were drifting closed and she knew it was her body's need to escape her thoughts and worries about Highway and the memories of being chased in the dark.

"If you don't go to bed you're going to find yourself face-first in the rest of the pizza," Jimmy observed.

"You're right." She scooted back from the table and stood.

"I'll walk you to your room," he said, also getting up from the table.

"That isn't necessary," she protested, knowing he wasn't finished eating.

"But it is. I need to check and make sure windows are locked and you need to sleep with your bedroom door open so that I'll hear if anything goes amiss."

His words reminded her once again that the danger hadn't passed; it had only potentially been postponed. She was acutely aware of him stopping at the coffee table to grab his gun and then walking in front of her down the hallway to her bedroom at the end.

Where the rest of her house was done in warm, earthy colors, her bedroom was an explosion of deep, lush purple…the color of royalty and befitting a princess.

Thankfully, Jimmy made no comment as he headed to the single window in the room and checked to make sure it was locked securely. He then turned and walked back to where Sheri stood just inside the doorway.

"Remember, door open all night and don't hesitate to call for me if you hear something ominous or just get the willies." He stepped closer to her. "Or if you just need some reassurance."

He stood so close to her that she could smell the woodsy scent of his cologne, feel his body heat radiate outward to steal some of the chill from hers.

His eyes darkened, and somewhere in the back of her mind she knew she should step away from him, but her feet were frozen in place as he raised a hand and gently stroked it down the side of her cheek.

"Sweet dreams, princess," he murmured.

She saw the kiss coming. He leaned forward and for just an instant his intent gleamed boldly from his eyes. Before she had an opportunity to process what was about to happen, his lips were on hers.

Achingly warm, soft and sensual, his mouth took complete possession of hers. It was definitely a friendly kiss, but so much more than just friendly.

It was hot, it was breathtaking and it was like nothing she'd ever experienced before. She instantly got lost in the sweet sensations that flamed through her entire body. She wanted to kiss Jimmy forever.

With an abruptness that startled her, he broke the kiss and stumbled back from her, his eyes glazed with a heat that was both thrilling and unexpected.

Without saying a word, he turned on his heels and walked away from her, disappearing back into the kitchen as she remained standing, stunned by her visceral reaction to the kiss.

She finally moved toward her bed where she drew down the purple comforter and turned on the lamp on the night table. She shrugged out of her robe, turned off the overhead light and then got into bed.

As she turned off the small lamp next to her, she tried to forget the kiss that had just occurred. She particularly needed to forget her reaction to it.

The last thing she wanted to do was feel an attraction to a man she was certain wasn't the prince she was waiting for. Jimmy could stay on her sofa for the rest of tonight, but tomorrow he had to go.

If he kissed so sinfully she didn't even want to imagine what it might be like to make love with him. She tossed and turned and finally fell asleep with the taste of pepperoni and sweet temptation in her mouth.

Chapter 9

Jimmy returned to the kitchen and tried to eat another piece of pizza, but all he could think about was the taste of Sheri's lips, the feel of her so soft and yielding in his arms.

He shouldn't have kissed her.

But he hadn't been aware that he was going to kiss her until he had actually taken her mouth with his. And he hadn't considered that the consequence of that single kiss would be the desire to repeat it and more.

He wrapped up the last of the pizza, put it in the refrigerator and then cleaned off the table. He checked the back door to make certain it was locked. He also noticed that Highway's doggie door had latches on it as well, and he made sure they were in a position that would keep any animal or man from crawling inside.

With the kitchen clean and secure, he wandered back to the living room and sat on the edge of the sofa, trying not to think about how kissing Sheri had been a mistake he wanted to continue to make.

From the moment she'd come into the kitchen wearing only that lavender nightgown and robe, desire for her had sprung to life inside him. He'd wanted to let the pizza burn while he swept her up in his arms and carried her to one of the bedrooms where he could make love to her until dawn appeared in the eastern sky.

She'd been quite clear that she was waiting for a prince in her life, which he wasn't. They'd both agreed that a friendship between them would be nice. She wasn't offering a friends-with-benefits kind of deal and he shouldn't be thinking about such a relationship.

What he should be thinking about was who had been in the woods. Was the attack on Sheri somehow tied to Ramona's unexpected reappearance in town? To Liz Marcoli's disappearance? Or had Sheri made a deadly enemy she was unaware of?

He leaned against the back of the sofa, a headache beginning to pound in the center of his forehead. What would have happened had he not come here to find Sheri? What would have happened if he'd just decided he'd been stood up and had gone on home?

Would he instead have found Highway dead in the woods and Sheri also vanished? Or would he have found both the dog and Sheri dead at the hands of an unknown assailant? Thank God he had decided on the action he'd taken.

The pounding in his head increased as he thought

of Sheri running through the woods, helpless and terrorized. Why? Like both of his partners, Jimmy believed that one of the most important aspects of a case was motive. If the motive could be figured out, then suspects would eventually come into clearer view.

He'd have to wait until morning to grill Sheri more thoroughly on who might have a beef with her. He also wanted her to repeat everything that had happened. It was possible by morning something that had happened—a sound...a scent—might be remembered that she hadn't thought of in the aftermath tonight.

But he'd known she couldn't handle anything more tonight. She'd worn her weariness, her worry for Highway like a crown too heavy on her head. Hopefully after a good night's sleep she'd be able to help identify anyone who might have an issue with her.

He got up and grabbed his gun and moved to the kitchen window where the clouds that had been so heavy earlier in the evening had finally blown away, leaving behind a near-full moon that spilled down on the lawn and the encroaching woods.

Was he out there now? In the darkness of the forest? Watching her home? Plotting another attack? His fingers tightened around the butt of his gun.

"Not tonight," he muttered to himself. Nobody would get through him to get to Sheri this night. What he had to figure out was how to keep her safe every night after this one.

He'd offer himself up as her personal bodyguard and move in here, but after sharing that kiss with her he knew that probably wasn't the best idea.

It was possible that if Dr. Cusack could identify the poison or tranquilizer that had been used on Highway it might be a lead to a potential suspect.

He left the kitchen and returned to the living room, realizing it was going to be a long night.

And it was.

He spent the long hours alternating between thumbing through one of the romance novels that were on a bookcase and getting up to walk through the house, peering out windows and doors.

More than once he checked in on Sheri, who was a tiny bump beneath a plush purple throw. Each time he stood in her doorway she appeared to be sleeping soundly and for that he was grateful. The last thing he wished on her was nightmares of what she'd endured.

She was going to need all of her strength to get to the bottom of this, as was he and his partners. They already had two unsolved cases on the books…Agnes Wilson, who had disappeared two years before and Liz Marcoli, who had now been missing over three months.

He couldn't stand the idea of an open case where Sheri was the victim. The problem of trying to figure out how to maintain her safety until they resolved this issue kept him awake through the wee hours of the morning.

At six o'clock he made a pot of coffee and sat at the kitchen table as the sun slowly slid upward above the tops of the trees.

He didn't expect Sheri up for another hour or two. He hoped she'd stay here today, but he had a feeling she'd open her store and keep business as usual. Maybe that would be for the best, to keep her busy and her thoughts off Highway and the mad dash through the woods.

He knew that several of the officers from the night before intended to be back here around eight this morning to comb through the forest in hopes of finding something that might have been missed the night before.

It was possible they might be able to set up some sort of rotation between Jimmy and his partners and a couple of other officers to make sure that Sheri was never here alone again until this was all resolved.

He'd have to sell the idea to Chief Krause, but with Ralph Storm breathing down Krause's neck, Jimmy had a feeling the last thing his boss would want would be another crime at the beginning of the height of tourist season.

It was just before seven when Sheri stumbled into the kitchen, her eyelids at half-mast and wearing a slightly cross expression that instantly identified her as not a morning person.

She barely glanced at him as she beelined to the coffeemaker. He remained silent, watching as she poured herself a cup of the brew and carried it to the table. Her slender legs were on display beneath the thin lavender bathrobe she wore and he tried not to notice how lovely she looked.

After she'd taken her first drink he decided it was safe to engage.

"Not a morning person, huh?"

She held up a finger and took another sip of her coffee, then leaned back in her chair and offered him a sleepy smile that stirred him deep inside.

"Actually, I love the mornings, after I've had my

first couple sips of coffee," she admitted. She took another drink and eyed him over the rim of the cup. "And to be honest, seeing you sitting here made it impossible for me to pretend that everything that happened last night was a dream."

He gazed at her sympathetically. "Sorry to burst your bubble."

"It's okay. I suppose you want to ask me again who might hate me enough to hurt my dog and try to grab me in the woods."

"It would be nice if you came up with a list of names," he said.

"A list? I'm having trouble coming up with a single name." She narrowed her gaze. "Your eyes are red. Did you stay up all night?"

"Guilty as charged. Depending on what happens today I'll manage somehow to catch a few hours of sleep."

"I can tell you what my plans are for today. Within the next hour I plan on calling and checking in on Highway and then I'm showering and getting dressed and heading into the store for business as usual." She raised her chin slightly, as if expecting him to protest.

"I figured that would be your plan. I'll drive you to the store and then when it's time for you to leave I'll pick you up and bring you back here." He said the words as a statement of fact.

She set her cup down on the table, her gaze remaining thoughtfully on him. "Okay, I'll let you be my personal chauffeur to and from work." Her eyes darkened and a faint dusty pink filled her cheeks. "But no more slumber parties."

"It was the kiss, wasn't it?"

She nodded and looked toward the nearby window. "I won't deny the fact that I liked your kiss, but that's why we shouldn't put ourselves in a position where it might happen again." She gazed at him once again. "You aren't the right man for me and I doubt that I'm what you're looking for in a woman."

"I'm not particularly looking," he said. "But if you say no more slumber parties, then that's the way it will be."

That just meant he was going to have to get creative in how he intended to make certain that nobody nefarious crept up to her house in the middle of the night.

There was no way he was going to let her stay in this isolated cottage in the woods all alone, especially after dark, until whoever had attacked her was behind bars.

Chapter 10

By the time Frank, Steve and several other officers showed up to begin the search of the woods, Sheri had showered and dressed and was ready to head to the store.

Jimmy had suggested more than once that maybe it would be a good idea for her to just stay home today, but she needed work to keep her mind occupied so she wouldn't think about the frantic run through the woods, her beloved dog or that crazy, wild unexpected kiss.

Besides, she sold ammunition for the shotgun at the store and she was going to pick up a couple of boxes to bring home so that she wouldn't spend her time alone in the house unarmed.

She'd called the animal clinic where she was told that Highway was just starting to regain consciousness, but Dr. Cusack wanted to keep him a couple more days to administer IV antibiotics and fluids. The tech Sheri had spoken to also said they wanted to make sure that Highway would be comfortable walking with his new cast before sending him home.

"What I'd like you to do is spend some time this morning making a list of all the people you interact with at the store or everywhere else," Jimmy said as he pulled into the Roadside Stop's back parking lot next to Jennifer's car. "I also want on that list any other hunters you might have had issues with in the past, vendors who are in and out, and past employees that might hold a grudge."

"That's going to be quite a long list," she said.

"We have to start somewhere, Sheri," he said.

"I see you've already started by contacting Jennifer to be here early?" She raised an eyebrow at him.

"I don't want you spending a minute here alone. If you can't staff the store so that there's always somebody here with you, then call me and I'll get here immediately."

Her heart hitched a bit. "This is serious, isn't it, Jimmy."

"Deadly serious," he responded, no hint of a spark in his dark eyes.

"I'm getting ammunition for my shotgun." She narrowed her eyes and raised her chin, expecting him to rebuke the very idea, and surprised when he didn't.

"Call me if anything unusual happens today," he said as she opened the car door to exit. "And if for any reason you can't get in touch with me, call Dispatch and they'll have somebody out here as quickly as possible."

"I'm sure I'll be fine here at the store." She got out of the car and with a wave of her hand, she headed inside.

Jennifer greeted her, a worried frown on her pretty face. "Sheri, are you okay? Detective Carmani told me about what happened last night. How's Highway doing? What are the cops doing to find the man?"

Sheri smiled and held up a hand. "Whoa, one thing at a time." As she and Jennifer sat on the stools behind the counter, Sheri filled her in on everything that had happened, although she didn't mention the mind-blowing, knee-buckling kiss she'd shared with the Italian lawman.

"And now I'm tasked with making a list of anyone and everyone in my life with the hopes that somebody on that list is the person who is after me," she finished.

"Sheri, I can't imagine a person in the world who would ever want to hurt you. You're the sweetest, most generous woman in the entire town of Wolf Creek," Jennifer gushed with obvious hero worship.

"Jennifer, for goodness' sakes, don't put me up on any pedestal. I'm sure there are people I've angered in one way or another, I just have to figure out who they might be." Sheri sighed, the task ahead of her nearly overwhelming. "Why don't you straighten some shelves until we get some customers?"

As Jennifer got up, Sheri pulled out a legal pad that she kept beneath the counter for doodling or making notes to herself about inventory or staff hours.

She turned it to a blank piece of paper and stared at it, tapping the end of a pen on the counter. How did anyone really know the impact they had on others as they went about their daily life?

Had she unintentionally ignored somebody? Had she hurt somebody's feelings by a throwaway comment? She came into contact with a lot of people during a busy workday, but she just couldn't imagine evoking the kind of rage that had chased her through the woods.

She finally wrote the first name—Travis Brooks, although she didn't believe the tavern owner was responsible, despite the fact that she'd held him at gunpoint. She'd known Travis for years and he'd never shown any indication that he had a bad bone in his body.

Sure, she'd heard stories about him occasionally getting stupid drunk with customers and dancing on the bar or wandering the streets until one of the cops picked him up and took him home. But he wasn't a bad guy and she certainly didn't believe he was a monster.

It was just after ten and she'd managed to write down three names. She was in the break room in the back when she heard the familiar clip-clop of a buggy approaching. A glance out the back door showed Abraham Zooker parking his horse and buggy in the area specifically designated for Amish visitors and their horse-drawn buggies.

It was a dirt area to the side of the asphalt parking and had a hitching post for the horses to be tied to while left unattended. There were hitching posts in front of many of the businesses on Main Street to accommodate the old-fashioned way of travel.

She watched as he wrangled a wooden nightstand

out of the back of the buggy, and greeted him with a warm smile while he carried it toward the back door.

"I see you've brought me another piece of beautiful furniture," she said.

The older man returned her smile. "And I would hope that it will be welcomed here."

Sheri stepped aside to allow him entry through the doorway. "Of course it's welcome. You know I love selling your pieces, Abraham, and the tourists and locals love to buy them." She followed him inside. "You can go ahead and put it with the rest of the furniture inside the store."

He carried the piece easily, as if it weighed little more than a sack of onions, and set it next to a coffee table. He straightened and tugged on his long salt-and-pepper beard.

"Anything new in the case of your aunt?" he asked.

Sheri's heart constricted. "No, nothing, although the case is still open and active."

"Your family has suffered so much in the last couple of months." He reached out and took one of her hands in his. His hand was dry and calloused and smothered her smaller one. "I continue to pray for you all every night."

"Thank you, Abraham. We can use all the prayers we can get. And things are well with you?"

He dropped her hand. "Things always go well with me," he replied. "A simple man finds simple pleasures." He started toward the back room to leave. "I will check in with you next week to see if anything has sold."

Sheri told him goodbye, watched as he returned

to his buggy and then pulled out of the back parking lot to the sound of horse hooves and creaking leather.

She went to the counter where against her own personal judgment she wrote Abraham's name on her list. Following his name she added Abraham's brother, Isaaic Zooker. Isaaic provided the variety of cheeses that was particularly popular with the tourists. The two brothers were in and out of the store often, delivering wares or picking up money their sales had earned them.

The list began to grow longer as she thought of all the people who provided services and goods that kept the Roadside Stop successful.

With each name she wrote, a well of denial made the strokes of her pen. She couldn't imagine any of these people being the man in the woods.

It pained her to write down not only her mother's name, but also Louis Harper, the mystery man who had supposedly been responsible for Ramona's sobriety and well-being over the past four years.

Even though she couldn't imagine Ramona wanting to harm Liz or hurt Sheri, she reminded herself that she knew very little about the woman who was her birth mother.

The morning passed with customers coming in and Jennifer and Sheri working side by side to keep things running smoothly. Between customers Sheri returned to her seat behind the cash register and worked on the growing list of names she felt would be no help at all to the officials investigating the events of the night before.

At noon Jason King came in—his youthful face held the same stress lines it had the last time she'd seen him. He leaned against the counter, as if too tired to stand up straight.

"Things no better at home?" Sheri asked sympathetically, knowing there was no way she was writing down the name of a seventeen-year-old Amish boy on her list.

"A little better. The young ones are with Elizabeth Yoder this afternoon for a couple of hours. People are doing their best to help." He offered her a tired smile. "I just decided to walk over and buy a bottle of orange juice and relax for a bit. Da would skin me alive for not being out in the field or taking care of my siblings, but it seems like all I do is take care of the young ones and work the field. I need to just be at rest sometimes."

Sheri motioned him to the three tables and chairs next to a long industrial cooler where she sold cold drinks, prepared sandwiches and a variety of food that tourists occasionally sat and ate before heading back on the road.

"Go sit. The juice is on me."

"I can't let you do that," he protested as he moved toward one of the tables.

"You can and you will," Sheri said firmly. As he slumped into a chair she set a cold bottle of juice in front of him.

"How's your father?"

Jason screwed off the lid and took a long drink before replying. "I think he's starting to come around a little. I mean, I miss my ma, too. But six months is a long time to carry grief."

Sheri thought of her aunt. "Sometimes you carry grief for a lifetime, but you have to put it into a place where it no longer brings you to your knees. You have to find the strength to keep on living."

Jason nodded. "I'm hoping my da gets to that place soon."

"So, tell me how everyone else is doing," Sheri asked.

For the next thirty minutes Jason talked about life at the settlement, about social gatherings and his friends and a simple existence that spoke of humility and faith.

When he finally left the store he appeared more relaxed and prepared to go back to the responsibilities that the death of his mother had placed on his young slender shoulders.

Sheri returned to her seat behind the register and once again pulled out her list of names. While she'd made it clear to many of the hunters in the area that her property was off-limits, Travis was the only person she'd ever pointed her shotgun at.

She was at a loss as to any other names to add and she couldn't imagine anyone on the list who would be capable of hurting Highway or her. She couldn't begin to guess what she might have done to any of the people on the list that would inspire the kind of demonic rage that had tried to get her, that had hurt Highway.

At two Abe arrived to take over his shift that would last until closing. Abe, who had loved her aunt Liz's cakes and pies. Abe, who had confessed to asking Aunt Liz out on a date only to be rejected by her.

Abe had always told Sheri that among the three sisters he thought she was most like her aunt. Abe had lost his wife several years ago. Was it possible he'd had something to do with Liz's disappearance? Was it possible because Sheri was so much like her aunt he now had his sights on her?

As he worked in the back room unloading a shipment of Wolf Creek shot glasses and mugs that had arrived, Sheri wrote his name down and then threw her pen aside.

She hated this. She hated that she had to look at friends and coworkers with a skeptical gaze, that this whole process would make her second-guess her relationships with everyone in her daily life.

It was nearly three when Officer Richard Crossly walked in. He was also a frequent customer. A tall, muscular man with nearly white hair, he talked about retiring at least once a week.

"How you doing, Sheri?" he asked as he grabbed one of the turkey club sandwiches from the cooler. "I heard you had some excitement at your place last night."

"Enough to keep my heart beating a little too fast even this morning," she told him.

He added a can of pop to the sandwich on the counter. "Have you heard from anyone if they've found anything in the woods today? I heard they were doing a search, but I haven't talked to anyone…been out on the highway writing speeding tickets all day."

"I haven't heard from anyone, either." She rang him up and took his cash. "But I hope they find something. I'm going to be armed and dangerous from now on at the cottage and if anyone tries to hurt me or my dog again they'll have hell to pay from me personally."

"Ah, nothing like a gun-toting gal to get *my* heart

racing," Richard said with a laugh. "Hopefully, some-body will figure it all out before we have to arrest you for manslaughter."

As he ambled out of the door, Sheri thought for several long moments and then added his name to her list. It felt strange to write down the name of a member of law enforcement, but Jimmy had told her to write down the names of regular customers and Richard was just that.

Jimmy called her at five. "I'm on my way to pick you up," he said.

"Did you sleep?" she asked, remembering the raw redness of his eyes that morning.

"Yeah, I got a couple hours of shut-eye," he re-plied.

"Did they find anything in the woods?"

His hesitation was her answer. "No," he finally said.

She squeezed her cell phone more tightly against her ear as fierce disappointment swept through her. "I'll be ready when you get here."

She hung up and went into the back room. Jennifer had gone home when Abe had arrived and Michael had come in an hour earlier to work until closing with Abe.

Both of the men were in the front of the store wait-ing on customers. Sheri walked to a sturdy metal cabinet and unlocked it. She withdrew two boxes of shotgun shells and placed them in a bag, then re-locked the cabinet.

She and Abe were the only people who had keys to this particular cabinet and only the local hunters knew that Sheri kept ammunition for sale in the store.

She couldn't allow a dark-eyed, hard-chested, lush-lipped detective to stay in her house for protection. If she held on to her dreams of the perfect prince eventually finding her, then she couldn't get any closer to Detective Hottie from Philly.

She was armed and dangerous with the shells for her gun, but she also knew from the single kiss they had shared that he was hot and dangerous to the dreams she'd made for herself long ago.

Jimmy had dropped Sheri off at the store that morning and then had gone home to sleep, confident that his partners and the other officers would conduct a thorough search of the heavily wooded area behind Sheri's house.

When he'd awakened and checked in with Frank, he'd been disappointed to learn they'd found nothing of evidentiary value anywhere in the woods.

He'd also spoken with Dr. Cusack earlier, who had told him that Highway's blood results had come back and the dog had been injected with a near-life-threatening dose of Xanax.

Jimmy had a feeling that whoever had administered the drug probably didn't have a prescription for it and, in any case, attempting to access that kind of information would mean breaking all kinds of privacy laws. He also knew how easily drugs could be obtained on the streets, on the internet and through friends. The drug was a lead that would be almost impossible to follow.

The only thing he could hope for was that Sheri had made a list of people where they might at least begin an investigation of sorts.

As he pulled up to the front of the Roadside Stop, he couldn't help the way his heart quickened in anticipation of the sight of her. When she'd left that morning in her tight jeans and a brown T-shirt with gold lettering that emphasized the gold of her eyes, he'd been in a near state of arousal just looking at her.

He didn't want to care about her. He didn't want to truly care about anyone, but from the moment he'd met her three months earlier, something about Sheri had touched him in a way that no other woman had ever done before.

Maybe it was because she was so small and appeared so vulnerable, but it also had to do with the way her hair fell in such soft waves around her shoulders, how her amazing golden eyes lit as if with a source from within.

In all honesty, he had no idea why he was so attracted to her, why the very sight of her welled up a protective instinct he'd never felt for any other person. He just felt so good, so right whenever he was with her.

He knew that in following through on his attraction to her, he'd experience heartbreak, rejection and abandonment issues for the second time in his life, and he told himself over and over again that he wasn't willing to go there again.

Still, as she left the store and headed toward his car, he couldn't help the way he felt, as if his world was about to be right, at least for as long as he'd be in her company.

"Hey," she said as she slid into the passenger seat and placed a white plastic bag at her feet on the floor.

"Hey yourself," he said. "How was your day?"

"Could have been better," she replied.

He knew she was probably referring to the fact that nothing had been found in the woods to help them in investigating who'd attacked her.

"Did you make a list for me today?"

"I usually try to do what I'm told when a law enforcement agent asks something of me," she said with a teasing tone.

He thought of all the things he'd like to ask her to do for him, to him, and tightened his hands on the steering wheel. "Then how about I drive through and get Chinese and we go to your house and talk about the list while we eat?" he suggested, shoving the other sexy ideas out of his head.

"Sounds like a plan," she agreed. "Although I can't imagine the people I listed having anything to do with what happened to me and Highway last night."

"We never imagined Steve's old girlfriend would try to kill Roxy," Jimmy countered. "Right now as far as I'm concerned everyone in your life except me, my partners and your sisters are potential suspects."

"Wow, you're definitely the suspicious type," she said.

"I prefer to think of myself as the cautious type," he returned as he headed down Main toward Chang Li's restaurant.

"And that's what I like about you," she said. "Especially when it comes to my safety."

Forty minutes later the two of them were seated at Sheri's table, plates full of sweet-and-sour chicken, sesame beef and broccoli, and crab Rangoons before them.

They had decided to eat first and then talk about

the names on her list afterward. Their dinner conversation revolved around her childhood with her aunt
and her sisters. He found himself laughing again and
again as she confessed to the schemes Roxy would
talk them into and the chaos that often resulted in
the house.

"We definitely were the ornery three musketeers,
and Aunt Liz had the patience of a saint," she said as
she reached for a second crab Rangoon.

"Speaking of that, have you heard anything more
from Ramona?" he asked.

"No, but Marlene told me today she'd decided to
have a meet with her. Roxy is still adamant that she
wants nothing to do with Ramona." She took a bite
and chewed thoughtfully and Jimmy tried to keep his
gaze away from her mouth, a mouth he knew was
not just sweet and giving, but also held a fiery heat
that had stunned him.

"Aunt Liz was such a good mother to us, none of
us really missed having Ramona in our lives. Did
you have any mother figures at all in your life?" she
asked curiously.

A hard knot instantly formed in his chest as his
thoughts shot back in time, back to when he was eight
years old. He'd been so hungry to belong to somebody permanently, so needy of love that would last
forever and fate had finally answered his prayers.

"Jane Brickman." Even her name falling from his
lips shot a stunning ache through his chest. "I met
her and her husband, Lenny, when I was seven years
old. They started coming regularly to my foster home
to visit with me."

He was pleased that his voice remained cool and

calm as he spoke of the couple he'd loved so much. "They visited me frequently and then after about a year they began taking me out for day trips to the zoo, to the movies, wherever they took me I was just happy to be with them. They were kind and gentle people and I grew to love them deeply." His voice cracked slightly.

He paused, swallowing against the emotions he'd suppressed successfully for so many years. He leaned back in his chair and raked a hand through his hair. "Sorry, I've never really talked about this to anyone before." He shoved his plate aside, his appetite gone.

"Jimmy, if you don't want to talk about it…"

"No, it's okay." He straightened in his chair. "It happened a long time ago and I think I need to talk about it. Anyway, it came to the point where I was spending weekends with Jane and Lenny. They'd even decorated a bedroom in their house just for me. It had a bedspread with a big race car on it and shelves filled with books and toys. When they finally told me they were about to begin the adoption process to make me their very own son forever, I cried. I'd never known what happiness was until that day."

He felt the weight of Sheri's gaze on him as he stared at the wall just above her head. Memories cascaded through his mind, memories of snuggling into that bed beneath the race car, Jane's gentle kiss good night on his forehead and Lenny tossing him up for an impromptu piggyback ride.

"But something happened," Sheri said softly. "Something bad."

The memories shattered as he gave a curt nod and swallowed against a weight of emotions he'd kept suppressed for years. "Jane was on her way to the grocery store when a drunk driver slammed into her car head-on. She was killed instantly." His stomach twisted, churning the Chinese food he'd just eaten. "My foster mother told me about Jane's death. I never saw Lenny again."

He finally looked at Sheri, surprised to see her eyes shimmering with tears that could only be for him. "I had the dream, you know, of having a family, of finally belonging. I was so sure it was going to happen for me and then it was just gone. I later heard that Lenny had moved away and was suffering from severe depression."

"And after that?" she asked softly.

"After that I was a very angry nine-year-old who became hard to place because of my aggressive, nasty disposition. For the next nine years I was moved from place to place, fighting authority, lost in a rage, until I finally reached eighteen and was given a change of clothing, a hundred dollars and told it was time to make my own way."

"You didn't get any counseling when Jane died? Nobody addressed the issue of your terrible grief?" she asked, her voice thick with emotion.

He finally looked at her with a wry smile. "I was lucky to get dinner most nights."

"Oh, Jimmy." She reached across the table and covered one of his hands with hers. Her tiny hand radiated warmth to the cold place that had taken up residence in his heart as he remembered the little boy he'd once been. A child who'd almost had what he wanted most of all in the world, and then it had all been snatched away.

"To be honest, I did have some great foster parents, but by the time I was placed with them I was already out of control, running with a rough crowd and trying to be the biggest badass in the whole city of Philly. I wouldn't let anyone close to me."

He pulled his hand from beneath hers, already feeling as if he'd said too much, cracked open parts of his heart that he'd never shared. "We have more important things to talk about than my past. You said you had a list of names for us to take a look at?"

Things had become too personal for him. It was time to step back to a level of professionalism where he had the job to try to figure out who had chased her the night before, who would want to hurt her.

For the next three hours they pored over the list she had made, talking about her relationship with the people on it. "No previous boyfriends? Past relationships?" he asked when they'd gone over the list for the second time and come up with no real person of interest.

"I've only had one past relationship and that was almost a year ago."

"Why isn't his name on the list?"

She shrugged. "I honestly didn't think about him. I haven't seen him since we broke up. I can't imagine he'd have anything to do with this."

"Who broke off the relationship?"

"I did." Shutters seemed to fall in her eyes. They went flat, completely unreadable. "I thought he was my blond prince, but he was really just a mean, hateful man who thought it was amusing to make fun of me."

"Make fun of you?"

"Whenever he was irritated with me, he'd call me S-s-stuttering S-S-Sheri, too s-stupid to s-speak." Her cheeks flamed with color. "I put up with it for three months and finally had enough and walked away."

"How did he take it?"

"Fine. I'm sure he immediately found another woman to verbally abuse." The color in her cheeks faded and her eyes took on a sparkling life once again. "Jimmy, Eric never had enough passion toward me to love or to hate me. I'm pretty sure he wasn't the man in the woods. Eric was slender and the man in the woods was bigger."

"I'm still going to check him out," Jimmy insisted. He didn't intend to leave any stone unturned until he found out who had attacked Highway and Sheri.

By the time they'd finished talking about each person on the list yet again, it was after nine and Sheri had stifled several yawns.

"Are you sure you don't want me or somebody else staying out here with you for the night?" he asked after they'd cleared the table.

"I've got bullets for my gun and I know how to use it," she said, a determined glint in her eyes. "I won't be taken by surprise again, so I'll be fine here alone." She walked with him to the front door.

"Then I'll pick you up in the morning to take you to the store. I don't want you driving the mountain road alone right now."

"Okay, I'll see you in the morning." She opened the door and stepped back, giving him plenty of room to leave without coming too close to her.

"Good night, princess," he said, and stepped outside. She closed the door behind him and he heard the reassuring sound of her bolting the door.

He got into his car and drove about half a mile down the road where there was a small area for a car to pull off onto a shoulder easement nearly overgrown and half-hidden by the woods.

He parked, got out of the car and opened his trunk where he had earlier stored a flashlight and a blanket.

If she thought he was going to leave her to her own devices tonight after what had happened the night before, then she was apparently delusional. There was no way he was going to allow her to be in that cottage surrounded by woods all alone.

It took him only minutes to hike back to her house and head to the backyard where he remembered seeing a colorful hammock tied between two trees. It would be the perfect place for him to plant himself.

He'd always been a light sleeper and there was no way if he snoozed in the hammock anyone would approach Sheri's house from the woods. He also wasn't concerned about Sheri shooting him. He'd bet his own gun that Sheri Marcoli was incapable of pointing a loaded gun at anyone and pulling the trigger, no matter what the circumstances.

If she'd had the guts to shoot anyone that shotgun would have been loaded the day she'd pointed it at Travis Brooks. He was rather pleased with himself for coming up with the idea of spending the nights right under her nose, in her own backyard until they had the attacker behind bars.

He took a dive into the hammock and it promptly twisted and tossed him on the ground. He landed with an *umph* and picked himself up and tried it again with the same results.

For a long moment he sat on the ground, wondering why he thought himself capable of guarding Sheri when he was being beaten up by a damned hammock.

He tried one final time, easing into the night-cooled canvas with success. As the hammock swayed to a faint night breeze, he thought of the people Sheri had put on her list.

Was the attacker there? Or was he somebody who hadn't even made it on Sheri's radar? What had he wanted with Sheri? There were so many questions and absolutely no answers.

One thing was clear, whoever had been in the woods wasn't done with Sheri yet. Jimmy felt it in his gut that danger still lurked around her. He could almost feel the malevolent forces that lingered in the nearby woods and he could only hope that when the time came the foster kid from Philly had what it took to save the beautiful princess from evil.

Chapter 11

Saturdays were always the busiest day in the shop and today was even busier than usual. Sheri was grateful for the constant stream of customers that kept her focus away from monsters in the woods, her precious Highway's recovery and the disturbingly sexy Jimmy Carmani.

For the past three days she and Jimmy had fallen into an easy routine. He picked her up each morning to bring her into work, and then reappeared at around five to take her back to her place. They usually picked up fast food to eat at her house while he told her about the progress the police were making on her case, which was basically none.

He left the house by nine each evening and Sheri made sure her newly loaded shotgun was next to her bed when she went to sleep. She'd only had a nightmare once, reliving the wild chase through the woods, terror banging painfully in her chest until she'd awakened gasping for air and grateful to discover that it was just a bad dream. She'd survived the real deal.

Tonight she would sleep easier, for Highway was finally coming home. She and Jimmy were picking him up on their way to the cottage after work and she couldn't wait to get him back where he belonged.

Dr. Cusack had not allowed her to visit him during his convalescence, insisting that seeing her would only upset Highway and set back his recovery time and adjustment to the cast on his front leg.

It had been agony for her, not being able to see him, not being able to assure herself that he was really okay, but she'd had to trust that Dr. Cusack had Highway's best interest in mind.

She couldn't wait to wrap her arms around Highway's furry neck and to have him sleeping next to her bed, his faint snores creating a nighttime lullaby in the bedroom that gave her a sense of security and hopefully kept any further nightmares at bay.

"You and Detective Carmani seem to be getting pretty close," Jennifer said as she stood next to Sheri during a lull in customers.

"He's my guard dog while Highway is at the vet's," Sheri explained. "At least I don't have to let him out to run in the yard occasionally."

Jennifer giggled. "Personally I think Detective Carmani is panting after you."

Sheri swatted Jennifer on the shoulder. "Don't be ridiculous," she said.

"I'm just saying." Jennifer moved two steps away

so that she was out of swatting distance. "He's definitely a hunk."

"He's short," Sheri said. *And he's not blond and he doesn't have blue eyes,* she thought.

"He might not be as tall as his partners, but he's plenty tall enough for you."

Sheri tried not to think about how well their bodies had fit together in that unforgettable kiss they had shared. Jimmy wasn't really short, he just wasn't a six-foot prince.

"There's nothing going on between us. He's just doing his job," she said firmly, unsure if she was trying to convince Jennifer or herself.

Jennifer raised an eyebrow, obviously not believing a word Sheri said. "Guess I'll go straighten some shelves before the next flurry of customers arrive."

"That's right, make yourself useful," Sheri muttered.

As Jennifer disappeared down one of the aisles, Sheri mentally cursed her for bringing up Jimmy. Since the night he had told her about his childhood loss, she'd felt herself getting too close, caring too much about him, yet she was convinced he wasn't the right man for her.

He himself had told her that he didn't know how to love, that he wasn't looking for a forever relationship. When the right man walked into her life it wouldn't be with the burden of defending her. He wouldn't be a man who saw Sheri as a potential victim.

Jimmy was just wrong for her, but that didn't stop her from wondering what it would be like to kiss him again. It didn't stop her from fantasizing what it might be like to make love to him.

On some level she found him fascinating. When they talked about his day over dinner, he was able to recount interviews and discussion with Frank and Steve almost verbatim, without using notes to refresh his memory.

He was sharp, quick-witted and often made her laugh with stories of his work and his life in Philly. He'd helped her fill bird feeders, thrown out their leftovers for the raccoons and put out fresh squirrel corn without complaint.

He was just easy to be with and he made her feel good whenever she was around him. Something about the way he gazed at her made her feel special.

Drat the man anyway, she thought as she headed for the back room to get a cup of coffee. She nearly jumped out of her skin as she saw William King standing in the back doorway.

"Mr. King," she greeted him with a hesitant smile. "I don't see you often here in the store."

"No, but apparently you see too much of my son." The man's blue eyes were pale, nearly colorless and without any friendliness at all.

"He does come in occasionally," Sheri said slowly. She wasn't going to lie about Jason's visits to the store.

"He talks too much."

"He's overwhelmed since his mother's death," Sheri replied.

It was obviously the wrong thing to say for William's eyes narrowed even more. "He's becoming enamored with the English ways and he has no business sharing personal things outside of his own people. I would have you turn him away should he come here again."

"As you wish," Sheri conceded. As much as it broke her heart for the young Jason, she would not go against his father's wishes. She'd always been close to the people from the Amish settlement and she would not get between a father and his son and the ways of their people.

William tipped his straw hat and then stepped out of the building. A moment later, Sheri heard the sound of his buggy pulling away.

William had been angry with Roxy months ago when the family would go into town and Jason would spend some time with Sheri's sister in front of her restaurant.

He was obviously terrified that his eldest son would turn his back on his faith and become English. The result of Jason becoming English would be that he would never be allowed to see or speak to his family again. He would be cast out and never mentioned again in the community.

Fear and grief can make a very angry man, she thought as she poured her coffee and then decided to close and lock the back door of the shop. If any vendors showed up, there was a doorbell they could use to announce their arrival. She suddenly wasn't comfortable leaving the door open and unattended. She didn't like the idea of just anyone being able to wander inside the storeroom.

She returned to the front counter with her coffee and once again her head filled with thoughts of Jimmy. His story of his loss with Jane and Lenny had nearly broken her heart.

At least when Ramona had abandoned them, she hadn't thrown them into the foster care system but had assured them a place where she'd known they would be cared for and loved.

Maybe she should be grateful to Ramona for knowing she wasn't in a mental or physical state to raise any children and had made the ultimate sacrifice in giving them away.

Or perhaps Sheri was giving Ramona too much credit. Maybe dropping off her children for Aunt Liz to raise had simply been a matter of selfishness on Ramona's part. She hadn't wanted to be saddled with any baggage.

And who was this Louis Harper from Arizona? Was he here in town with Ramona? Did he have some kind of a beef with her children?

Sheri felt nearly schizophrenic by the time Jimmy came to pick her up. Her thoughts were shooting in a thousand directions and she was having trouble sustaining any one thought for any length of time.

The first thing she did when she slid into his passenger seat was tell him about her visit from William King. "I know it sounds crazy, but he lost his wife a month or two before Aunt Liz disappeared. I keep wondering if maybe he decided to take Aunt Liz as a replacement wife."

"That does sound a bit crazy," Jimmy said. "I mean, somebody at the settlement would have seen Liz by now if she were at the Kings' house. Surely Jason would have told you that your aunt was living at the settlement."

"But maybe William has her locked up in a barn

or a shed where nobody can see her." Sheri laughed at her own words. "Maybe I've truly lost my mind."

"We've been out to the settlement a dozen times, Sheri, and nobody there has seen your aunt. Besides, what would any of this have to do with you being attacked in the woods?"

"I never professed to have any answers. I'm just filled with silly thoughts today." Thoughts that included her aunt chained like a farm animal in a barn, her mother killing her aunt so she could take her rightful place as mother to the girls she had abandoned so long ago, and finally visions of her and Jimmy in bed together, naked and gasping as they made love.

"Silly thoughts," she muttered to herself. She sat up straighter in the seat as they approached the animal clinic. Highway would bring her sanity back. He would bring back some sense of safety and security by his mere presence.

She nearly leaped from the car before Jimmy had brought it to a full stop, her eagerness to see Highway bubbled up inside her.

Dr. Cusack was waiting for her, Highway on a leash with his front leg in a sturdy plaster cast. He yipped with excitement at the sight of her and she fell to her knees in front of him.

Wrapping her arms around his neck, she buried her face in the familiar scent of him as he nuzzled her arm and then licked the underside of her jaw. "My sweet Highway," she said as happy tears blurred her eyes. With the first greeting out of the way, Sheri finally got to her feet and smiled at the vet.

"So, he's good to go?"

"I don't think I could keep the two of you apart another day," Dr. Cusack replied with a smile. "I'll need to see him again in about four weeks. By then we'll X-ray that break and make sure it's healed and then we can get the cast off him as soon as possible."

Highway bounded to the door, the cast not hindering him at all as he looked at the door and then back at Sheri, silently demanding she get him out of there as quickly as possible.

Jimmy had remained in the car with the air-conditioning running and as she and Highway left the clinic, Jimmy hurried out of his seat and opened the back door.

Highway jumped in and lay down as if he'd been there a thousand times before. Sheri slid into the passenger seat and turned to check on her baby. "I'm so glad to see you," she said, loving the way his ears perked forward and the bright gleam of intelligence and love that shone from his eyes.

Thank goodness the tranquilizer hadn't left any long-term effects. Highway appeared to be himself, smart and strong and ready to get on with life despite the small hindrance of the cast on his leg.

She turned around and buckled in. "I can't wait to get him home where he belongs."

Jimmy smiled at her. "You look happier at this moment than I think I've ever seen you."

"I'm just so grateful that man didn't succeed in killing my dog."

"And I'm grateful he didn't succeed in catching you."

Jimmy's gaze was filled with a warmth that made Jennifer's words pop back into Sheri's head. The warmth of friendliness, that's what it had to be, not the heat of lust.

Roxy inspired lust in men. Marlene inspired lust in men. Sheri was far too ordinary to arouse that kind of intense emotion in any man. Jennifer was just plain wrong and the kiss she and Jimmy had shared had been nothing more than a strange anomaly based on timing and circumstance.

"Burgers?" Jimmy asked.

"How about we just head on to my place and I'll do omelets or something?" She was eager to get Highway settled in where he belonged.

"I wasn't sure you could cook anything," he teased.

"Simple I can do."

"Omelets sound good to me," he said.

The rest of the drive was completed in silence. Jimmy appeared to be concentrating on something inside his head and Sheri welcomed the peace and quiet after a long day of chatting with customers at work.

Once inside the cottage as Highway sniffed in every crack and crevice, as if to assure himself that all was well, Jimmy set the table and Sheri fried up bacon and then made vegetable omelets.

The silence between them continued until they were both seated at the table, Highway like a big black furry throw rug next to Sheri's feet.

"Maybe I just scared a hunter who was obviously hunting out of season," she said, finally breaking the silence. "Maybe he kicked Highway and had darts or something for his hunting and used that on him, as well."

"If that were the case, then I'd think once he'd

neutralized any danger from Highway he'd run away from you rather than after you," Jimmy reasoned. "Tomorrow we're going to check out William King's place. I know he had a beef with Roxy before and he was obviously angry when he came to see you today. Maybe he has an issue with the entire Marcoli clan."

"That just seems so crazy," she said, trying not to notice how well his white shirt fit across his broad shoulders, how right it felt for him to be seated across from her at her dining table. "To be honest, I think I don't want to spend time tonight talking about crime or suspects at all. I'm tired and I'm just looking forward to snuggling in with Highway."

"Then we'll finish eating and I'll get out of here," Jimmy replied.

She eyed him carefully to make certain she hadn't irritated him, but he appeared fine with leaving early and allowing her a night to herself and her furry buddy. Easy, he was so easy to be with and he always seemed to want whatever was best for her.

For the rest of the meal she talked about the people who had come into the store that day, telling him where they were headed, where they were from and what they had bought.

"You wouldn't believe how popular those stupid hats with the stuffed wolves are with people passing through," she said.

"So, people take a little tacky piece of Wolf Creek with them when they leave," he said with a grin.

He told her that he and his partners had eaten breakfast that morning at Roxy's Dollhouse restaurant and that her sister had vowed that she'd kill all of them if anything else bad happened to Sheri.

By the time they'd finished the meal and cleared off the dishes, she was ready for a quiet night, and with a goodbye to Jimmy, she was left alone with Highway.

The first thing she did was change into her nightgown. Then she grabbed a romance novel from the bookshelf and curled up on the sofa with Highway like a buddy pillow next to her. Thank goodness her sofa was wide in the seat to accommodate both her and her furry friend.

She didn't want to think. She just wanted to stroke Highway's fur and lose herself in a book that she knew would end with happy ever after.

The hero in the book was the epitome of the hero in her fantasies, blond with chiseled features and the courtly manners of a prince. Of course he was madly in love with the heroine and would die for her if necessary.

It wasn't reading romance novels that had formed the fantasy of a prince for Sheri. Her fantasy had been born in the days when she'd been a young girl and an outcast due to her stutter.

She'd also fantasized that her unknown father was secretly a king of some exotic foreign country, although she had no idea how Ramona would have had contact with any royalty. But during those days her fantasies were so much nicer than her daily reality as a stuttering outcast with no friends.

She read until almost ten and then placed the book down and went into the kitchen to recheck the back door to make sure it was securely locked.

Highway limped next to her and when he got to the door he lowered his head and released a guttural growl. The hairs on Sheri's nape raised as she quickly turned off the kitchen light and then returned to the door to peer outside.

A full moon cast down a ghostly light that illuminated the yard. She saw nobody standing in the shadows or lurking by the edge of the trees.

"What is it, boy?" she murmured, and placed a hand on the top of Highway's head. He yipped, his body tense, and then she spied what was making Highway react defensively.

He was in the hammock and she immediately knew it was Jimmy. She opened the back door and squeezed out, not allowing Highway to follow her. She got halfway to the hammock when he sat up, his eyes gleaming like those of a trapped animal.

"You're lucky I didn't put a bullet through your sneaky heart," she exclaimed.

"You don't even have your gun with you," he said. He shifted his weight and was promptly dropped on his butt to the ground. Sheri stifled a giggle as he quickly got to his feet and glared at her.

"That mutt gave me away, didn't he?"

"That's his job. Have you been sleeping out here every night?" He hesitated and in that hesitation she had her answer. She released a sigh, not knowing if she was irritated or secretly pleased by his obvious show of caring. "Since you're busted, you might as well come inside and at least have the comfort of my sofa."

"That sounds like a great idea," he said. "A hammock is furniture made by the Devil meant to drive a man mad."

Sheri laughed, but as they walked together back

toward the house, She had a feeling that inviting him back inside was probably a terrible idea.

Jimmy stood in the bathroom, a towel wrapped around his waist as he finished up shaving. For the past three nights he'd been on Sheri's sofa and for the past three nights he'd suffered agonizing, stimulating erotic dreams of being with her in her bed.

An internal tension was building inside him with every minute that he spent in her home, in her very presence. The scent of her seemed to be permanently burned into his nose, the sound of her laughter etched inside his brain. He'd never felt this way before. He'd never been so acutely aware of another human being. It felt far too good for comfort.

During the days he worked with his partners in an attempt to solve not only the case of the man in the woods, but also continue the investigation into Liz Marcoli's disappearance.

Everywhere they went they hit dead ends. How did you find a shadow in the woods? How did you find a woman who had disappeared over three months ago when the trail was arctic cold?

They'd driven out to the settlement and had a talk with William King. They'd also done a deeper investigation into Louis Harper, the man who had been Ramona's personal savior. He was a successful businessman who had no criminal record and seemed completely aboveboard.

Harper was still in Arizona. According to a phone conversation he'd had with Steve, he and the rehab facility staff where Ramona worked had been instrumental in encouraging her to face her past, to seek out the daughters she'd abandoned.

He'd just put his razor down when the bathroom door flew open. He whirled around in surprise to see an even more shocked Sheri standing in the doorway.

"Oh…I didn't know you were in here," she said. Her gaze started at his freshly shaved jawline and slowly tracked down the near-naked length of him.

Her gaze heated him and flickered licks of fire that warmed blood to places that would only prove embarrassing. He grabbed the towel to make sure it stayed in place as she remained standing in the doorway.

"You have tattoos." Her gaze lingered on the barbed wire tattoo around his left biceps and then moved to the outline of a detective shield that rode his right biceps.

"Uh, yeah."

She looked gorgeous with her shiny hair bed-wrestled and a faint stain of color on her cheeks. She was clad only in her short lavender nightgown that clung to her curves like a second skin.

"Sheri." Her name released from him, sounding half-strangled as a wave of lust, of immense want, roared through him. "You need to back away and close the door."

Her golden eyes had deepened in hue and her tongue slipped out to moisten her lower lip. Jimmy felt his mind fall into a place where there were no consequences, where his need to have her overrode all common sense.

And still she remained in place, as if waiting. But waiting for what?

"Sheri, if you don't leave now I won't be responsible for my actions."

Her breath visibly hitched in her chest, her breasts rising and falling as her nipples became hard against the silk material of her thin nightgown. "I don't think I want you to be responsible for your actions right now." Her voice was a mere whisper. "I don't even think I want to be responsible for my own actions right now."

She took several steps toward him in the tiny room and then placed her palm over the frantic beat of his heart. She grabbed his hand and placed it over her own heart, which beat just as fast, just as frantically as his own.

"What are we doing, Sheri?" he asked, the warmth of her skin through her nightgown a burning fire that radiated through him.

"I don't know, but I don't want to stop."

That's all he needed to hear. With one hand still grasping at the towel at his waist, he reached for her with his other arm.

She wrapped her arms around his neck as their lips found each other's. Hot and eager, their tongues battled as she pressed her body more tightly against his.

The kiss seemed to last both an infinity and a mere second. He broke the heady contact, needing to maintain control, yet not wanting to, desperate to manage the situation when all he wanted to be was wildly out of control.

"Come to my bed, Jimmy. Come and make love to me." Her voice was husky, breathless and her eyes were the color of glittering, polished amber.

"I'm not your prince."

She smiled, an alluring temptation that simply fired him hotter. "Right now I don't need a prince, but I do need you." She reached out and grabbed the hand that wasn't holding the towel over what had become an almost painful arousal.

He stared deep into her eyes, seeking a part of her that didn't want to follow through, a place that might be resentful when they were finished with what apparently was about to happen. He found nothing but desire shining there and he could do nothing to deny her...or himself.

He allowed her to pull him out of the bathroom and down the hallway to her bedroom. It was still early enough in the morning that the only light was the faint stir of dawn as they entered her bedroom.

The bed was a jumble of lavender sheets and purple spread, and as they fell together on top he was surrounded by her scent, the fragrance that had muddied his head for a couple weeks.

He had no idea where his towel went, but when he reached to embrace her once again, he was naked. It didn't seem fair that she still had clothes on, so he grabbed the bottom of her nightgown and swept it over her head and then tossed it to the floor. She wore nothing beneath it.

For a moment he simply gazed at her beauty in the golden glow of dawn. She was pint-size perfection, her small breasts in perfect proportion to her tiny waist and slender hips. Her skin glowed in the faint light spilling in through the window and exposed a smattering of freckles on each of her shoulders.

She stole his breath away.

He wanted to tell her how beautiful she was, but he didn't have the words. Instead he drew her against him and kissed her deep and long, her warm naked curves fitting against him as if they'd been made to mold together.

Her hands caressed up and down his back, as if memorizing each muscle, every sinew, and as she continued his want of her grew bigger, brighter, burning out the last of any rational thought he might entertain.

He slid his lips from her mouth down the sweet curve of her jaw and then nipped his way down her throat. She moaned and the sound of her pleasure only torched his higher.

Moving downward, he teased one of her nipples with the tip of his tongue. She moaned again and moved her arms up to tangle her hands in his hair.

Her body squirmed beneath his as if she were eager for him to touch her, to kiss her everywhere, and he complied, languidly loving her body with his tongue, tasting her skin like forbidden fruit that would never be offered again.

He was ready to take her, to have her hot and fast to satisfy his own need, but he also wanted to make this an experience she'd never forget. He wanted to set the bar high for any prince who would eventually come after him.

"You're driving me crazy," she finally gasped as his fingers stroked the inside of first one silky thigh and then the other.

"I want you crazy...crazy for me." He took her mouth with his in hard demand as his fingers slid across her warm, moist center.

Once again she moaned and raised her hips to meet his touch. Her fingernails lightly scratched across his back, an erotic sensation that made him fight for self-control.

Her pleasure first and then his own, he reminded himself. He wanted her sated, breathless when he finally sought his own release.

He moved his fingers more quickly against her sensitive flesh, watching her face, feeling the tension that built in her body. Her head thrashed against the pillow, her hair spilling first one way and then the other.

And then she was there, rippling shudders rushing through her as she cried out his name. While she was still gasping from the force of her climax, he positioned himself between her thighs, his gaze meeting hers as he slowly entered her.

Her eyes were like those of a wild jungle animal, golden flecks sharp and glittering with bold invitation and a renewed hunger. Surrounded by her heat, he was almost afraid to move, fearful that with a single stroke he'd be finished and this moment would end.

Still, his body moved without his mind in charge, pulling back slightly and then stroking more deeply into her. The pleasure was mind-blowing and she encouraged him, grabbing on to both sides of his hips to guide him.

Faster, more frantic they moved together, their breathing wild and irregular and escaping on moans and gasps. He realized he couldn't hold back any longer and was grateful when he felt her body stiffen and shudder at the same time he released.

He collapsed just to the side of her, not speaking until he could finally find his voice. "I thought you weren't a morning person," he finally said.

She leaned up on one elbow to gaze down at him. "I wasn't until now." She reached out and traced her fingers over the barbed wire tattoo. "Tell me about this."

"I got that when I was eighteen and thought I was going to be the biggest badass in Philly. I was training in martial arts and running with a gang of guys who now are probably dead or in prison. I consider it a badge of shame."

She frowned. "Why?"

"I was at a bad place in my life when I got it. A couple of years ago I thought about having it removed, but then decided I needed it as a reminder of where I'd been and how far I've come since then."

"And the other one?" She reached across his chest to touch the tattoo in the shape of a shield. As she did her body was warm and comforting on his.

"The day I was accepted into the police academy I knew I wanted a detective's shield, so I got the tattoo to remind myself of my goal."

"There must have been a lot of personal and emotional growth between the two," she said as her hand moved from the tattoo to lie in the center of his chest. "Like a battle between good and evil that happened right here in your heart."

He nodded, wondering if she had any idea how absolutely gorgeous she looked at the moment, with her lips slightly swollen from his kisses, her hair a chestnut tangle and her eyes still glowing with residual sexual fulfillment.

As much as Jimmy wanted this moment to go on forever, he knew it couldn't. He had to ask the question that burned foremost in his mind.

"So, what happens now? We didn't exactly plan for this to happen."

A frown once again streaked across her forehead. "No, we didn't plan it. But now we get up, we have coffee and we go on with our lives." She worried a hand through her hair, as if to attempt some kind of order. "This was one-time magic, Jimmy. We both know we aren't meant to be together for any long-term relationship and we'd be fools to pretend otherwise."

He was surprised to discover that her words hurt just a little bit. One-time magic, and yet already he wanted to repeat it. He rolled away from her and sat up. "Of course you're right."

He found his towel on the floor and once again wrapped it around his waist. "Coffee is made. I'll meet you in the kitchen." He started to leave the room but paused as she called his name.

"I think I'll be fine here now that Highway is back. He alerts me to anyone coming close to my house and I have my gun and a phone to call for help." She sat up and grabbed the sheet to hide her breasts. "It's been two weeks since I was chased in the woods. Maybe we all overreacted and there's really no danger lurking around."

She was not only kicking him out of her bed, but also kicking him out of her house. He merely nodded and continued to the bathroom. It took him only minutes to wash up and dress, and then he headed into the kitchen and poured himself a cup of coffee.

He stood at the back window and stared beyond the clipped grass and toward the forest where the early sun couldn't begin to penetrate the primal tangle of trees and bushes.

Had they all overreacted? There had been no threat to Sheri at all since that night in the woods. Yet there was no way he thought she'd surprised a hunter.

The facts read more like an attempted abduction. Besides, she'd scarcely been alone since the night of the attack. The perp hadn't had another chance to attempt to get her again. The danger wasn't gone. It was simply waiting.

Despite knowing there were no facts to back him up, his gut instinct told him that the attack on Sheri was somehow not only tied to Liz Marcoli's disappearance, but Agnes Wilson's, as well.

His gut told him that they had a serial kidnapper working their town. More, he had the feeling that the same perp could potentially be a serial killer.

There was a malevolence he smelled, he tasted in the air, and his biggest fear was that evil had chosen Sheri as his next victim.

Chapter 12

It had been an awkward, quiet breakfast and ride in his car and Sheri had been grateful when he'd finally dropped her off at the store.

She had known that making love with Jimmy was wrong on all kinds of levels, but when she'd seen him standing in the bathroom, that white towel precariously balanced on his slim hips and his magnificent chest bare, she knew she had to have him.

She'd been fighting the sexual chemistry that sparked in the air between them since the night they'd shared the kiss, and that morning she'd simply decided to stop fighting.

He'd wanted her, too. She'd seen his desire the minute she'd stepped into the bathroom, had seen his heat in the depths of his eyes.

"Good morning," she greeted Jennifer as she stepped into the store.

"Back at ya," Jennifer said. She was planted on one of the chairs behind the register, a cup of coffee next to her.

"If you can hold down the fort for me for an hour or so, I've got some paperwork that needs to be done in the office this morning," Sheri said.

She felt the need to be alone, to process the early morning lovemaking and her ambivalent feelings toward Jimmy. Besides, she really did need to take care of writing checks and ordering inventory.

"Not a problem," Jennifer said. "As you can see, the place is quiet for now."

"If things get busy, come and get me," Sheri instructed. The large back room not only held a huge storage area with shelving, but also had a restroom and a small enclosed office.

Sheri went into the office, closed the door behind her and sat at the desk. Even though she'd showered before dressing for the day she imagined she could still smell the scent of Jimmy lingering on her skin. It was the scent of minty shaving cream, cool, fresh soap and very hot male.

She punched the button to awaken her computer and then leaned back in the comfy leather chair and closed her eyes.

For several long moments myriad thoughts flittered through her head. Had she really just startled a hunter in the woods that night? Did Jimmy make love with such mastery with all the women he'd been with before?

Why would a hunter be wearing a ski mask in June

and why tranquilize her dog? Why not just beat feet out of the area? Was Aunt Liz dead or alive? Why, even knowing he was wrong for her, did she want to make love with Jimmy again?

Her eyelids snapped open and she sat forward and grabbed the mouse, moving it to bring up the program she needed to check and order inventory.

For the next hour she kept her concentration strictly focused on business, refusing to allow it to wander anywhere else. She ordered supplies, wrote out paychecks and studied what had sold well and items that weren't moving over the past couple of weeks.

The ring of her cell phone interrupted her work. It was Marlene. "Sheri, can you come to the Dollhouse tomorrow evening around eight-thirty?"

"Sure. What's up?"

"Roxy has finally agreed to meet with Ramona, but she wants you and me to be there."

Sheri smiled into the phone. "Is that so that we can keep Roxy from committing bodily harm on the woman who gave her birth?"

"Something like that," Marlene said with a laugh. "Actually, I just think Roxy needs our support. We both know she has the most baggage where Ramona is concerned and she wants us there when she meets Ramona after all these years."

"I'll be there," Sheri replied.

It would be nice if Roxy could somehow make peace with Ramona, she thought after she'd hung up. It would be nice if they all could find peace. Ramona would never be a mother to any of the girls she'd abandoned, but she could have a role of some sort in all of their lives. Sheri still hadn't figured out exactly what role Ramona should play in her own life.

By the time she left the office the store was busy with customers. "I was just about to call you for help," Jennifer said.

"Why don't you work the floor and I'll man the register," Sheri suggested.

For the next couple of hours there was a steady stream of customers that kept both Sheri and Jennifer jumping. Sheri was grateful for the distraction.

By one o'clock, the store had emptied and Sheri told Jennifer to head to the back room and grab some lunch. When Jennifer had disappeared, Sheri remained in the chair behind her register, her thoughts once again going to Detective Jimmy Carmani.

He was nothing like what she'd envisioned for herself when it came to a lover, a husband or a lifetime partner. But he did stir her in ways she'd never felt before.

It wasn't the words he spoke to her or the things he did, rather it was the way she felt when he looked at her, the security that washed over her whenever she was in his presence. Being around him made her want to be a better person, made her want to be sociable and funny just to hear the sound of his deep, rich laughter.

She stiffened slightly as she saw a white panel van pull to a stop outside and a familiar man step out of the driver's door. Edward Cardell. What was he doing here? He'd been a major suspect in Liz's disappearance and was still considered a person of interest.

Sheri had met him only twice before, once at the police station and another time when he had come into Roxy's restaurant while the three sisters were having a late lunch together. That had been three weeks ago.

She attempted a pleasant smile as he walked through the door. He was a nice-looking older man who had secretly been dating Liz at the time of her disappearance, secretly because Liz hadn't wanted Sheri and her sisters to know that she was seeing somebody.

"Good afternoon, Sheri," he said.

She nodded, wondering what he was doing here. He didn't shop in the store, their paths didn't cross on a regular basis. To add salt to the wound, soon after Liz was gone, Edward had started seeing Liz's best friend, Treetie Burns, further damning himself in the eyes of Liz's nieces.

"I just wanted to stop by to tell you that I just heard that you've been through some traumatic experiences lately and I'm sorry that your aunt isn't here to support you." His eyes radiated compassion.

"Thanks, but I'm doing just fine," she said, not able to let go of the thought that it was possible he was the very reason her aunt wasn't with them. As far as everyone knew he was the last person to see Liz before she'd disappeared.

"I didn't expect anything less of you," he said. He remained several steps away from the counter, not attempting to invade her personal space. "She spoke of you so often. Of all of you, she always believed you were the most like her, strong in spirit and able to handle whatever life threw your way. She worried more about Roxy and Marlene, but she always felt in her heart that you would be okay no matter what."

"Why are you telling me this now?" His words stirred emotions Sheri didn't want to tap into, emotions like deep grief and overwhelming sorrow.

He shrugged. "I was up at the cabin fishing for a few days and when I got home I heard about you having problems with somebody. I just…I felt the need to tell you."

"I appreciate you stopping by," she said, but she knew her voice didn't hold the sentiment of thankfulness.

He sighed. "You still think I did something bad to your aunt, don't you?"

"I don't know what to think," she answered honestly. "The only thing I do know is that until we have answers as to what happened to her, there aren't many people I trust."

"I understand. I'm only sorry I didn't get to meet you girls in the company of your aunt instead of under such terrible circumstances."

Thankfully at that moment the buzzer rang, indicating that somebody was at the back door. Jennifer appeared in the storefront. "Cheeseman Zooker is here with a delivery."

"I have to take care of this," Sheri said to Edward.

"Then I'll just see you around," Edward said.

With Jennifer once again manning the front of the store, Sheri hurried into the back room to deal with the unpleasant Isaaic Zooker. He was known as Cheeseman in his community because his family provided the product not just to Sheri to sell to tourists, but also to Roxy for use in her restaurant.

Isaaic was a tall, well-built man. He might have

been handsome beneath his beard and the brim of his straw hat, but Sheri had never seen him smile.

He brought a variety of cheese—cut, sliced, cubed and already packaged and priced for Sheri to sell in the store. She took a small percentage of the sales and that worked to everyone's satisfaction.

"What do you have for me today?" she asked him, eager to put the conversation, the very unexpected appearance of Edward Cardell in the store, behind her.

"Cubed bacon cheddar, sliced pepper jack…" As he listed the cheeses he pulled each one out of the woven bag he'd carried and placed them on the picnic table where the staff usually took their breaks.

"I'll put them in the display case and probably within the next two or three days they'll all be gone. Your cheeses are always a big hit with the tourists."

He nodded, his dark eyes lingering on her. "You are doing okay?"

The question surprised her. He'd never asked her anything personal or shared anything of his own life with her. "I'm fine."

His gaze looked down at the floor. "You are one of the best of the English. I would be saddened if anything happened to you."

"Thank you, Isaaic," she replied, her heart touched by his unexpected words.

"Good day to you, then," he said, and within the blink of her eyes had disappeared out the back door.

The afternoon had been filled with surprises, she thought as she heard the familiar sound of horse hooves and the jingle of reins as Isaaic left the parking area. Surely the rest of the day would bring no more unexpected visitors or unusual conversations.

At least the unusual events had kept her mind off Jimmy, who would be arriving to pick her up in the next hour or so. What was she going to do about Jimmy?

She'd told him she didn't need him to be her bodyguard in her home anymore, and now she needed to tell him that she didn't want him bringing her to work and picking her up each evening.

It was time to cut the cord. They'd gotten too close, driven together by circumstances beyond their control. She needed to distance herself from him.

She felt confident in her ability to protect herself with Highway back home to alert her to anyone getting close to the house, and her shotgun.

Jimmy might not believe her capable of shooting the gun to harm somebody, but Edward was right— she was strong and capable of doing whatever was necessary to keep herself from harm's way.

"How's Highway doing?" Jennifer asked, as if she'd plucked a piece of Sheri's thoughts.

"He's doing great. The cast on his leg hasn't slowed him down a bit and I always know where he is in the house by the thudding sound he makes when he walks. I'm happy to have my snuggle buddy back."

"I thought maybe you'd gotten yourself a new snuggle buddy," Jennifer mused.

"Don't even go there," Sheri threatened with a mock tone.

"Sheri, someday you're going to have to stop looking for your fairy-tale prince and start looking at real men who would love you."

Sheri shook her head. "I've been dreaming about my prince since I was a little girl. I know he's going to find me. All I have to do is be patient."

"Maybe it's time for a grown woman to put away childhood dreams," Jennifer advised.

"I'm only twenty-six and I'm not ready to put aside anything yet," Sheri protested. "I have time for my prince to find me."

As Jennifer moved away from the counter and Sheri stocked the fresh cheese that Isaac had brought, she pulled forth a vision of the man she was certain was her own special prince.

She frowned irritably as she realized the vision in her head wasn't of a blue-eyed blond prince, but rather a picture of a dark-haired, hot Italian with tattoos on his upper arms.

Liz knew that time was running out for her. The meals had stopped coming altogether, as if she'd already been deemed unacceptable for whatever reason she'd been kidnapped and held. Now she was locked away in an underground bunker and apparently forgotten.

Was this the way it had happened to the person buried in the back wall? Had the captor lost interest, forgotten about his prisoner and stopped delivering food?

Had that person slowly starved to death and then been buried in the wall when the captor had found his caged bird dead?

At least she had water. Liz knew that the body could go without food for some time, but water was vital to staying alive.

Still, it was getting more and more difficult to hold on to any mere tenuous thread of hope. She spent most of her time sitting in the chair and remembering the past, embracing the love she'd found with three little girls after the unexpected death of her husband.

Ramona had given her a gift, had created in Liz a will to live when she'd had none. The only thing Liz regretted was the pain and sorrow her girls must be feeling now as each day passed and she was absent from their lives.

Of course, Liz had brought them up to be strong and self-reliant. There was some comfort in the knowledge that they would survive her death.

Hopefully Roxy would curb her sharp tongue long enough to find a man to love her and Marlene would get past the wounds her marriage and divorce had created. Sheri would find her prince and they would all live happily ever after. That's what Liz hoped for them. That's what she prayed for.

She had stopped praying for herself to be rescued long ago, realizing after all this time it probably wasn't going to happen. Nobody knew where she was or who held her captive. She didn't even have the answers to those questions.

But she knew now that for whatever reason she'd been kidnapped and held, she'd been deemed unworthy and the price for that was death.

There were moments when her gaze would drift to the earthen wall across the small area where she'd found the bones of a human hand. Somebody had been buried in that wall, probably some other woman judged as unworthy.

She only hoped that when death came it was swift and as painless as possible.

Chapter 13

It had been a long morning for Jimmy. Haunted by memories of the dawn lovemaking with Sheri, knowing there would be no more intimate dinners, special moments or physical contact with her had given him a headache he'd battled all day.

It was like he was a drug addict and she was his drug of choice and now he was going through physical withdrawal pains. He'd been stupid to allow himself to get so close to her. He'd been foolish to let her burrow so deeply under his skin.

He was in love with her. The knowledge hit him like a lightning bolt out of a cloudless sky. He loved Sheri Marcoli. He hadn't believed that he could love, but he felt the rightness of knowing that it was love that filled his heart, that trembled in his very soul for her.

For several long moments he'd sat at his desk, savoring the alien but wonderful emotions that filled him up. If he looked forward, envisioned his future he could see himself in her cottage, sharing her life, being not just her best friend, but also her lover and her forever partner.

On top of discovering he was in love with a woman who wanted the complete opposite of him, Chief Krause had been in a foul mood.

He'd called the detectives on the carpet for a dressing-down in the Wilson and Marcoli disappearances, beating them up for this latest issue with Sheri.

"This is a small damned town," Krause had yelled, his face red with frustration. "How hard can it be to find a bad guy? You all have had two years to find out what happened to Agnes Wilson and over three months to find Liz Marcoli. And now somebody is chasing another Marcoli woman through the woods in the middle of the night and beating up her dog. Get out there and beat feet until you come up with some answer on at least one of these cases."

The three detectives had left the station for lunch with their ears still ringing from Krause's harsh criticism. Frank and Steve had decided pizza sounded good for lunch, so now Jimmy sat with them at The Pizza Place, the same restaurant where he'd planned a date with Sheri that had never happened because she'd been running for her life from some unknown perp.

"I don't know what Krause expects from us," Steve said, his blue eyes holding more than a hint of frustration as he reached for a piece of the large hamburger pizza in the center of the table.

"Miracles, that's what he wants," Frank said. "We've chased down every road available, talked to practically everyone in town in an attempt to get a handle on things and we've come up with nada."

"Storm must be chewing on his butt again. I swear, I wish that man would run for governor or something and get him out of town."

"I've heard rumors that that's exactly what he's planning to do. One more term as mayor here and then he has bigger political fish to fry," Frank revealed.

The last thing Jimmy wanted to discuss was Ralph Storm's political aspirations. "I can't stop feeling like somehow what happened to Sheri and what happened to Liz are related," he finally said.

Both of his partners looked at him blankly. "How on earth do you make that kind of leap?" Steve asked. "There's no evidence that anyone was chasing Liz around before she disappeared."

Jimmy shrugged. "Maybe the perp got lucky and grabbed her on his first try. I just know that several people have talked about how alike Sheri is to Liz, that of the three sisters, Sheri had the same qualities as Liz."

"So, if somebody took Liz and killed her maybe they're looking to replace her with a younger model?" Frank asked with a raised eyebrow.

"Something like that." Jimmy took a bite of his pizza, tasting nothing but cardboard as his thoughts continued to tumble around in his head. He chewed, swallowed and then sighed. "I don't know, it just popped into my head. Maybe it's just a crazy, desperate idea."

"At least it's an idea," Steve said. "If we were to pursue this idea, do you know anyone specifically who has mentioned that Sheri is a lot like Liz?"

"Abe Winslow," Jimmy replied.

"But we checked his cabin in the first couple of weeks after Liz disappeared and didn't find anything." Frank reached for a second piece of the pie and then frowned. "Unless he had Liz stashed someplace else up around his mountain cabin. Besides, he had an alibi for the time Liz went missing."

"Yeah, he had some relatives that vouched for him, relatives that might have lied. Maybe we need to look at good old Abe a little closer," Steve said. "We know he admitted to asking Liz out for a date and that she turned him down. That might be a motive for him to kidnap her if he had some sort of unhealthy obsession."

"He's been a widower for a long time now," Frank added. "Maybe he figured the only way to get a woman to live in that dump he calls home was to kidnap one."

"Maybe the mountain search should have gone higher and wider," Steve said. "Krause wants results, but he's the one who called off the search into the mountains."

Jimmy said nothing, listening as his partners jumped on his bandwagon of speculation. He tried to stay focused on the conversation but thoughts of Sheri kept intruding…intimate thoughts, inappropriate thoughts.

"We definitely need to take another look at Abe."

Steve's statement drew Jimmy back to the conversation at hand.

"Anyone else you can think of?" Frank asked Jimmy.

"Let me talk to Sheri when I pick her up at the store later and maybe she'll have a few more names of men for us to look at again," Jimmy said.

The rest of the lunch was spent talking about Marlene's progress in getting her bakery up and running and Roxy redecorating Steve's son's bedroom.

"Tommy has decided he's too old for horses and now he wants a big-boy room decorated with police stuff. Roxy is excited to make it just the way Tommy wants it." Steve shook his head, his eyes soft as he apparently thought of the woman in his life and his son.

They spoke of mundane things, of life with the women they loved and the conversation reignited an old hunger inside Jimmy, a hunger for a place where he belonged with somebody who would love him forever.

He wanted that place to be with Sheri, in her enchanted cottage with Highway. He could easily imagine wintry nights with a fire glowing in the fireplace, Sheri snuggled on the sofa with him, and Highway at their feet, legs moving in sleep as he happily chased rabbits in his dreams.

He was obviously out of his mind. What he needed to do was start some regular workouts at Ling's Studio, get back some of the discipline and training that would center him, allow him to stop himself from entertaining foolish fantasies.

By the time they got back to the station, they were all called to the scene of a domestic dispute. Two patrol cars were already parked in front of the neat ranch house when they arrived.

Joe Jamison got out of his patrol car like a bear awakened from hibernation. "Shelly and Roger Geiger appear to be having an argument that has escalated. Shelly is locked in the bathroom and Roger is trying to get inside. She has her cell phone and has told us he's already beaten her and that he has a collection of guns inside the house. We decided to wait for backup before approaching."

Every cop knew that one of the most dangerous situations they faced was the unknown of a domestic disturbance. As Jimmy pulled his gun to head around the back of the house, he found it ironic that he'd just shared lunch with two men who had gotten their love life right and now he was at a house where the two people inside had apparently gotten it all wrong.

It took an hour to get the situation under control. Joe Jamison managed to talk Roger into coming out of the house where he was immediately put in handcuffs and placed in the back of the patrol car.

Shelly came out as well, her nose bloody and screaming that she didn't want Roger arrested and threatening to sue the police for abuse even though it had been her loving husband who had busted her nose.

"Geez, people can be so screwy," Steve said as the three of them headed back to the station.

"I have a feeling this won't be the last time we're called to their house," Frank grumbled.

"How do you know when it's right?" Jimmy asked from the backseat of the car. "Steve, after you and Roxy get married who is to say in a couple of years we won't be at your house settling an issue."

Steve flashed Jimmy a grin in the rearview mirror. "I don't have to worry about that happening. Roxy would kill me long before any cops could get to my house," he said with a laugh.

"Seriously," Jimmy said. "How do you know when you meet the woman who is going to be your partner through life? The one who will always have your back and be at your side?"

"You just know," Frank replied. "When you love somebody it should be easy."

"It's not just about love and passion, although you certainly need to have that, but it's also about respecting each other and kind of having a mutual admiration thing," Steve said. "Do I smell a romance in the air?" Once again his gaze flicked to Jimmy in the rearview mirror. "Those Marcoli women, they can be pretty irresistible, just ask us."

Jimmy felt his cheeks warm. "Unfortunately, the last of the Marcoli sisters is waiting for a prince to give her a happy ever after, and we all know that's not me."

Frank turned in his seat to look at Jimmy. "Sometimes women don't really know what they want until you tell them. Jimmy, if you really care about Sheri, then you need to let her know."

In his years in law enforcement Jimmy had faced many frightening, dangerous situations, but the idea of speaking to Sheri about his feelings for her absolutely terrified him.

"I'll see you all tomorrow," Sheri said as she saw Jimmy pull up front.

"Don't worry about us," Abe assured her, and winked at Michael. "We'll try not to eat all the cheese and drink too many beers before we close up tonight."

Sheri grabbed her purse from beneath the counter. "In these days of high unemployment, new staff is always easy to find," she said teasingly, and then dashed out the front door.

The moment she slid into the passenger side of Jimmy's car she realized she'd spent far too much of the day anticipating seeing him again.

She wanted her prince, but she couldn't stop thinking about Jimmy. She told herself it was because of the role he'd played in her life. He'd been her protector, the person who had held her while she cried. He'd been trying to solve the case of her missing aunt. Surely what she felt toward him was the warmth of friendship and gratitude. It couldn't be anything more than that.

"Good day?" he asked as she buckled her seat belt.

"Not bad, what about you?"

"Interesting," he said, and told her about Krause going ballistic and then the domestic dispute they'd responded to.

Sheri shook her head in disbelief when he told her about Shelly not wanting to press charges against the man who had given her a bloody nose. "Some women just can't leave. It's sad," she exclaimed. "And speaking of sad, I guess Roxy has decided to attempt a meeting with Ramona. I'm supposed to be at the Dollhouse tomorrow night for a big family reunion. I just hope we all get through it without blood being spilled," she said with a small laugh.

"I'm sure it will all be fine," he said. "I have a few more questions for you. Do you want to drive through for some food and we'll talk while we eat? I promise I'll take off as soon as we're finished."

"I can always do Chang Li's," she replied, although she knew she shouldn't be encouraging this, encouraging him. *But he has questions to ask me,* she told herself and she assumed the questions were related to the investigation. It would be nicer to talk about things over sesame chicken and egg drop soup.

"Do you cook?" she asked once they had left the drive-through window of Chang Li's and were on their way to the cottage.

"I'm a bachelor, of course I cook," he said. "If I have the time I can make a mean spaghetti sauce or a great pot of chili. I can cook a roast so tender it will make you weep." He flashed her a quick smile. "I did a lot of cooking when I was in foster care."

She nodded and stared out the passenger window. For some perverse reason she'd hoped he couldn't cook. It would have been a definite negative strike against him and she desperately needed to think negatively about him in order to keep her fantasy, her dream alive.

She was grateful when they reached the cottage and she could leave the car that smelled of him. Outside the air smelled of fresh pines and sweet flowers, not of familiar cologne and even more familiar male.

Highway greeted them at the door and she was dismayed to see that he appeared to be as happy to see Jimmy as he was to see her.

She carried the take-out bags into the kitchen where he got out plates and silverware, then pulled two diet sodas from the refrigerator.

It was all so familiar, all too easy, as if they'd been

living together for months and she wasn't sure why but suddenly it irritated her, he irritated her. He aggravated her because she liked him here.

"So, what did you want to talk to me about?" she asked once they were seated at the table across from each other.

"You mentioned to me that lots of people who know you believe that you're a lot like your aunt. I want to know who the men are who have mentioned this to you," he said.

She looked at him in surprise. "As a matter of fact somebody said that very thing to me today."

"Who?" Jimmy took a bite of his chicken and gazed at her curiously.

"Edward Cardell."

Jimmy raised a dark brow. "He came into the store?"

"Yeah, surprised the heck out of me," Sheri admitted.

"What did he want?"

"He said he'd heard that I'd had some trouble and he wanted to tell me that he was sorry to hear about it." She frowned thoughtfully. "It was kind of weird. He's never been in the store before."

She watched Jimmy chew slowly, his brow creased in thought. Drat the man. Why did he have to be so handsome? Why couldn't he be the blond-haired, blue-eyed prince she'd been waiting for?

"I think maybe we'll have another chat with Edward," he finally said. "Can you think of anyone else who has mentioned that you remind them of Liz?"

"Just Abe and now Edward. Why are you asking

me this?" She suddenly felt ill at ease by the conversation.

"It was just part of a theory we kicked around today." He looked down at his plate, as if unwilling to meet her gaze.

"What kind of a theory?" Sheri's heart beat an unsteady rhythm. Had they come up with something? Had they found out something that had to do with Aunt Liz? "Jimmy, you're scaring me."

His gaze shot up to meet hers and he immediately reached for her hand across the table. "Sorry, I didn't mean to frighten you." He squeezed her hand and then released it. "We're kicking around the idea that maybe somebody kidnapped your aunt Liz and for one reason or another is now after you because you're so much like her."

She studied him for a long moment as his words tumbled in her brain and finally locked into place. "S-so your th-theory is that s-somebody kidnapped A-Aunt L-Liz and probably k-killed her and now that p-person is trying to r-replace her with me." She bit her tongue hard in an effort to halt the stutter.

"It's just a theory, Sheri," Jimmy said softly. His gaze was soft, so tender as it lingered on her. "It's only one of many theories."

She shoved her plate aside, her hunger gone along with any irritation she'd felt toward him. Rather she was filled with the need for him to hold her, to make sense of a world that no longer made any sense.

"Your newest theory scares me more than I already was scared," she confessed.

"That wasn't my intention."

Sheri scooted away from the table and went to

stand by the window and stared out at her backyard. She drew several long, deep breaths in an effort to control the emotions that suddenly felt wildly out of control.

"Sheri?"

She heard the sound of Jimmy's chair scooting back from the table and tensed. She relaxed when she felt his presence behind her but he didn't touch her in any way.

Leaning her head against the windowpane, she closed her eyes. "Even though I thought I was preparing myself for the possibility that Aunt Liz is dead, your new theory leaves no room for her to be alive."

She opened her eyes and her tears of grief blurred her vision. She heard the thump of Highway's cast as he came to where she stood. He gave a soft whine, as if sensing the depths of her sadness. "If you think the man who chased me in the woods might want me to replace Aunt Liz, then that means for sure she's dead."

"Our theory could be wrong," Jimmy said softly. "We've had lots of wrong theories about everything." He placed his hands on her shoulders and she wanted nothing more than to turn around and fall into his arms. She needed to weep the sadness, the fear out of her heart, out of her very bones.

But she had to stop using him, somehow she had to stop needing and wanting him. She straightened her shoulders and shrugged off his hands. As he took a step back from her she turned and faced him with renewed strength.

"You've gotten your question answered, now let's

finish our meal." She stepped around him, not meeting his gaze, and returned to the table.

While they finished the dinner, she told him about Isaaic Zooker being nice to her, that Michael Arello was working out nicely at the store and he repeated what Steve had mentioned over lunch about Roxy redecorating Tommy's bedroom.

"I'm not sure who's going to get to the altar first," Sheri said. "Steve and Roxy have been talking about a wedding, but I have a feeling it's very possible Marlene and Frank will sneak one in while Roxy is still dithering about all the details. She wants it to be the biggest social event the town has ever seen."

"Why doesn't that surprise me?" Jimmy asked drily.

He fell silent then, concentrating on the food and occasionally looking at her with dark eyes and an expression she couldn't read.

It was obvious he had something else on his mind, but she wasn't sure she wanted to know what it was. She didn't want to explore further theories about Aunt Liz. She didn't want to talk any more about what had happened to her and Highway. She was tired of it all.

What she wanted to do was get him out of her space, him with his handsome face and beautiful eyes. He commanded the space around him wherever he was and in the small interior of her kitchen his natural power and maleness was nearly overwhelming.

They finally finished the meal and he helped with the quick cleanup of the kitchen and then she walked him to the front door.

"I'll drive myself to work tomorrow," she finally

said as he opened the door. He jerked around and opened his mouth in what she knew was going to be a protest, but she held up a hand to halt whatever words he was about to speak.

"It only makes sense. I'm meeting Roxy and Marlene and Ramona at the Dollhouse right after the store closes, so I'll leave the store and go directly there. I imagine our meeting won't take long and I'll be just fine. Besides, we can't keep up your babysitting of me forever."

"I haven't minded," he said.

"And I've appreciated it, but I'll take the shotgun with me in the truck. From now on it will go wherever I go. Highway will keep me safe here. You have more important things to do than take all the extra time driving me back and forth to work every day. I'll be fine without you."

His dark eyes studied her and he remained as still as a statue. "Unfortunately, I'm not sure I'll be fine without you." He drew in a visible deep breath. "I'm in love with you, Sheri."

Chapter 14

He hadn't intended to say the words. He'd decided that he'd never tell her how he felt about her, but it just slipped out and the result was exactly what he expected.

Her eyes opened wide and the faint smile that had been on her lips fell away. She reeled backward and stumbled to the sofa. "Oh, no, Jimmy. You can't be. You're obviously just confused."

He left the door and tossed a bright yellow pillow from the chocolate-brown chair across from the sofa and sat, loving her with his gaze, with every fiber of his being. "I might be many things, Sheri, but I'm not confused about what I feel for you."

"We've just been spending so much time together, almost acting like husband and wife. You've played such an important role in my life for these last couple of weeks, You're mistaking love for something else…fondness…friendship…" She floundered as she stared at the coffee table.

"Sheri, look at me." He waited until she lifted her gaze to meet his. "I'm not mistaken and I'm not confused. I know I'm not the man you want in your life, but I had to tell you how I felt about you."

He should have kept his mouth shut, he thought. Telling somebody you love them shouldn't put such pain and misery on their face. "I think I fell in love with you a little bit the very first time you came into the station with your sisters to talk about your aunt's disappearance. I feel magic when I'm with you."

"I can't cook. I'm cranky in the mornings," she protested.

"As I recall, you can be quite magnificent in the mornings," he said with a teasing tone.

Once again she broke eye contact with him as her cheeks flared with color. "That shouldn't have happened. It obviously gave you the wrong idea and made you believe that you're in love with me."

"Making love with you was incredible, but that's not the only reason why I love you. I love the way you make everyone feel welcome when they walk into your store. I like how your eyes reflect your emotions and that your smile melts something inside me. I love talking to you about everything and nothing."

"Jimmy." The single word sounded as if she was in agony and when she raised her eyes to look at him once again, the agony was in her gaze. "Stop. Please stop. It's just wrong. We've gotten too close under the circumstances. I've obviously been giving you mixed signals and for that I'm sorry."

He'd hoped that she'd have some kind of an epiphany, that she'd suddenly realize her idea of a handsome prince was foolishness and that she was really in love with him. But she obviously didn't feel the same way about him as he did about her.

He stood and forced a smile. "I guess the good thing about this is that I've always feared that I wouldn't know how, that I wouldn't be capable of loving anyone. The bad thing is I fell in love with the wrong woman."

He didn't wait for her to reply, but rather stood and hurried to the door. When he reached it he turned back to her. "Don't worry, Sheri. This doesn't change anything between us. I still intend to watch over you, to make sure you stay safe. I will still be working the investigation with every fiber of my being. The only thing that will change is that I now realize I can't go back to being your friend anymore. I'm in too deep to be satisfied with just being a friend."

It was the longest speech he had ever given in his life and when he was finished he walked out the door, into the warm evening that did nothing to take away the ball of cold that had formed like a lump in his chest.

He should have never spoken his feelings aloud, he thought as he got into his car. He should have never confessed his love for her. Maybe if he'd waited, maybe if he'd given it more time, she would have eventually developed a tremendous love for him.

Even as he thought it, he knew it probably wasn't true. Sheri was waiting for a fantasy and he hoped her prince showed up soon. She deserved a prince to bring her happy ever after, to love her the way she needed to be loved.

What he'd learned from all this was a reconfirmation that he wasn't meant to have love in his life, that he'd been marked by the very abandonment at the beginning of his life as a man who would want and not have. It was time to stop wanting and just accept the fact that he would always be alone.

He stood deep in the woods and watched the back of the cottage. The moonlight flooded down on it, painting it with silvery light.

His need, his desire had grown so big he could scarcely think about anything else anymore. His head was filled with only Sheri and his need to take her, to possess her.

He clenched his hands into fists at his sides as he thought of the dog. He'd thought he'd killed the beast that night in the woods. Using a wooden stick to slam into the dog's leg, he'd heard the snap of bone and when the dog went down it had been relatively easy to plunge the syringe into his hide and empty it.

He'd been certain the dose had been lethal. He'd obviously underestimated the strength of the dog.

He had also underestimated Sheri's skills, her speed and her will to survive. His hands clenched tighter as he thought of how she'd fought him. That whole night had been a failure of mammoth proportions.

Detective Carmani had been vigilant in keeping an eye on Sheri since then and now the devil dog was back. Sheri would be too smart for him to attempt to take her from the woods once again.

He needed a new plan. He had to have her. The old one wouldn't last much longer and he wanted Sheri in the bunker before Liz died.

His brain clicked and whirled with suppositions, with possibilities and when he finally had a plan that seemed viable, he smiled in the darkness.

Soon, sweet Sheri. Very soon she would join her aunt in the bunker and then he'd kill Liz and begin the training to make Sheri his perfect partner, the wife he needed.

He loved her. The words haunted Sheri's sleep and stayed in her head the next morning as she got ready to head into the store. She wished he hadn't told her. Life would be so much easier at the moment if she hadn't heard those words from him.

He loved her and she was confused. He was nothing like what she'd dreamed of, nothing like the man who was supposed to appear in her life and be her future.

But his smile made her warm, his laughter tickled her, too. There was a part of her that wanted to heal all the wounds he'd ever experienced and another part of her that wanted to make love with him again and again.

Was she in love with him? She was so confused, unwilling to give up a dream and yet drawn to a red-blooded real man who could potentially be her happy ever after?

She needed some time to sort it all out in her head. The very last thing she had expected was for Jimmy to tell her that he was in love with her.

True to her word, when she left the cottage she

carried the shotgun to her truck and placed it in the passenger seat next to her. As she left the cottage she looked for any vehicles following her, for anyone lurking about the property, but saw nothing suspicious.

She didn't relax until she made it to the store and walked in with her shotgun in hand.

"If this is a stickup I can tell you the owner is really going to be mad," Jennifer said from her perch behind the register.

"Just a little precaution since Jimmy isn't bringing me into work anymore," Sheri explained, storing the gun under the counter.

"I have some bad news for you," Jennifer said.

Sheri mentally groaned. Just what she needed... bad news on top of everything else that was troubling her mind. "What bad news?"

"Abe isn't coming in tonight. He called and said he's sick with the flu."

Sheri sighed in relief. At least it was bad news she could live with. "I have to leave here around six. Are you available to close with Michael tonight?"

Jennifer shook her head. "Sorry, I'm usually available any night, but tonight I can't. We've got a family reunion to attend and my mother would kill me if I didn't go."

"I'm not really comfortable leaving Michael in charge of closing up by himself," Sheri said with a frown. "It's not that I don't trust him, but I just don't think he's ready to take care of closing out the register and making sure things are locked up."

She shrugged her shoulders. "I'll just hang around to close up shop tonight. I'm meeting my sisters at the

Dollhouse around eight-thirty, so I'll just work the evening hours and then head on over there."

"It's going to be a really long day for you," Jennifer said.

"That's okay. I've done it plenty of times before." Besides, today of all days she welcomed the extra work which would hopefully keep her from thinking of Jimmy and his shocking confession of love the night before.

At that moment the first customers arrived and the business day officially began.

Thankfully it was a busy day, with people stopping in on a regular basis. She and Jennifer were kept hopping until just after noon when there was the usual lull in the store.

Sheri holed up in her office, leaving Jennifer instructions to come and get her should the traffic get busy again. As Sheri eased down into the office chair, her thoughts went back to Jimmy.

Her feelings for him were a tangled mess that she didn't know how to begin to sort out. On some level she knew she could love him, could be in love with him if she'd only allow it.

But the idea of releasing a long-held fantasy, of trusting a real flesh-and-blood man to take care of her heart was almost as terrifying as the idea of the man who had chased her through the woods.

It didn't help that she'd once believed Eric to be the prince she'd sought and he'd turned out to be the worst kind of warty toad.

Was the real problem that she was afraid to try again, afraid to trust any man again? It was so easy to trust a man who wasn't real, who was only a figment of her imagination. She twirled a strand of her hair as she continued to ruminate on all matters of the heart.

Maybe the real problem was that she'd never truly believed that a man could love her. Oh, she knew she was well liked and respected by a lot of the men she worked and interacted with on a daily basis, but deep in the very core of her she'd never really expected a man to love her.

She couldn't cook. She stuttered, and her own mother hadn't loved her enough to clean up her lifestyle and keep her. Was it any wonder Sheri had decided the only man for her was a fantasy prince?

What had Jennifer told her the other day? Something about it being time to put away childhood fantasies and look around for a real man who could love and respect her.

Was it time? Was Jimmy the prince she'd always dreamed about, just in a different packaging? Was he the man who held her lifetime of happiness in the palm of his hand?

She was grateful when Jennifer called out that she needed help up front, grateful to put her confusion behind her and take care of customer needs.

Jennifer left at one and Michael showed up for his shift right on time. "I'm glad to see you're taking the job seriously," she said to him when they were alone.

Outside a rain shower began, assuring her that for at least a little while it was doubtful there would be any customers.

"I like working here," Michael said. "It's cool to talk with everyone who comes through. I like finding out where people are going and where they're coming from. I've never been anywhere but here and sometimes I think about taking off and seeing other places."

"Where would you go first?" Sheri asked.

"Florida," he answered without hesitation. A twinkle appeared in his eyes. "You know, the beach and all those bikini-clad babes."

Sheri laughed. "Now you're showing your age."

"Hey, I'm a healthy male without a girlfriend. I like thinking about babes."

Sheri shifted positions on her chair and looked at the handsome young man. "And why don't you have a girlfriend? I mean, you aren't that hard to look at."

He flashed her a grin and then frowned thoughtfully. "I got kind of a bad reputation when all that stuff was going on with the kids in the cabin. Everyone knew Roxy and Marlene had both fired me for stealing. I wasn't ready to tell anyone about the kids yet." He shrugged. "It definitely put a damper on my love life."

"But you turned out to be a hero, Michael."

The police had placed Michael on a persons-of-interest list when Roxy was being threatened and he'd been followed to the old cabin in the woods where the cops were surprised to find three young orphans who Michael had been caretaking for while he tried to prepare them for foster care.

"I do kind of have a crush on somebody," he admitted.

"And who would that be?"

"Jennifer."

"Ah, so you like those older women," Sheri teased.

"She's only a year older than me," he protested. "That's not so old."

"Have you told her how you feel?"

He looked at her horrified. "No way. I mean, it takes a lot of guts to tell a girl you like her. I'm not ready for that yet." He pointed out the window. "Look, the rain has stopped and the sun is shining again."

"That means hopefully the rest of the afternoon and evening we'll have more customers," Sheri said. "I think I'm going to do a little dusting." She grabbed a rag and a spray bottle of polish from beneath the counter, once again seeking some kind of activity that would drive thoughts of Jimmy out of her brain.

As she worked to dust the shelves and rearrange the furniture provided by Abraham Zooker, she couldn't help but think about what Michael had said—how it took guts to tell a woman how you felt about them.

Jimmy had taken that leap of faith the night before and had been shut down soundly. It had taken courage for him to speak of his love for her. She knew from his past that he'd been vulnerable, that it had taken an enormous courage for him to speak words of love to her. And she ached for his heartache, a heartache she'd provided.

The rest of the day she stayed busy, and at seven forty-five Sheri went into the bathroom to brush her hair and freshen up for the meeting between Ramona and her sisters.

She hoped things went well. She didn't want any drama, just some sort of resolution for them all. Hopefully the meeting tonight would not only answer some questions for her about the role she wanted Ramona to play in her life, but also bring peace to Roxy and Marlene where their birth mother was concerned.

How she wished Aunt Liz was here to guide them all through the murky waters. How she wished she could talk things over with her aunt, tell her about Jimmy and the fact that he believed himself in love with her. That there was a little part inside herself that believed she might be in love with him.

But Aunt Liz wasn't here and all she had to depend on was her two sisters. They had both found the love of their lives in the past couple of months. Maybe tonight after Ramona left, Sheri could talk to them about Jimmy and her confusing feelings for him.

Surely they would be able to counsel her on all things of the heart, on her want of Jimmy and her need for her fantasy prince.

By eight she turned the Open sign to Closed and locked up the front door. She told Michael he could go ahead and take off, and then she grabbed the shotgun and her purse from behind the counter.

As she walked out the back door she noticed that the late-afternoon sunshine was warm on her shoulders and had dried up any reminder of the earlier brief rain.

Michael pulled out of the lot with a wave and disappeared from sight. Sheri unlocked her truck, leaned forward to put her purse and the shotgun on the passenger seat and before she could straighten up to get into the cab she felt a sharp sting in her neck.

She slapped at the stinging skin, thinking it must have been some sort of a biting gnat or insect.

And that was her last conscious thought.

Chapter 15

"You've been unusually quiet all day," Steve said to Jimmy when it was almost time for the three detectives to take off for the night.

"I've been going over all the files again on the Wilson and Marcoli disappearances," Jimmy said. "I think our next step has to be to look at any men who live alone. If he's keeping these women alive someplace, then he can't be living with anyone else."

He didn't add to his partner that he'd been seeking immersion into anything that would keep his mind off of his broken heart.

"That's a pretty tall order," Steve said. "Life is hard here in Wolf Creek, especially in the winters. We have a lot of singles and widowers living around here."

Jimmy nodded. "I know, but my gut is telling me

this man is taking these women for a specific reason. If we were dealing with a serial killer, the odds are that he'd leave the bodies someplace where we would find them. But this." He gestured to the open files in front of him. "This just feels like something different. Why haven't we found their bodies?"

He scooted back in his chair. "Most serial killers want their work to be found. They want social buzz and they feed off a community's fears. But we've never found Agnes's or Liz's body. There's been no taunting contact with authorities."

"It just means our perp isn't necessarily the norm," Steve pointed out.

"True, but maybe it's worth looking into?"

Steve nodded. "First thing tomorrow morning we'll have Frank get on the computer and get a list of all the men around here who don't have partners. In the meantime, why don't you join me and Frank at the Wolf's Head Tavern for a couple of beers and burgers. The ladies are going to be tied up with their family reunion thing and so we figured we'd bachelor it at the tavern."

Jimmy shoved away from his desk, eager to spend time with anyone to prevent him from thinking about what had happened the night before and what a fool he'd made of himself. It had been more than humiliating that he'd actually believed he had a chance with Sheri. It was hard to swallow that his feelings for her hadn't been reciprocated.

"Sounds good to me. Are the two of you ready to go now?"

Frank appeared beside Steve. "Yeah, let's get out of here."

The mood in the squad room had been sober all day as everyone was aware of Krause's continuing foul mood. Normally the squad room was not only filled with officers working, but also joking back and forth with each other. Krause's mood had put a pall on what had already been a depressing day for Jimmy.

A half hour later the three men were seated at a table in the dimly lit tavern with a pitcher of beer as a centerpiece and frosty glasses of brew poured all around.

They'd ordered food but for the moment were content to sit and sip the cold beer. "Hell of a day," Steve finally said with a deep sigh.

"Hell of a couple of months," Frank said.

"At least with this new theory of yours we have something to do," Steve said to Jimmy.

"And we'll make sure we interview every man at the station where Krause can see that we're actively working our butts off," Frank said. "He acts like we're nothing more than Keystone Kops bumping into light posts."

"He's just frustrated," Jimmy defended. "As all of us are."

"Why aren't you with Sheri tonight?" Steve asked curiously. "I thought you were her main man."

"She fired me last night as her personal bodyguard," Jimmy informed him, hoping the forced lightness in his tone gave nothing away of the utter heaviness that was in his heart. "She's got a loaded gun and Highway back in the house and insisted she could take care of herself from now on."

"At least you know she'll be safe and sound with

her sisters later this evening," Frank said. "I'm glad I'm not required to attend that particular family reunion."

"That makes two of us. Roxy is definitely a mess about it. I'm just glad she actually agreed to meet with Ramona. If nothing else, hopefully it will bring a sense of closure to her," Steve said. "She has some dark memories where Ramona is concerned. Maybe this meeting will finally ease some of them."

"Too bad we can't bring some closure to them all about Liz," Jimmy added.

"Nothing jumped out at you when you were looking at the files today?" Steve asked.

"Nothing that we haven't already explored at least twice before." Jimmy released a heavy sigh. "I just hate the idea that we've got some creep in town preying on women and it might be somebody we consider a friend or the seemingly normal guy next door."

"Isn't that the way it usually is? You arrest a serial killer and all of his neighbors tell the reporters how normal he seemed. I think you might be on the right track with the idea of checking into all the single men in town," Frank said. "If nothing else it will give us a new list to look at, new people to question."

"If we could just get a damn break," Steve said in frustration. "If we could just find a lead to follow. We're good detectives. What in the hell are we missing?"

"Hell if I know," Frank replied.

Travis appeared at the table with burgers and fries for each of them. "Men's night out, huh."

"Something like that," Frank said as he reached for the mustard bottle Travis had brought with him.

"The food isn't as good as you'd get at the Dollhouse and I don't have any fancy pastries to offer you for dessert, but let me know if you need anything else," Travis said as he placed the ketchup bottle on the table. He sauntered back to the bar where several men were seated.

"Single man," Jimmy said, his gaze lingering on Travis. "And he and Sheri had an issue."

"Liz and her nieces ate and drank here a couple of times a month before Liz disappeared," Steve added, his gaze also going to Travis, who was now wiping down the long bar with a cloth in preparation for the night drinkers that would be arriving soon.

"But I checked him out pretty thoroughly when Sheri was attacked." Jimmy paused to drag a French fry through a pool of ketchup on his plate. "He lives in the small house behind the tavern, is here most of his days and nights and doesn't have the time or own any other property to keep a woman alive for any length of time."

"Besides, I've always considered Travis one of the good guys in town," Frank said. "I just can't believe he has anything to do with these crimes."

The three men fell silent as they dug into their burgers. In the silence a vision of Sheri once again appeared in Jimmy's head. Not a picture of her smiling or laughing but rather the startled and then dismayed look as she'd processed his words of love for her.

"Roxy thinks it's some crazy mountain man who has Agnes and Liz chained in his house, waiting on him hand and foot," Steve said.

"Sheri sort of had the same idea about William

King. He lost his wife two months before Liz disappeared and she thought he might have Liz chained in a barn or an outbuilding to be his new wife," Jimmy said, and then smiled, remembering how she'd laughed at her own idea.

"As far as I'm concerned there's no idea too far-fetched," Steve said.

"I told Sheri I was in love with her last night." The words fell from Jimmy's lips before he'd realized he intended to say anything to his partners. His cheeks immediately flamed with heat and he wished he could recall the words.

Steve and Frank both looked at him in surprise. "You're in love with Sheri?" Frank asked.

Jimmy hesitated and then gave a curt nod.

"I knew it," Steve said triumphantly. "I swear I saw it every time you said her name, each time I saw the two of you together. There was that snap of energy between the two of you. I knew you were getting in deep with her."

"Yeah, well apparently it was a one-way deal," Jimmy muttered, unable to hide the misery that crept into his voice.

"She cut you down?" Steve asked in surprise.

"At the knees," Jimmy said with a painful wince.

"It's that prince thing, isn't it?" Frank grabbed the mustard bottle and squirted another dollop on the last of his burger as he shook his head ruefully. "Marlene told me she's been waiting on some fairy-tale prince to fall in love with."

"I knew I wasn't what she was looking for," Jimmy said. "She'd told me all about the prince thing the first time we had any real personal interaction. I was stupid to allow my feelings for her to get so out of control. You two bozos don't help you know, all happy in love. You make a man want what each of you has for himself."

Steve frowned. "I could have sworn that she had feelings for you. Deep feelings. Roxy and I even talked about it, how unusual it was for three sisters to find love with three detectives who were partners."

"So unusual, it didn't happen," Jimmy said. "At least not mutually."

"I don't know, the Marcoli sisters are all pretty hardheaded. Maybe you just need to work harder, convince her that she doesn't need some fantasy prince in her life, that all she really needs is you," Steve said. "I'm telling you, buddy, she feels something for you and I have a feeling she just needs a little more convincing."

Jimmy frowned thoughtfully and dragged another fry through his ketchup. Did he really want to go through another rejection with Sheri? Did he really want a woman who he had to convince was in love with him?

"I don't know. I think maybe it's best at this point that we just leave things the way they are," he finally said as he stared down at his plate.

"Coward," Frank said softly.

Jimmy's head jerked up. "I'm not a coward, I'm just a realist. I already spilled what was in my heart for her and she rejected me. What's the point of doing it all over again?"

"Because you do love her and we both know that coming from your background love is especially important to you," Steve argued. "And besides, women like men who fight for their love. Lord knows I had to fight for Roxy to finally realize how much she loved me."

"And Marlene wasn't exactly an easy catch," Frank said. For a moment his blue eyes went hazy, as if remembering his fight for his lady's love. "I say if you want Sheri, if you really believe you can give her what she needs forever, then go after her."

"But, you might want to wait until after the family drama is over tonight," Steve advised. "Who knows what kind of emotional turmoil we all might have to deal with after their meeting tonight."

"I haven't decided to do anything yet," Jimmy replied. Even though he'd half expected Sheri to reject him last night, he hadn't realized how utterly devastating it would be until he'd gone back to the silence of his own apartment.

He'd felt like that lost little boy again, happiness, love and family within a mere finger's reach and yet he'd been denied the very thing he wanted, he needed most in his life. The need to belong.

There was a part of him that didn't want to try anymore, that wanted to make peace with the fact that he would probably spend his life alone, chasing down criminals and casually dating random women to ease his loneliness.

And yet there was also a tiny part of his heart that refused to believe that dismal scenario would become the rest of his life. There was a tiny shard of hope inside him that still glimmered with a light difficult to ignore.

Maybe he just needed to give Sheri a little more time to process his profession of love for her. After all, it wasn't as if she didn't have other things to consume her at the moment.

She had to figure out her relationship with a birth mother she'd never known, she had an aunt who had been missing for months and she and her precious dog had been attacked by an unknown man in the woods. When he thought about it, maybe his timing just sucked.

Like Steve, Jimmy had believed there were times when he'd felt love radiating from Sheri to him. There had been times when he felt her smile was made especially for him, when her eyes had glowed not just with a sexual tension but with a hunger for his entire being.

Patience.

That's what he needed.

Unfortunately, that had never been one of Jimmy's strong suits.

Food.

Liz nearly trembled with joy when the doggie door opened and the tray was shoved inside, holding roast beef and red potatoes and green beans. She carried the tray with trembling hands to her chair and although she wanted to gobble the food down as fast as the fork could shovel it in, she fought the impulse, not wanting to make herself sick.

She'd thought she'd been forgotten. She'd believed that she'd never eat again, but now glorious food sat before her on a plain white plate. Along with the food was a cup of hot tea. Glorious, she thought, nearly salivating at the scent of the hot food alone.

Instead of inhaling it, she ate slowly, savoring each

and every bite. The roast was tender and juicy, the new potatoes seasoned and buttered to perfection. The green beans had a bit of a bite to them, but she ate everything on the plate, unsure when she would see any food again.

Maybe her captor had been out of town the past couple of days when there had been no food delivered. Maybe he'd been ill. Her blood chilled as she realized if anything happened to the man who held her captive, then she'd definitely die in this bunker slowly…painfully of starvation.

When she finished eating everything on the plate, she got out of the chair to carry the tray to place it back at the little door so that it could be retrieved and hopefully returned again in the morning with breakfast. As she bent down, a wave of dizziness struck her.

She drew several deep breaths and then straightened, wondering if maybe she'd eaten too fast after all. She stumbled back to her chair and half fell into it, the small room beginning to spin in circles inside her head.

Drugged, she thought someplace in the back of her head where her brain was still functioning. Her eyelids were heavier than they'd ever been and even as she worked to keep them open, she couldn't.

The food had been drugged and she'd eaten every bite and now she couldn't open her eyes, she couldn't even lift an arm.

Was she still breathing?

She fell into the darkness that called to her.

She had no idea how long she was out cold, but consciousness came back slowly in small increments.

She became aware of the faint scent of lilacs and the uncomfortable position she was in on the chair.

Her mouth was unbelievably dry and her limbs still felt a heaviness that was abnormal. Her brain was wrapped in cotton and she shook her head and sat up straighter in the chair in an effort to orient herself from the fog.

She remembered the food and the unconsciousness that had resulted. Why had her food been drugged? What had been the motive? There had to be a reason why she'd been knocked out cold. What could it be?

She frowned and in the silence she heard the faint wisp of another's breath. Her heart banged against her ribs as she realized she was no longer alone in the bunker.

Her gaze shot wildly around the room and when it landed on the single bed in the corner, she cried out in horror.

No! Her brain screamed in denial even as she got to her feet and rushed to the side of the bed. *No, please don't make this be,* her heart cried as she fell to her knees.

Liz's sweet Sheri lay on the bed, small and still. Liz wanted to rage at the person who had brought her here, at the fate that had placed Sheri in the sights of the madman who now held them both captive.

What on earth did their captor have in store for them? Why had he taken Sheri? She shouldn't be here. She should be feeding her animals in her backyard, laughing at Highway's antics, not in this bunker where death was buried in the wall and the fear of the unknown reigned supreme.

Chapter 16

The men lingered at the tavern after they'd eaten, sharing another pitcher of beer and talking about crimes both past and present.

Jimmy certainly had no reason to rush home. There was nobody…nothing waiting for him there. Neither Steve nor Frank were apparently in any hurry, either, with the family meeting at the Dollhouse set to begin at any minute.

"I just hope we don't get a call from dispatch to head to the Dollhouse to break up a brawl. I'd hate to have to arrest my own soon-to-be wife for assault," Steve said half-seriously.

"Roxy isn't going to assault anyone," Frank assured him. "Not with both Marlene and Sheri there to stop her. Besides, we all know Roxy has a tough exterior but is as soft as a marshmallow on the inside."

"We all know Roxy has a lot of baggage where her mother is concerned. Maybe this will be a good thing and if nothing else they can figure out what kind of a role they want Ramona to play in their lives," Jimmy said.

"If any," Frank added.

"Ramona might have an easier time getting into their lives now that they're all missing their aunt Liz," Jimmy said.

"According to Ramona she didn't know Liz was missing when she first turned up in town. It was only after she heard some town gossip that she realized what was going on. I checked her out and she was still in Arizona when Liz went missing," Steve said.

Jimmy checked his watch. It was eight-thirty. The family reunion should have begun. "I just hope they all get what they need from each other tonight," he said.

Fifteen minutes later his cell phone rang. He dug it out of his pocket and frowned as he saw Roxy's name on the caller ID.

"It's Roxy," he said to the other two men and then he answered. "Roxy, what's going on?"

"Is Sheri there with you?"

The question caused Jimmy's heart to plummet to the floor. "No, I thought she was with you at the Dollhouse."

"She never showed up and it's not like her to be late. I've tried to call her a couple of times, but her phone keeps going to voice mail." The simmer of worry in Roxy's voice exploded into full-blown terror inside Jimmy.

"I'll check at the store, maybe she got hung up,"

Jimmy said. "I'll call you back if I hear from her and you call me if she arrives there." He disconnected the call, trying to fight against an overwhelming sense of dread.

"What did she want?" Steve asked.

"Sheri never made it to the Dollhouse and she isn't answering her cell phone," Jimmy said as he stood, his heart beating far too fast. "She should be there by now. She told me she was going there directly from the store. I'm going to the store to see if she's still there."

"We'll go with you," both of his partners chimed in.

They paid their bill and then got into their separate cars to head toward the Roadside Stop. The hamburger and fries Jimmy had eaten before now roiled around in his stomach with a faint sense of nausea.

Why wouldn't she be at the Dollhouse with her sisters? She'd been so certain she could take care of herself. He clenched and unclenched his hands on the steering wheel, telling himself that it was possible she'd had customers who'd come in late and had decided to wait on them rather than hurry them out the door.

He never should have listened to her when she'd told him she'd be fine. He should have insisted that he keep driving her to and from work, making sure she got home safe and sound every day.

Don't jump to conclusions, he counseled as he hit the highway that would take him to the store. Maybe there was a perfectly logical explanation for her lateness to her meeting with her family.

Still, he couldn't help but remember that the last

time he'd thought she was just late she had actually been being chased by a crazy man through the woods.

That doesn't mean she's in trouble now, he tried to console himself. But in his heart, in his very soul, he knew that nothing within her control would make Sheri late to the meeting with her sisters and her mother.

A glance in his rearview mirror let him know that Steve and Frank were just behind him. Their presence gave him little comfort. He wouldn't be comforted until he knew Sheri was okay.

As he pulled up to the store he saw the Closed sign in the window. So, she'd shut up shop for the night. It wasn't until he pulled around to the employee parking area and saw her bright yellow pickup parked there that alarm bells screamed in his head.

He stomped on his brakes, cut his engine and was out of his car in a flash. He raced to the driver's door of the truck and mentally reeled as he saw both the shotgun and her purse in the passenger seat. Oh, God, the worst had happened. She was gone.

A hand fell on his shoulder, firm and solid and he turned to see Steve, his blue eyes calm and steady. "You can't lose it now, partner. She needs you to be at the top of your game."

Jimmy nodded, although he felt as if he couldn't draw a breath and he feared if he didn't breathe he'd pass out.

Gone.

She was gone, and it was just like Agnes two years ago, just like Liz over three months ago. She was gone as if the wind had simply blown her far away.

"I'll get my kit," Frank said, and walked back to his car where he opened the trunk to retrieve what he'd need for taking fingerprints.

"We need to find out who was with her when she came out here to leave," Steve said calmly.

His calm tone grated on Jimmy. He wanted to punch something. He needed to throttle the person who had somehow, someway, managed to make Sheri vanish.

He drew several deep breaths, fighting against the anguish, the sense of hopelessness that already cascaded through him, stealing all the warmth from his body. "It would have been either Abe or Michael. They always worked the evening shift."

Steve stepped away from Jimmy and pulled his cell phone from his pocket. As he made the necessary calls, Frank opened his kit on the ground next to the driver's door of the truck.

Jimmy watched helplessly as Frank pulled on gloves and then began to process the outside of the door. Frank worked slowly, methodically, as he should and yet Jimmy wanted to scream at him to hurry, that every minute that passed took Sheri farther away from him.

Steve walked back over to Jimmy. "Abe called in sick today and Michael was with her when she closed up the store. He said when he pulled out of the parking lot she was just getting ready to get into her truck. That was just a few minutes after eight."

"So, she's already been missing almost an hour," Jimmy said as he looked at his watch. An hour. It was an eternity in a case like this.

"I've got men on their way. We'll do a general search of the area and see what we can find," Steve said.

"It's going to be dark soon and that's only going to make any search more difficult," Jimmy said. Once again he felt sick to his stomach, terrified for the woman he loved.

It didn't matter that she didn't love him back, nothing mattered now except that she be found safe. He didn't need to wrap his arms around her if that wasn't what she wanted, but he needed to know that she was okay for anyone else who loved her to hold her.

Within minutes two patrol cars pulled in. Big Joe Jamison departed from the driver's seat of one and Chelsea Loren and Wade Peterson got out of the other car.

Steve walked over to greet them and fill them in while Jimmy watched Frank move to the interior of the car. Jimmy could stand around watching no longer and so he began to walk the area around the truck and then moved outward, looking for signs of tire tracks that might indicate what kind of a vehicle had carried Sheri away.

It would have been easier had the rain stuck around, but the heat of the evening sun had dried the asphalt and no tire tracks were visible.

He found nothing in or around the parking area. As his mind spun over past details and conversations, he yanked Steve aside. "I want somebody to head to Abe's and make sure he's really sick and doesn't have Sheri there with him. We also need to check out Edward Cardell. He was in the store and told Sheri how much she reminded him of Liz. Maybe he really is some kind of a creep."

Steve took notes as Jimmy continued to access the files in his mind, seeking a name, a face who might be responsible for Sheri's disappearance.

Work it like any other crime, Jimmy told himself. *Don't think about the fact that it's Sheri who is missing. Just think without any emotion involved.* "You might see if you can get somebody to go to Judge Bishop's house and obtain a search warrant for William King's place."

Steve looked at him curiously. "William King?"

"His wife died before Liz disappeared and Jason has been in the store several times talking to Sheri about his father not being himself, not working the fields and disappearing for long periods of time. We need a warrant for every building on his property," Jimmy said.

What had sounded crazy at the time now took on a new form. Nothing was too crazy to check out now that Sheri was gone.

"I'll get the ball rolling." Steve walked away and once again got on his phone.

Night was falling far too quickly, filling the parking area with deep shadows that would only make things more difficult for any searchers. Jimmy didn't want night. He needed sunshine and daytime so that there were no shadows to hide wherever Sheri had been taken.

But it was impossible to hold back the night, and with the night came despair because Jimmy had no idea how to find Sheri, just like they hadn't been able to find Agnes Wilson or Liz Marcoli.

* * *

"Sheri? Sheri, honey, wake up."

The voice came from far away...a familiar voice that instantly soothed her. But the darkness of her mind was soothing as well and she wasn't sure she was ready to leave it.

"Sheri Lynn, it's time for you to get up and talk to me."

There was only one person who ever called her Sheri Lynn and that was Aunt Liz, but she was missing...she was dead. *Am I dead?* Sheri wondered.

If this was Heaven, it smelled funny, like dank earth and stale air. She fought against the darkness, curious as to what she would see if she opened her eyes. Would Aunt Liz be there with angel wings?

Her eyes fluttered and she felt a soft, warm caress on her face. "That's it, baby. Open your eyes so I can see those beautiful peepers of yours," Aunt Liz's voice said.

Sheri opened her eyes and stared at the woman kneeling at her side. Her heart leaped with happiness as she saw the familiar, beloved face. "Aunt Liz!" She sobbed a gasp of happy relief and sat up.

Liz joined her on the small bed and the two hugged and wept. For Sheri all that was important at that moment in time was that she was back in her aunt's arms and that Liz was still alive.

After the initial hugging and crying was over, they finally unwound from their embrace and continued to sit side by side as Sheri looked around with a frown.

"Where are we? What is this place?" Besides the cot where they sat there was a chair with a standing reading lamp behind it, empty wooden shelving and a stool and shower stall.

"I don't know." Liz worried a hand through unkempt hair. She looked like a wild woman with her hair longer than Sheri had ever seen it and with no style or order to the salt-and-pepper strands.

She'd lost weight and wore a shapeless pale yellow shift and her eyes burned with an intensity Sheri had never seen before.

"But who brought you here?" Sheri asked, trying to make sense of the half earthen, half concrete small room. "Who is keeping you here?"

"I don't know," Liz said. "I woke up here and meals are delivered to me through that little door and I've never seen who is on the other side."

Sheri looked at the small doggie-like door and immediately thought of Highway. A hysterical burst of laughter bubbled to her lips, but she swallowed it down and instead released a gasp. She'd though Highway could keep her safe. She'd believed possessing a shotgun would keep harm away and yet here she sat in some hole under the ground with the aunt she'd believed was dead.

"Did you see who brought me in here?" she asked, a headache tightening her forehead as she tried to make sense of it all.

Liz shook her head. "I was unconscious. I got a meal, and it had been at least a day…maybe two that I hadn't been fed. I ate everything on the plate and then I almost immediately got dizzy. He'd obviously drugged the food. He brought you in here while I was out. I never saw him."

"You keep saying 'him.' How do you know it's a

man? Has he spoken to you? Has he told you why you're here?" Sheri struggled, trying to gain as much information as possible in a world gone mad.

"He's never spoken a word to me, but I know it's a man. He wears gloves when he shoves the food tray through the door, but he has big hands. It's definitely a man."

Liz's eyes filled with tears once again. "I can't believe you're here. As much as I wanted to see you again, I never wanted it like this…I never wanted you here with me."

"We've all been looking for you since the day you disappeared," Sheri said. "It's been almost four months now. The police searched everywhere but they didn't have any clues to follow."

Liz's eyes widened in surprise. "Four months? I knew it had been a long time but I had no idea it had been that long. It's easy to lose track of time in here. What happened, Sheri? How did he get you here?"

Sheri rubbed two fingers across her forehead in an attempt to ease her headache and access her memories. "I was at the store getting ready to leave. I was meeting Roxy and Marlene at the Dollhouse. Ramona is in town."

"Ramona?" Liz looked at her in stunned surprise.

"She's been clean and sober for four years and I guess as part of her personal journey she wants to make amends to all of us. Anyway, I was supposed to meet them all tonight. I was just about to get into my truck when I felt a sharp sting in the back of my neck." She frowned. "I thought it was an insect, but it must have been a needle. I—I d-don't remember anything a-after that until now."

Liz grabbed one of Sheri's hands and squeezed. "I remember the early morning that I was taken. I got up as usual, I baked and was getting ready to take the goodies to the Dollhouse when something happened…but I don't know what happened or how I came to be here. I don't even remember anyone being at my house, or speaking to anyone that morning, but somebody was there, somebody who obviously drugged me and brought me here."

Sheri raised her wrist to see what time it was, how long she'd been missing, but her watch was no longer on her wrist. "He took my watch," she said.

A rise of renewed panic swept through her as she realized she didn't know how long she'd been gone, how many minutes or hours both she and Aunt Liz had been unconscious.

"It's okay." Liz squeezed her hand once again. "Time has no meaning here. Tell me what I've missed while I've been here. Are Roxy and Marlene all right?"

Sheri's headache began to abate as she told her aunt about the events of the past four months. She talked about Roxy falling in love with Steve and Steve getting his little boy back. She told her about Marlene and Frank falling in love and Marlene preparing to open her own bakery on Main Street.

While she told her aunt everything that had happened, she tried to keep her mind off the hopelessness of their situation. She knew better than anyone that the police had no leads, that whoever held them captive in this underground bunker had flown far under the radar.

"And what about you, Sheri. Did your prince find you since I've been gone?"

A wealth of emotion swelled in Sheri's chest as she thought of Jimmy. "He found me, and I didn't recognize him. He wasn't anything like I'd imagined and so I turned him away."

A sob escaped as Sheri thought about what a fool she'd been, hanging on to childhood fantasies when her prince had been right in front of her eyes all along.

Jimmy, with his beautiful dark eyes and rich black hair. Jimmy, with his easy laughter and ability to comfort and make her feel safe. He'd been a prince and she'd taken his love for her and cast it aside because he didn't fit her stupid childish vision.

Once again Liz wrapped her arms around Sheri as she stuttered and stumbled over her words, telling her aunt about Jimmy and realizing how important he'd become in her life, in her heart. "He was right under my nose all the time and I couldn't see him," she cried. "And now it's too late."

"We can't give up hope now," Aunt Liz said firmly.

"I don't know who's going to take care of Highway." Sheri tried to pull herself together as she straightened and stood. "Why are we here? What does this man want from us?" And more important, how could they escape?

She looked around the room more carefully, seeing no way to get out, no means of escape except through the door that she knew was locked and too thick for them to break down.

She stared at the earthen wall on the far side of the room. "Don't look over there," Liz said, a new tension in her voice.

Sheri turned and gazed at her aunt. "Why? What's over there?"

"Bones. Human bones. I think maybe I found Agnes Wilson."

As Liz's words sank in, Sheri shuddered, a new despair grabbing her by the throat and making it difficult for her to breathe.

"We've got to get out of here," she murmured more to herself than to her aunt.

"I've had four months to try to figure out a way out and so far I haven't discovered any escape," Liz said flatly. "I knew I was trapped here. I also believe whoever is holding us isn't going to let me live now that you're here."

Sheri once again stared at her aunt. "I've grieved for you once and I refuse to grieve for you again." She raised her chin and ignored the banging of her headache. "Eventually he'll have to come for you, if that's his plan, and when he does we have to fight him together. We have to make sure that we aren't separated."

And somehow, some way they had to buy time so that her prince could ride to their rescue.

Chapter 17

While they were waiting on a search warrant for the King property, Jimmy decided to drive to Sheri's place to make sure there were no clues, no signs of anything amiss there.

He'd gone past panic, beyond terror and into a zone where his emotions were tightly locked away. If he allowed them out he knew he'd be no good to anyone. He'd go completely insane.

Frank rode with him. He needed to pull some prints at Sheri's to compare to those he'd lifted from the truck. The two men rode in silence, for which Jimmy was grateful. He had no words to speak, couldn't think of anything but the aching hole inside him, the frantic terror that clawed at his insides.

It was now almost midnight and he'd already heard that officers had checked out Abe Winslow, who appeared to have the flu and that there was no sign the older man had left his cabin all day or any indication that Sheri had ever been there.

Michael Arello had also been questioned at his parents' home, but had nothing to add other than what he'd already told them, that Sheri was fine and was in the process of getting into her truck as he'd pulled out of the parking lot to go home.

In fact, Michael had been devastated by the news and had instantly asked what he could do to help, insisted that he be assigned to a search party or whatever.

Roxy, Marlene and Ramona had shown up at the shop, adding to the chaos of the scene as they asked questions, offered help and apparently put aside any familial issues that might exist between them. In times of crisis families pulled together, even fractured families.

Jimmy had been grateful to take off from the store, eager to get the warrant in hand and head to the settlement to check on William King, whose own son had indicated that he'd been acting secretive and aloof for the past couple of months.

Joe was supposed to call him when they had the warrant in hand so things were in progress, but Sheri was still missing with no clues as to where she had gone or who had taken her.

Despite his attempt to forcefully shove his emotions away, to remain cool and calm and professional, he couldn't stop the frantic pounding of his heart or the catch in his breath whenever he allowed himself to feel her absence.

When they reached her cottage, Jimmy pulled out

the key ring he'd retrieved from Sheri's purse on the passenger seat of her truck. "I'll need to lock up Highway before you come in," he said to Frank. "He's not friendly with strangers and I can't remember the word Sheri used to indicate that somebody is okay."

It took him agonizing seconds to find the right key that unlocked the door behind which Highway was barking and growling, obviously smelling Frank… the stranger.

Jimmy slipped through the door and closed it quickly behind him. Highway immediately halted the barking and his tail began to thump in obvious happiness.

"Hey, boy," Jimmy said around the huge lump in his throat. He patted Highway's head and then went down the hallway to Sheri's bedroom, knowing that the dog would follow him.

He pointed Highway to the rug at the foot of the bed and then he slipped back out of the room and let Frank into the house. "I'll be back in the bedroom with Highway. Just knock on the door when you're finished," Jimmy said.

Without waiting for Frank to reply, Jimmy went back to the bedroom and fell to his knees at the edge of the bed. The purple bedspread smelled of Sheri, that sweet floral scent of lilacs and a hint of vanilla.

He remembered holding her in his arms, the way they fit together so well. He couldn't forget making love to her, the soft moans that had escaped her lips, the passion that she'd shown him.

He didn't care if he never made love to her again. He just needed her to be safe. He needed to know she was here with Highway, filling the bird feeders and laughing at the squirrel antics.

This room smelled of love. It smelled of home and as Highway nudged his arm, he turned and wrapped his arms around Highway's neck, unable to staunch the raw sobs that ripped from the very core of him.

He burrowed his face in Highway's thick neck as he released the tears of terror that had burned inside him since the minute he'd gotten the phone call from Roxy.

Sheri. Sheri, where are you? His heart cried out in terror, in frustration. *Highway needs you here. I need you here.*

He didn't know how long he clung to the dog that Sheri loved before he finally managed to pull himself together. Still seated on the floor, he swiped his face with the back of his hand as he once again computed everything Sheri had ever told him about anyone in her life and mentally scanned the files from Agnes Wilson's and Liz's disappearances.

Who was behind all this? Was it the same perp in all three crimes or were they unrelated? Two sixty-something women, and now Sheri, just vanished from the face of the earth.

A soft knock on the door pulled him to his feet as Highway growled a warning. "Jimmy, I'm finished and I just got a call from Joe that we have our warrant for the King place."

Jimmy placed a shaky hand on Highway's head. "She'll be back, Highway." It was a promise he prayed he could fulfill. "Go on outside to the car, Frank," he said through the door. "I'll meet you out there."

He waited to give Frank enough time to leave the house and then he opened the door and he and Highway left the bedroom. Before leaving the house, Jimmy made sure there was food and water for the dog and that the doggie door that led to the fenced run outside was unlocked.

Highway would be fine until Sheri returned, and if she didn't return soon, Jimmy would come back here to check in on the dog. Sheri would want somebody taking care of her baby.

He relocked the house and then hurried to the car where Frank was in the driver's seat with the engine running. "Joe and a couple of other officers are going to meet us at the Kings' to execute the search warrant."

"She's got to be there, Frank. She's just got to be," Jimmy said, his composure slipping once again. He balled his hands into fists as rage built up inside him, a rage directed not only at the unknown perp, but also for himself, for not being more vigilant, for not making sure that the princess was safe from all harm.

By the time they reached the Amish settlement there were already three patrol cars parked in front of the King home. William King stood on his front porch, his arms crossed and an expression of anger twisting his features. His son, Jason, stood next to him, looking frightened and younger than his seventeen years.

As Jimmy got out of the car, Joe walked over to him. "We've told Mr. King that we are here to execute a search warrant of the premises, but we waited for you to begin the search. Needless to say, King is not a happy camper. Chelsea is inside the home with the younger children, trying to keep them from being frightened."

Jimmy nodded, set his shoulders straight and approached the stern-looking bearded man on the porch. "Detective, there is obviously a mistake here," he said to Jimmy. "You have awakened me and my children in the middle of the night, disrupted our household for nothing. I have done nothing wrong and I certainly don't have a woman hidden anywhere here or anyplace else."

"Just let us do our job and we'll be out of here as quickly as possible," Jimmy said.

William stepped aside and indicated that Jimmy and anyone else could enter his home. While Jimmy began inside, the other officers fanned out with high-beam flashlights to check the barn and other out-buildings.

A wild-goose chase, Jimmy thought as he and Frank moved slowly through the three-bedroom ranch house, lit only by an occasional lantern and their flashlights.

It was simply furnished and in one bedroom Chelsea was seated on the floor with the four young King children surrounding her and several kerosene lanterns lighting a small circle as she told them a story.

As her gaze met Jimmy's her blue eyes were filled with worry, with compassion and the unspoken knowledge that the woman they sought wasn't here in the house.

He quickly looked away, not wanting to see the helplessness he felt in the very depths of his being reflected in her eyes. He couldn't allow himself to falter. He couldn't allow himself to break down until Sheri was back where she belonged.

If not here, then where? Jimmy fought against a hopelessness he'd never felt before. Agnes Wilson… missing for two years. Liz Marcoli…missing almost four months. And now Sheri Marcoli…how long before she became a cold case on somebody's desk?

No. She wouldn't be like the others. She couldn't be. He couldn't allow that to happen. They had to find her tonight, she needed to be found as soon as possible. He refused to lose another woman he loved.

When the house was finally cleared, Jimmy stood on the porch next to William King as the teams of officers began to check in. The barn was clear. The shed was clear. Nowhere was there a sign that Sheri was or had ever been anywhere on the property.

"Maybe you should speak to Cheeseman Zooker. He has a soft spot for Sheri," William said. "Although you know this isn't our way." The anger had left William's eyes, leaving behind a deep weariness. "We do no harm to others. I'll admit I've been guilty of placing too big a burden on my son, but not of something as heinous as kidnapping anyone."

He placed a hand on Jason's shoulder and looked at the young man. "I have been quite selfish in my grief over my wife's death. I have spent long hours isolating myself from my loved ones. I have spent weeks…months walking in the forest in despair, but I've not taken a woman to replace what I have lost. Nobody could replace my late wife."

Without a word Jimmy headed back toward the car. He wanted to tear down every building on the settlement, raze the entire town of Wolf Creek, burn the trees of the forest and on the mountain in an effort to find Sheri.

Sheri and Liz were still seated side by side on the bed when the sound of a lock being turned in the door clicked audibly.

Liz wheezed in a breath and Sheri grabbed her hand tightly as she realized it wasn't the little doggie door that had been unlocked, but rather the door itself, indicating that they were about to meet their captor.

They'd made a plan of sorts, that Liz would attack from the front and Sheri would attack from the back. Although Liz was weak from her captivity, she still had her wits and the will to fight.

The door slowly creaked open and Sheri gasped as she saw the tall, broad man who stood there, silhouetted in the light that shone from just behind him.

"Abraham? Abraham Zooker?" Sheri stood on shaky legs as she faced the man who made beautiful furniture, who had come into her store often, a man she had fondly considered a friend.

Sheri's first thought was that there was no way any plan of attack would work against the strong, big furniture maker. She and Liz would be nothing more than pesky flies to be swatted away.

"I am here to take your aunt." Abraham took a step into the bunker.

Sheri's insides trembled with terror, but she forced a smile at the man who was obviously mad. "Abraham, what am I doing here? Why have you brought me to this place and where are we?"

"I built this room into the earth of my basement. You're in my home, Sheri. I've brought you here to teach you how to be my wife. I tried to teach your aunt to be quiet and obedient, but she's been like a hound from hell, screeching obscenities day and night, never calming, never quieting enough to learn anything. And now she is nothing more than a burden and she must be gone."

Sheri's mind reeled, and bile rose up the back of her throat. Abraham wanted her to be his wife? His gaze was soft as it lingered on her. "Agnes was my first mistake and Liz was my second. I thought I could make them into the proper wife that I deserve, but then I realized you are already so close to being right. You have the gentle spirit, the sweet soul that I hunger for."

"You keep away from her, you filthy pig!" Liz screamed, her pale face mottling red with fury.

Abraham looked at Sheri. "You see? She is unmanageable. She is uncivilized." He took another step and held out a hand to Liz. "Now it is time."

"Abraham, stop it right now," Sheri exclaimed. "It isn't time for anything." She tried to staunch the horror of the situation that chilled her to her very bones. She needed to be strong. She knew she needed to try to play his game in order to assure not only her own survival but also that of her aunt's.

She at least had to buy them some time, and hope and pray that somehow Jimmy and his detectives could find something that would lead them here.

Abraham frowned and tugged on the end of his tangled beard. He dropped his hand to his side and tilted his head to look at Sheri once again. His eyes were dark pits, unfathomable but with a faint sheen of madness.

She pasted a soft smile on her lips. "You know how important family is to our kind. I will learn obedience and how to be a proper wife much better with my aunt as my guide. In any case, we have not finished our visit yet. It's been months since I've seen her and I would ask you for more time with her now. We have a lot to talk about, a lot to share before we say goodbye again."

Abraham once again pulled on his beard, as if contemplating her request. Sheri pressed her advantage. She took a step closer to him and placed her palm in the center of his broad chest, fighting against the wave of nausea that tried to take hold of her.

"Please, Abraham. It would please me so much to have more time with my aunt." She looked up at him with a pleading gaze.

His cheeks colored faintly and she drew her hand back, unable to touch him for another minute, another awful second. "We will leave things as is for the rest of the night and talk about it again tomorrow," he finally said.

"Thank you, Abraham. I appreciate it," Sheri said, and bowed her head humbly.

He gave her a curt nod and then stepped out of the room, closed the door and locked it once again. Sheri nearly fell as she wobbled her way back to where Liz sat trembling on the bed.

"I feel like I'm going to throw up," Sheri said.

Tears filled Liz's eyes. "I always knew you were strong, but I didn't realize just how very strong until right now. You just saved my life." Liz wrapped her arms around Sheri.

Sheri leaned her head against Liz's shoulder, knowing that really all she'd accomplished was to get her aunt a temporary stay of execution.

Before they pulled away from the King residence, Jimmy pulled out his cell phone and called Officer Richard Crossly, who had stayed behind at the store.

"We're still out here at the settlement and just finishing clearing the King property. We're on our way to Isaaic Zooker's place but I wanted to check in to see if there's anything new there."

"Nothing," Richard reported.

Jimmy pressed the phone closer against his ear and closed his eyes. He wasn't sure what he'd hoped... that Sheri would magically reappear from the place she'd vanished? That somebody had dropped her off and the whole night would have been just a terrible misunderstanding.

But he knew that wasn't going to happen. Sheri wasn't going to suddenly be back where she belonged. She needed help, and he didn't know what to do except what they were doing, search everywhere until they found her.

"Thanks, Richard," he finally said.

"Sheri's sisters and mother have gone back to the Dollhouse. I think they're planning a search party of their own," Richard said.

"Get an officer over there with them so they don't do anything stupid. The last thing we want is them to stumble on something and destroy evidence or confront a man who is potentially a killer."

"I'll head over there myself," Richard said. "We've done everything we can here at the store."

With a murmured goodbye, Jimmy hung up and pocketed his phone as Frank started the engine to head to the Zooker place.

"Looks like we've awakened everyone in the area," he said.

Jimmy stared at the other homes where faint glows indicated lanterns at the windows, just inside the doors. Yes, the whole settlement seemed to have been awakened by the police presence on their land.

The gossip would be in full swing by the time the sun came up. His heart squeezed tight. He didn't want the sun to rise without Sheri being found.

Jimmy didn't know much about Isaaic Zooker. He knew the man had never married and had a reputation in town for being particularly antisocial. He was well-known for his variety of cheeses that he produced and sold both to the Dollhouse and in Sheri's store, but Jimmy had never heard any real gossip about the man.

When Roxy was trying to put together a list of people who might want to hurt her, Isaaic had been on her list. She'd told Steve that the man hated her and gave her the creeps. But the local talk was that Isaaic hated everyone and everything English.

Certainly the man responsible for Agnes's and Liz's disappearances, if they were connected, would have to be antisocial. The detectives had already discerned that the person they sought would probably have to live alone.

Jimmy sat up straighter in the seat, a new buzz of anticipation filling him as he realized that Isaaic

Zooker fit many of the characteristics of the man they sought.

Had the man who had been delivering cheese to the Dollhouse and Sheri for the past several years developed an unhealthy obsession with Liz who provided the homemade fresh pastries and pies for the restaurant? Had that obsession for some reason now transferred to a younger woman—Sheri? Where did Agnes Wilson fit into the scenario?

So many possibilities, so little evidence to prove anything. With no trails to follow, only suppositions and theories, despair battled with hope in Jimmy's heart. Just like the battle that had once been waged between good and evil when he was trying to decide between cop or thug.

He reached up and rubbed the area where the barbed wire tattoo had been etched into his biceps. Evil had lost that particular battle. He hoped that evil would not prevail now.

As they pulled up to Zooker's white, neat ranch house, he also stood on his porch, the moonlight illuminating him, along with a lantern he held in one hand.

"There is trouble?" he asked as Frank and Jimmy approached where he stood.

"Sheri Marcoli is missing. We believe she's been kidnapped and we're checking the area."

Isaaic's dark eyes widened and a small gasp escaped him. "Sheri is one of the few English I like and respect."

"Then you wouldn't mind if we come in and took a look around your home?" Frank asked.

"You're welcome in my home," Isaaic replied.

"But I would never do anything to hurt Sheri." He stepped aside to allow them entry into a neat and tidy, simply furnished living room. Lanterns illuminated the room from their perch on the fireplace mantel.

"When was she kidnapped?" he asked.

"Sometime this evening," Jimmy told him. "And if I have to I'll tear down every standing building in the entire town to find her."

Isaaic nodded. "I would expect no less from you for her." He motioned them toward the hallway. "I will light the way for you." As they moved from room to room, Isaaic lit lanterns to glow in each bedroom and in the small bathroom.

He preceded them back down the hallway and into the large kitchen, where he lit more lanterns and the scent of cooked pork lingered in the air.

Hours. It had now been hours that Sheri had been gone. Had she been carried away far into the mountains? By now she could be in another state or she could be as close as the house next door.

"What about your brother, Abraham Zooker. Has he ever said anything unusual about Liz or Sheri Marcoli?" Jimmy asked.

Isaaic's face bleached of color, matching the white shirt he wore. "I have no brother." His slender face tightened with tension. "I once had a brother, but he turned his back on our ways. He's become English and is no longer a member of this community, of my family."

"How has he become English?" Jimmy asked curiously. He knew that Abraham had been shunned for a while for apparently using more than what was allotted to each person for water. But he hadn't realized the shunning had turned into an excommunication.

"He uses his water at will and he now also uses electricity." Isaaic's words came quickly, as if forced from a pressure cooker. "Oh, he pretends he does not. We see his lantern glow in the house after dark, but we have also seen the electric lights that spill from his basement window deep into the night."

"Is it possible he's working on his furniture building at night in his basement?" Frank asked.

Isaaic shook his head. "He has his shed for his work. His tools are there and that's where he does his work. Bishop Yoder tried to counsel him, but he wouldn't listen. He changed after his wife died. He stopped interacting with the community, went to church only sporadically."

"When did his wife die?" Jimmy asked. He hadn't even realized that Abraham had ever been married.

"Almost four years ago. She just dropped dead in the middle of the kitchen floor from a massive heart attack. She was a good wife, obedient and kind and he seemed lost without her." Isaaic's eyes were filled with sadness. "And now he is lost to us all forever."

Almost four years ago. That would have been just before the time that Jimmy had started working for the Wolf Creek Police Department. Her death must have happened in the months right before he'd arrived in town.

But what had every nerve in Jimmy's body jumping was Isaaic speaking of electric lights shining from the basement windows in Abraham Zooker's home.

Why would an Amish man have electricity in his

basement? Did he watch television there? Was he surfing the internet? Or was it possible he was keeping somebody down there? Was it possible the man who made beautiful furniture had Sheri in his basement at this very moment?

Chapter 18

Liz had been right, time had no meaning as Sheri and Liz remained sitting on the cot, talking about all the life that had happened since Liz had disappeared.

Sheri told her about the frantic search, how they'd initially believed Edward Cardell had taken her to the old fishing cabin in the woods and had killed her.

Liz laughed, her laughter holding an edge of sadness. "Edward could never hurt a fly. He's a very nice man."

"Since you've been gone he and Treetie have become an item," Sheri said, her disapproval rife in her voice. "I can't believe that either of them would betray you like that."

Liz patted Sheri's leg. "It isn't a betrayal and none of you girls should be mad at either one of them. Edward and I had a nice relationship. It was easy and comfortable, but he was never going to be a permanent fixture in my life. He and Treetie are much more suited to each other and I hope they find happiness together."

Sheri studied her aunt's face in the dim light. For the first time Liz looked every year of her age. Dark circles were evident beneath her eyes and lines of stress creased her forehead.

"Are you mad at Ramona for saddling you with us when you could have found another husband and built a different kind of life for yourself?"

"Heavens no, I was never angry with her for bringing you girls to me. I knew I was never going to be anyone's wife again and each one of you brought a joy into my life that I never thought I'd get to experience. But I was disappointed in the choices Ramona made with her life, that she'd left holes in little hearts because she couldn't pull herself together. At least she did the right thing in recognizing she couldn't be the mother you all needed. Some mothers never recognize that and do irreparable harm to the children they raise in chaos."

"She'll never be a mother to me," Sheri said. "No matter how many times she apologizes, no matter what she says about those years in her life, you'll always be my mother."

Liz patted her leg once again. "I would hope that if it's true that she's clean and sober and working on building a bridge to you girls, that you'll open your hearts to allow her in somewhere in some fashion."

"You know we're in bad trouble," Sheri said after a long moment of silence. "The police have no leads as to where we are. Abraham has been quite careful and has left no clues or evidence behind."

"I've known I was in bad trouble for some time," Liz said. "I just wish you weren't here with me. I wish you were in your backyard with Highway running circles at your feet while you feed your woodland creatures and feel the warmth of the sun on your face." A sudden sob escaped Liz's lips. "Your being here is my worst nightmare come true."

Sheri hugged her aunt. "I refuse to give up hope. If I can somehow fool Abraham into thinking that I am the right woman for him, then maybe I can manipulate him into allowing you to stay alive. I can work myself into a position where he will trust me and then someway I'll figure out an escape plan."

"No prince riding to the rescue," Liz said as a statement of fact rather than as a question.

"There never was a prince riding to my rescue," Sheri replied. "Those were the fantasies of a stuttering young girl who felt like an outcast and needed a hero. I need to be my own hero and somehow I need to figure out how to get us out of this mess."

She shoved away thoughts of Jimmy that tried to intrude into her head. She couldn't think about him now. It made her heartache too deep.

He must hate her now. He'd handed her his heart on a shining silver platter and she'd thrown it back in his face, clinging to foolish dreams that had no place in the reality of a grown woman.

She had a feeling that Jimmy wasn't a man who took chances a second time. It had taken him an enormous amount of courage to speak of how he felt for her. She knew in her heart how difficult it had been for him to reach out for love again given his traumatic childhood experience.

He would be doing his job now, attempting to find her, but it would no longer be love driving him, it would be duty. But she had certainly never considered Abraham a potential suspect in her aunt's kidnapping, so there was no reason for any of the lawmen to consider him, either, other than the fact that she had put his name on her list of people she interacted with on a regular basis.

She had the terrible feeling that if she and her aunt were going to be saved, then it was up to her. She had to somehow get into Abraham's head, figure out how best to interact with him and then pray that sooner or later she could escape.

The idea of pretending to care about Abraham, of touching him in any way, made her want to throw up, but if pretending that she was the woman he'd waited for saved their lives, then she'd do whatever she had to do.

At least she didn't have to worry about Highway. If she never returned to her cottage, Jed Wilson would take the dog he had trained and love it as if it were his own. Highway and her sisters would grieve for her. It was possible even Ramona would grieve for the child she'd given away so long ago who had grown into a woman she'd never really gotten to know.

Once again she leaned into her aunt, comforted by Liz's presence, yet knowing if something didn't happen, it was possible neither of them would ever see the light of day again.

It was almost three in the morning when Jimmy and Frank knocked on Abraham Zooker's front door. The modest ranch house was set some distance from the others in the settlement and was dark, as if Zooker was unaware of the search activity that had taken place in the past couple of hours at his neighbors'.

Nervous energy bounced around inside Jimmy as he waited for Zooker to answer the door. The workshop was a solid wooden shed not far from the house. It, too, was dark and the door hung open, indicating to them that the interior was void of human presence.

They had spied no electric lights gleaming out of the small basement windows as they'd pulled up. The entire area was shrouded with darkness broken only by the moonlight that filtered down from the cloudless sky.

Jimmy knocked on the door, harder this time, the sound echoing in the otherwise silent night. "Coming," Abraham's deep voice came from somewhere behind the door.

A moment later he appeared in the doorway, a lantern in his hand and a confused sleepiness on his face. "Detectives," he said in surprise. "Why would you be on my doorstep at this time of the morning?"

"We'd like to ask you a few questions," Jimmy said, fighting the need to shove past the man and race to his basement to see what was down there.

"Questions that couldn't wait until sunup?"

"Questions that couldn't wait another minute," Jimmy said. "Are you going to invite us inside?"

"Of course, everyone is welcome in my home, although you'll have to excuse the mess. I spend most of my time in my workshop and things have gotten away from me here."

Even in the faint light from the lantern, Jimmy

could see that Abraham's words were an understatement. Dust lay on furniture and turned the brown sofa to a dusty beige. The air inside smelled stale, with lingering cooking scents of old oil and spoiled fruit and vegetables.

"Now, what questions can't wait?" Abraham asked as they stood in the middle of the living room.

"We hear you are no longer a member of the community, that you have become too English," Frank began.

"We've been told you're using electricity," Jimmy added.

"Ah, you've been talking to my brethren." Abraham moved to a light switch on the wall and turned it up. Nothing happened. "I'm afraid my reputation has been sullied by the fact that I no longer participate in the social gatherings. If you listen to my neighbors you'll hear stories of me watching pornographic movies and having the internet, but I am still a simple man living our way."

"Can we see the rest of the house?" Jimmy asked.

"I have nothing to hide here." He handed Jimmy the lantern and then lit another one on one of the dusty coffee tables.

Jimmy and Frank headed down the hallway, scouring the shadows of each room, flipping light switches that didn't turn on anything.

Had Isaaic been mistaken? Did he have a personal grudge that might have him pointing in the direction of his brother? Was it possible Isaaic had lied about Abraham having electricity?

By the time they returned to the living room,

Frank's cell phone rang and he motioned that he would take the call outside.

As he walked out the door, Jimmy looked at Isaac once again. "And now I'd like to see your basement."

"My basement?" Abraham's shoulders stiffened slightly. "But it is just a dusty, dirty place of storage."

"I'd still like to have a look around," Jimmy insisted.

Abraham shrugged his shoulders and tugged on his beard as if he couldn't imagine why Jimmy would make such a request. "As you wish," he said.

He led Jimmy to a door in the kitchen that opened up onto a wooden stairway. With the light of the lantern only the first couple of steps were visible.

Jimmy hesitated a moment and then began to descend the stairs. Frank still hadn't come back but Jimmy felt no fear, only a resignation that this was probably just another dead end. He was aware of Abraham's heavy footsteps on the stairs behind him.

When he reached the bottom he spied another light switch and flipped it up, stunned when light filled the room. He turned to look at Abraham in surprise. "Perhaps your neighbors aren't exaggerating about your English ways after all," he said.

The basement was relatively small, with dusty shelving and boxes of what appeared to be women's clothing stacked helter-skelter. Directly ahead of him was another door.

He frowned, mentally attempting to deduce how there could possibly be a door there. "Where does that go?" He turned toward Abraham just in time to see the older man lunging toward him with a long, thick piece of wood raised over his head.

Jimmy reacted instinctively, he dropped and rolled as the wood smashed into the concrete floor next to him and Abraham bellowed in rage.

Before he had a chance to draw his gun, Abraham attacked again. Jimmy jumped to his feet and managed to grab the end of the wooden stick Abraham wielded.

Never underestimate your opponent, his sensei's voice whispered in his head. Abraham was much older than Jimmy, but he worked with his hands and had the strength of a bull.

For a moment they were bound by each other's grasp on separate ends of the wooden pole. Jimmy used both of his hands in an effort to pull it out of Abraham's strong grasp, but it appeared to be an equal match.

"It's over, Abraham," Jimmy said between gritted teeth. "We know she's here. There are other police officers outside."

"She is mine." Abraham's pale blue eyes flared with madness. "She will be my wife. She will clean my house and cook my meals. She will be obedient and giving, and will warm my bed at night."

"You're crazy," Jimmy rasped, his arm muscles shaking with his efforts. "You can't make a woman be your wife. What did you do with Agnes Wilson? With Liz Marcoli?"

Sweat began to appear on Abraham's forehead as he continued in the standoff. "They were unacceptable…mistakes. But Sheri isn't a mistake. She already has all I need and she will give it to me freely in time. She just needs to be trained and then she'll be perfect." His eyes darted frantically toward the door that appeared to lead nowhere.

In that wild gaze Jimmy knew that Sheri was behind that door. She was mere steps away from him. All he had to do was neutralize Abraham and Sheri would be safe.

With an inhuman roar, Abraham managed to grab the wood from Jimmy's hand. Once again he raised it like a club and Jimmy blocked the blow with his forearms.

Pain crashed through his arms and up to his shoulders. He shook it off and kicked out to scissor-cut Abraham's legs, and the man fell with the force of a giant tree, the length of wood flying across the room.

Instantly he was on Jimmy, his breath sour and hot in Jimmy's face as his hands attempted to encircle Jimmy's neck. Jimmy wrapped his own hands around his neck, making it impossible for Abraham to get a firm grip. He knew that if Abraham did manage to grab his neck he was more than strong enough to strangle Jimmy to death.

At the same time he fought to keep Abraham from his throat, he pulled his legs up and kneed Abraham in the groin. There was no such thing as a low blow when you were fighting for your life.

Abraham brayed out in pain and rolled off Jimmy as the sound of footsteps running down the stairs filled the room. Frank appeared in the doorway, gun drawn and body tense.

"I've got this," Jimmy said as he got to his feet and then grabbed Abraham and yanked him up from the floor. Jimmy reached behind him for the handcuffs that were in his pocket and quickly snapped them into place around Abraham's wrists. He shoved Abraham toward Frank. "Now he's all yours. You can read him his rights when you get him out of my sight."

To the sound of more footsteps clamoring down the stairs, Jimmy approached the door that appeared to lead into the very ground itself. His heart hammered madly as he threw the dead bolt back.

Every officer who had arrived on scene fell completely silent as the door creaked open. There was a gasp from somebody behind Jimmy as the underground room was exposed.

Before he could take a step inside, before he could draw a single breath, Sheri was in his arms, sobbing. He held her tight, his heart pounding with his own relief. She was in his arms only a moment and then pulled away and reappeared with her aunt.

Suddenly chaos reigned as an ambulance was called and more officers arrived on scene. Jimmy was jostled to one side as he watched Sheri and Liz being led up the stairs, Chelsea on one side of them and big Joe Jamison just behind them.

"You okay?" Frank asked as the basement quieted and it was just the two of them left.

"Yeah, I'm fine." Together the two men went into the small bunkerlike room and looked around, careful not to touch anything. The whole room was a crime scene and would have to be processed as such.

"I already called in our crime scene guys," Frank said as if reading Jimmy's mind. "They should be here anytime."

"Can you imagine living in this room for four months?" Jimmy asked softly. "It's a miracle Liz didn't completely lose her mind in here."

The thought of Sheri being locked away down here in the bowels of the earth for any length of time shot a sense of horror through Jimmy.

He walked toward the back dirt wall where there were several lines drawn, as if Liz had been keeping time somehow by making marks. He froze as he saw what was unmistakably a skeletal human hand half-buried in the dirt.

He turned back to Frank. "I think I just found Agnes Wilson."

Frank walked over to where he stood and frowned. "He must have lost his mind when he lost his wife. Only a madman would do something like this." He clapped Jimmy on the back. "Let's get out of here."

In the distance the sounds of sirens created a sense of peace through Jimmy. They had been far too late to save Agnes Wilson, but Liz and Sheri would be fine with the love and support of Roxy, Marlene and Ramona. Their family was back together again.

He walked out of the house just in time to see Sheri and Liz being placed in the back of an ambulance. They would be whisked away to the Wolf Creek Hospital and checked out for any injuries or traumas.

They were in good hands and Jimmy's work here was done. The bad guy was behind bars, the princess had been saved and it was time for him to head into the station, fill out his reports and then go home to his toadstool, for no matter how badly he wanted to be with Sheri, he was the prince of nothing.

Dawn came and went with Steve interviewing Sheri and Liz after which a reunion at the Dollhouse took place with Sheri's sisters and Ramona.

Roxy manned the kitchen, fixing omelets and toast and thick bacon for everyone while the joy of having Sheri and Liz back where they belonged overflowed.

They both had been released from the hospital fairly quickly. Sheri with no injuries and Liz suffered only a weight loss that the doctor assured her wasn't an alarming issue. He jokingly told her she just needed to eat some of her own baked pies and cakes.

Sheri was beyond exhausted when at eleven the next morning she finally headed home to her enchanted cottage. Highway greeted her with frantic barks of joy and lavish licks that she tolerated even though she rarely allowed him to lick her.

She knew it had to have been Jimmy who had laid down the fresh food and filled up the water for her furry companion and her heart both ached and expanded with emotion.

It didn't take her long to shower and then change into a comfortable bright yellow sundress. She then collapsed on the sofa, with Highway next to her. As she stroked his fur and replayed the events of the time spent in hell with her aunt, of those moments of interaction with Abraham, she felt only the relief of rescue.

According to what the officers had told her, it had been Isaaic who had told Jimmy about Abraham having electricity and that was what had brought Jimmy and the others to the house where they were being held.

Sheri had been amazed to realize that Aunt Liz had been so close to them all during her captivity and she was appalled that the man who made magic with his hands in building sturdy, beautiful furniture was also responsible for the death of Agnes Wilson and would have killed her aunt in his quest for the perfect wife.

Jimmy.

His name reverberated through her brain. He'd fought Abraham to save her. She'd heard from the others that Jimmy had gone head-to-head with the big man in an effort to get through the door that separated her and Aunt Liz from safety.

She had glimpsed him only once as she'd been loaded into the ambulance, but hadn't seen him anymore after that. And why would he want to see her? He'd done his job and now he was ready to move on.

And why shouldn't he? She'd virtually shoved him away, out of her life because of her own stupidity. She was grateful to have her aunt Liz back. She was relieved to be safe in her own home, but for the first time since she'd moved in here, even Highway's gentle snores didn't soothe the regret of love lost, of an aching heart.

She'd been a fool, blinded by childish dreams and afraid to let them go. She deserved to be alone now. At least Abraham wouldn't be able to prey on any other women.

When she awakened again it was just after six in the evening. Highway had long ago abandoned the sofa for a more comfortable spot on the floor and as she sat up, he did the same, his ears pricked forward as if to anticipate something happening.

She got off the sofa and padded into the kitchen where she snagged a soda from the fridge and then opened the back door. Highway darted out, but even his silly romping in the grass couldn't drag a smile out of Sheri.

She settled into one of the lawn chairs on the patio, grateful that she no longer had to be afraid to be in her own backyard. The bad man was in jail, and her mother just might eventually become a friend instead of an anonymous stalker.

There should be peace in her heart, but instead it felt as if a huge chunk had been torn out. S-Stuttering S-Sheri had been looking for a prince to make her world right, to make all her peers accept her.

She knew now that her prince had been right beside her all the time and she'd been too blinded by her childish fantasies to see him.

She pulled herself up and out of her chair and went to the small storage shed where she kept the birdseed and squirrel corn. As she began to fill the feeders, Highway ran circles around her legs.

He suddenly halted, ears pricked forward as he stared at the side of the house. He gave a joyful bark at the same time that Jimmy came around to the back.

Her heart immediately jumped into her throat at the sight of him. He was clad in tight jeans and a white T-shirt and the evening sun played in his dark hair. At the sight of her his lips curved into a hesitant smile.

"You aren't going to sic that dog on me, are you?" he asked teasingly.

"And why would I do that? The way I hear it you saved him from having to live the rest of his life without me." She kept her tone light and easy to match his.

There was no reason to get excited just because

he was here. It was probably natural that he'd want some sort of follow-up or check-in with her after everything that had happened, after everything they had shared. A friend checking in on a friend, that's all it was, she told herself.

"I was just doing my job," he said. He stood some distance away from her and watched as she finished filling the last bird feeder. "How are you feeling?"

"Okay...grateful." She gestured toward the chairs on the patio. "Do you want to sit?"

"No, I'm fine." His dark eyes held her gaze for a long moment. "You look beautiful in yellow."

"Thank you." Self-consciously she ran her hands down the skirt of the sundress. So many words she wanted to say to him, so many words she wanted to take back. "Jimmy..."

He held up a hand to halt whatever she was about to say and took several steps closer to her, close enough that she could smell his fragrant cologne, a smell that evoked warmth and a feeling of security and love.

"I've been told by a couple of guys who know that you Marcoli women can be quite hardheaded at times."

She looked at him in surprise. As he took another step closer to her, she couldn't help the way her heart leaped alive, how her senses seemed to become more acute.

"I've been thinking about this prince thing of yours," he continued.

"I..."

He pressed his index finger over her mouth, a look of fierce determination on his handsome face.

"I know you've been waiting for this blond-haired, blue-eyed prince to give you a happy ever after. But, have you ever considered the possibility that your prince might not be over six feet tall, that he might not be blond-haired or blue-eyed?"

He didn't give her an opportunity to respond. He dropped his finger from her mouth and instead took her hand in his. "You know I'm an orphan and I've been doing a lot of thinking today. I think maybe my father was the king of some faraway country and my mother was queen. They had to give me up for my own safety because they were under siege and feared that if my true identity was known, then assassins would try to kill me."

Sheri stared at him, amazed by the fantasy he had spun in response to hers. "I believe I'm a prince, Sheri. In any case, at one time I thought I was the Prince of Philly. But, more important, I believe I'm your prince, the man who can give you your happy ever after."

He slammed his mouth closed and appeared to be holding his breath while he waited for her response. Lord, but she loved this man. Her love for him blossomed inside her like a flower to the sun.

"You know what I think?" she said.

His eyes remained dark and slightly anxious. "What?"

"I think I've been waiting for a prince when all I really needed was you, Jimmy Carmani. I think it's far past time for me to put away silly fantasies and build my fairy-tale ending with a hot, sexy detective who makes my heart sing whenever he's near."

Jimmy's eyes widened and he grabbed her by the

waist and drew her close enough that his mouth could take full possession of hers. She melted against him, heart wide-open, spirit soaring, for she knew this man was, indeed, her prince of men, her happy ever after.

Epilogue

It was pure chaos in the Dollhouse green dining room. It had been almost a month since Liz and Sheri had been pulled out of the bunker. Tonight they had all gathered because first thing in the morning Ramona was returning to Arizona.

In the past month Ramona had found peace with the girls she had abandoned so long ago. She would never be a mother to them, but she had become a friend. Even Roxy had finally accepted Ramona's olive branch, and during the past month the two had been busy working on planning Roxy and Steve's wedding that would take place in September.

"Have another piece of pecan pie," Aunt Liz urged Steve, who groaned and held his belly.

"I can't stuff another bite into my mouth," he protested.

Aunt Liz was back at home, baking goodies for Roxy to sell at the restaurant and enjoying just being with the people she loved. She was also helping Roxy with the wedding preparations.

Marlene's grand opening of her bakery was set for the next weekend and Sheri knew it was going to be a huge success. The black-and-pink awning above the door announced the chic little establishment as Marlene's Magic Bites.

At the moment, Sheri sat at the large table next to Jimmy, who had become as important to her as breathing. Each and every day her love for him only grew stronger and she knew he felt the same way about her.

Most nights he spent at the cottage and with his presence it truly was an enchanted place. He reached out and placed a hand over hers as if he could read her thoughts.

"You okay?" he asked.

She smiled. "Better than okay."

She'd had several nightmares since being rescued, but each time she'd been pulled from the horror by Jimmy's arms wrapped around her and his voice whispering soft comfort. She knew in time the nightmares would leave her, but Jimmy's arms would always be there for her.

Jimmy leaned toward her. "How much longer do we need to stay here and make nice?" he whispered.

"Do you have someplace else to be?" she asked.

His eyes lit with a desire that stole her breath away. "Yeah, in bed with my princess."

Sheri dabbed her mouth with her napkin and placed it on the table next to her plate. "I think we've been here long enough," she whispered back, love swelling tight in her chest. "Jimmy and I need to head out," she said as she got up from her chair.

Goodbyes were said all around and Ramona promised to call and write often. Together, Sheri and Jimmy stepped out of the Dollhouse and he grabbed her hand and tugged her hurriedly toward his car.

She laughed at his eagerness as her own grew. This was passion. This was love. In minutes they would be at the cottage where Highway awaited them and happy ever after was a reality.

* * * * *

H HARLEQUIN®

ROMANTIC suspense

Available August 5, 2014

#1811 CAVANAUGH STRONG

Cavanaugh Justice

by Marie Ferrarella

When her family is threatened, detective and single mom Noelle turns to her new partner, the sexy Duncan Cavanaugh, never realizing his promise to serve and protect includes her daughter and her heart.

#1812 DEADLY ALLURE

by Elle James

Special agent Nicole Steele gets up close and personal with former Special Ops soldier Dave Logsdon while hiding out on his boat. But can she trust him with a secret that threatens the nation?

#1813 UNDER THE SHEIK'S PROTECTION

by C.J. Miller

Sarah is shocked to learn her mystery lover is Middle Eastern royalty. When attempts are made on both their lives, she'll have to choose—walk away or fight alongside him, for her life and a future...together.

#1814 FATAL FALLOUT

by Lara Lacombe

When nuclear scientist Claire is targeted, FBI agent Thomas Kincannon is assigned to protect her. What should be an easy task is soon complicated as the assassin kidnaps Thomas's niece and offers an exchange: the little girl for Claire.

REQUEST YOUR FREE BOOKS!
2 FREE NOVELS PLUS 2 FREE GIFTS!

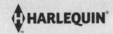

ROMANTIC suspense

Sparked by danger, fueled by passion

YES! Please send me 2 FREE Harlequin® Romantic Suspense novels and my 2 FREE gifts (gifts are worth about $10). After receiving them, if I don't wish to receive any more books, I can return the shipping statement marked "cancel." If I don't cancel, I will receive 4 brand-new novels every month and be billed just $4.74 per book in the U.S. or $5.24 per book in Canada. That's a savings of at least 14% off the cover price! It's quite a bargain! Shipping and handling is just 50¢ per book in the U.S. and 75¢ per book in Canada.* I understand that accepting the 2 free books and gifts places me under no obligation to buy anything. I can always return a shipment and cancel at any time. Even if I never buy another book, the two free books and gifts are mine to keep forever.

240/340 HDN F45N

Name	(PLEASE PRINT)	
Address		Apt. #
City	State/Prov.	Zip/Postal Code

Signature (if under 18, a parent or guardian must sign)

Mail to the **Harlequin® Reader Service:**
IN U.S.A.: P.O. Box 1867, Buffalo, NY 14240-1867
IN CANADA: P.O. Box 609, Fort Erie, Ontario L2A 5X3

Want to try two free books from another line?
Call 1-800-873-8635 or visit www.ReaderService.com.

* Terms and prices subject to change without notice. Prices do not include applicable taxes. Sales tax applicable in N.Y. Canadian residents will be charged applicable taxes. Offer not valid in Quebec. This offer is limited to one order per household. Not valid for current subscribers to Harlequin Romantic Suspense books. All orders subject to credit approval. Credit or debit balances in a customer's account(s) may be offset by any other outstanding balance owed by or to the customer. Please allow 4 to 6 weeks for delivery. Offer available while quantities last.

Your Privacy—The Harlequin® Reader Service is committed to protecting your privacy. Our Privacy Policy is available online at www.ReaderService.com or upon request from the Harlequin Reader Service.

We make a portion of our mailing list available to reputable third parties that offer products we believe may interest you. If you prefer that we not exchange your name with third parties, or if you wish to clarify or modify your communication preferences, please visit us at www.ReaderService.com/consumerschoice or write to us at Harlequin Reader Service Preference Service, P.O. Box 9062, Buffalo, NY 14269. Include your complete name and address.

HRS13R

"Hey, Cavanaugh, this should be very interesting. You're
partnered with The Black Widow," the slightly overweight
Holloway gleefully told him.

The unflattering nickname sounded like something an
irreverent journalist would slap on an elusive perpetrator, not
a label the police would put on one of their own.

"What are you talking about?" Duncan demanded, confused.

Holloway looked at him, obviously enjoying the fact that
for once he was the one in the know while Duncan was still
in the dark.

Grinning broadly, the detective laughed. "You really don't
know, man?"

Holloway leaned in, though he still failed to lower his voice.
"Well, rumor has it she's been engaged twice."

"Twice," Duncan echoed while looking at the woman who at that moment was meeting with the head of the vice department, Lieutenant Stewart Jamieson, before being brought out to meet the rest of them.

"She broke it off?" Duncan guessed.

Holloway shook his head, looking like the proverbial cat that had gotten into the cream. "Nope, she didn't have to. They both died. She didn't even get to walk up to the altar once." Pausing dramatically, Holloway gave it to the count of two before adding, "The first one left her pregnant."

Because he belonged to an extended family that could have easily acquired its own zip code, Duncan's interest went up a notch. "She has kids?"

"Kid," Holloway corrected, holding up his forefinger. "One."

"A daughter. Her name's Melinda. She's almost six. Anything else you want to know?" a melodious low voice coming from directly behind him said, completing the information.

Duncan turned his chair around a hundred and eighty degrees to face her. Up close the energy almost crackled between them. He would have to be dead not to notice.

Don't miss CAVANAUGH STRONG by *USA TODAY* bestselling author Marie Ferrarella, available August 2014 from Harlequin® Romantic Suspense.